Edited by Caitlin Lengerich

Cover Design by MiblArt

Interior Formatting by Grace Elena

 Created with Vellum

This is for everyone who lost someone and didn't know how to handle their grief. Everyone who tries to hide their emotions from the rest of the world, and only hurts themselves in the process. Everyone who feels like a burden when they talk about their problems.

You are not alone. You are not a burden.
There will always be light to cut through the darkness, you just have to be brave enough to let it.

I miss you everyday, Grandma.

BROOKE NOEL

chapter one

CLOTHES COVER every surface of my room.

The bed, desk, dresser, and floor are buried in everything that was in my closet and dresser drawers only an hour ago. A pink bikini top is draped over the TV, partially blocking the *Friends* rerun I have on for background noise but haven't looked up at once. I hold a pair of cut-off shorts in each hand, one slightly darker than the other, weighing which to add to the still-empty Vera Bradley duffel bag that I'd picked up at a thrift store earlier this summer. The same store where I found the white wicker dresser that now holds up the small TV.

I slump to the ground with a groan of frustration, throwing both pairs of shorts into the flood of garments surrounding me. Why is it this hard to pack? Maybe I'm not ready for this after all.

My head whips to the door when a chuckle sounds from the other side before it cracks open, only wide enough for Caleb to pop his head through. His eyes widen as he takes in the state of my room, and the pile of clothes blocking the door from opening any further.

"You do know you're only going to be gone for a weekend,

right?" he teases, but his face softens when I look up at him—my face full of anxiety.

After struggling to force back the swell of shirts and jeans, and almost tripping—which pulls a half-laugh-half-snort from deep in my chest—Caleb makes it over and drops down beside me. He sits there quietly, waiting for me to speak if I want to.

This is how it's always been with Caleb—never pushing me to talk about it, but always listening if I want to.

I sigh, looking down at my feet and letting my shoulders slump further over my legs that are cradled into my chest. "I don't think I can do this," I say into my knees.

"You were so excited for this last week, and you know all my mom has talked about is how excited she is to see you," he reminds me, as if I could forget Claire's squeal of delight when I told her I'd be joining the boys for the famous Dey Family Fourth of July Party.

"Well, last week I still thought I'd have my best-friend there with me." I glare at him, reminding him that he bailed on this weekend first. As newly appointed assistant manager, Caleb felt obligated to cover for George this weekend at George's Deli. George had claimed it was a family emergency, but considering he had some emergency mysteriously pop up most holidays over the last year, I doubted it was the truth. Caleb's just too kind to say no.

If it wasn't his best trait as a friend, I'd be more upset. But it's not in his nature to turn away from someone in need of help. He's compassionate to his core, which is why I know he's in agony that his decision is having a negative impact on me.

"Adam will still be there, he's your friend too." Just from his tone, and the way he emphasizes the word *friend*, I know there's a suggestive look in his eyes. The same look that shows up every time he mentions his older brother and me in the same sentence. Luckily, he never asks more about our flirty friendship, and I'm glad I'm looking down so he doesn't see how my breath catches just at the sound of his name.

Wanting to change the subject before he can pick up on just how strong my feelings are, I take a deep breath to steady my heart and look up at him with pouty lips. "But all of my Fourth of July traditions are with you."

"Isn't it weird to think that, since fourth grade, we've only ever watched the fireworks together?" he asks, and it launches us into a flurry of memories from previous years' parties. One of my favorites is the year we snuck onto the roof of his parent's house to get the best view of the fireworks, only to be scolded by our moms later when we needed help getting down. His dad pretended to be mad with them, but he's as big a fan of fireworks as us, so he shot us a thumbs-up and a wink when no one was looking.

By the time he leaves to let me finish, or *start* packing, I'm feeling much better. Caleb has always had a knack for putting a smile on my face, even when it's the last thing I want to do.

After throwing enough clothes to last me a week into my duffle bag, and dropping it next to the dining table on my way to the living room, I launch myself onto the couch next to Caleb. We both realize what's happening too late, and even though he tries to move out of the way, I barrel into him. His elbow connects with my ribs and leaves me gasping for air, while my knee drives into his thigh, sending him doubling over off the couch. The potted plants on the coffee table, that Caleb insists on keeping around—and alive since my green thumb is nonexistent —wobble in loud, echoing noises on the glass when he knocks into the leg.

I wheeze, curling into a ball and clutching my side on the cloudlike couch. It's the only piece of furniture we allowed Claire to buy—as a compromise. She originally insisted on furnishing the entire place since my mom's outstanding medical bills meant very little was left to me. But after losing her, I needed something that felt like mine, and while I love Claire's sophisticated style, thrift store furniture is more up my alley, and in my budget. Caleb let his mom furnish his room but backed me up in the communal areas of the apartment. I made an exception on the couch though, because the thought of what could've caused the stains on the used ones we saw terrified me.

"I think you grossly miscalculated that jump," Caleb groans from the ground. "I thought you were supposed to be the smart one."

I huff out a laugh then whimper when the movement brings on a new wave of pain. "I'm a math major, not a physics major, cut me some slack. Velocity and acceleration aren't my forte."

He's laughing as he sits up and pulls himself back onto the couch beside me. "Fair point."

We both get quiet, pretending to be focused on the TV, but I've known him long enough to know he's trying to figure out if it's worth bringing up the real reason I'm hesitant to go back to our hometown—to his parents' house in particular.

I don't want to talk about it though. Right now, being distracted is all that's keeping me together, so I sigh and say, "The fireworks really won't be the same without you."

The front door creaks open and Caleb smirks, raising his voice so the new person entering the apartment can hear. "Just get Adam to watch them with you, it'll almost be like having me there."

My eyes cling to him the moment he steps around the corner and the remaining pain in my ribs turns into flutters that cascade through my abdomen. Even though his light brown hair was recently cut, it's still a mess—in the way that hair can be a sexy mess when someone just rolls out of bed—but his brown eyes are bright with curiosity.

"First off, we might be related but we're nothing alike, so I doubt that." Adam smiles in jest as he drops onto the couch beside me. My heart races, until he slings an arm over my shoulders like he would to a buddy or a sister, and I fight to keep a smile on my face. "And secondly, what are we talking about?"

"In case you didn't hear, Caleb's ditching us this weekend," I blurt out before Caleb can say anything else about fireworks.

Adam Dey has one flaw and it's that he doesn't like fireworks.

Okay, fine, he has more than one flaw but who doesn't like to watch fireworks? It's criminal, really.

"I'm not ditching you," Caleb refutes. "I have a work obligation."

I roll my eyes playfully and use the opportunity to lean in closer to Adam to whisper, "Definitely ditching."

"Rylie!" Caleb tries to act frustrated, but his laugh is slipping through.

Adam glances between us, brows raised, until his gaze finally locks on me, and he leans in even closer, conspiratorially. "Definitely ditching," he agrees, and the two of us fall into laughter. Caleb's glare only lasts another second before he joins us.

"So, what's the real reason you can't come?" Adam asks.

"George had a family emergency," Caleb says, shrugging like it's no big deal, but one of Adam's eyebrows quirks up in question.

"Again?" Adam says, and I laugh because it's exactly what I said when he first told me a few days ago.

"And Caleb is too nice to say no," I chime in.

Adam and I look at each other with pointed expressions and say in unison, "Again."

We start laughing again when Caleb glares harder at us.

"I never thought a little, bald, Italian dude would have you whipped," Adam says, removing his arm from around me to mess with Caleb's hair. As the two of them fall into one of their brotherly quarrels, I can't help but smile at the familiarity of it all. Our age and location may change, but these moments with the three of us, laughing like this, never do and that's a comfort I need right now.

"We should get going, I told mom we'd be there for dinner." Adam stands, clapping his brother on the back one last time before looking at me. "Where's your stuff? I'll bring it to the car."

I point behind us at the table.

"And *you're* not whipped?" Caleb calls as Adam carries my bag out.

"No, I'm just being a gentleman for a lovely friend of mine," he says with a wink at me, and my heart skips a beat. I ignore the f-word and focus on the preceding adjective, the word repeating in my head like a catchy song. *He called me lovely.*

"Kiss-ass," Caleb grumbles when he sees the smile on my face.

Adam's laugh rings through the apartment as he walks out the door and the sound sends a chill through me. Caleb has always been around as a sort of buffer between us. Anytime my thoughts got out of control I'd be able to look at Caleb and ground myself—remind myself that Adam's my best friend's older brother, and nothing is going to happen between us. He doesn't even see me that way. But I'm starting to wonder what a weekend alone with him is going to do to me.

I guess I'm about to find out.

"Ry?" Caleb's voice pulls me away from my thoughts and I find his concerned gaze locked on me. "Call me if you need anything, okay?"

"I will." I pull him into a hug. "Thanks, Cale."

Adam pops his head in the door. "Ready?"

"Yup." I smile, ignoring the dread pooling in my stomach and growing by the second. "Let's go."

"Have fun, Ry," Caleb whispers before releasing me. "You deserve it."

I smile at him one last time before running out to the car and hopping in. Let the two-hour drive from Kasper Mountain College back to Lockney begin.

* * *

THE FIRST HOUR passes with us singing along to songs off a shared playlist the three of us keep updated just for this drive. It's been easy to smile and laugh with Adam—it always is—but with just the two of us here, the love songs feel more intimate than playful. Especially since I've caught him looking over at me too many times to count.

I raise my eyebrows and turn down the volume when I catch him glimpse over at me again. "What?"

"Nothing," he says, but I shoot him a glare until he glances over again. "Fine, it's just—" He pauses mid-sentence and sighs. "You know, you're not a bad singer."

I roll my eyes. "Why do we have this conversation every time we're in a car together?"

"Because I forget."

His response comes so quickly that I can't stop my cringe. Just what everyone wants to hear the person they're into say. *I forget about you.*

He must glance over again and read the hurt on my face because he quickly amends, "I don't mean that I forget you're a good singer, it's just that you're always better than I remember."

"Nice save," I mumble.

"I'm being serious." His voice is pleading for me to listen. "That's what I meant the first time, it just came out wrong."

I wish I knew which was the truth, but I'm scared to find out, so I drop it and quip back, "At least *one* of us is musically talented in this car." I'm already smiling again—around him it's too hard not to.

His shoulders sag in relief and he chuckles. "You really want to taunt the person who has your life in their hands at the moment?"

I smirk at the empty threat. "I'll take my chances knowing that you enjoy my company too much to do anything."

"Quite the gambler, I see," he grumbles in defeat.

I'm looking out the window, savoring my victory with a smug smile when I squeal because Adam's right hand has moved to my midriff and is tickling me. I can't move out of his reach, so I squirm and laugh until I'm gasping for air and begging for a reprieve.

His fingers slow their assault and I'm finally able to catch my breath. It's only then that I notice my top has ridden up in my struggle and his fingers are on my bare stomach. I can't breathe as he drags his fingers across my skin at a snail's pace, not breaking contact until he's traced a line across my waist. I iron-grip the sides of my seat and hope he can't feel my body trembling at the touch.

When his hand finally pulls away, I let out a stuttering breath. He left a blazing trail across me that's seeping warmth throughout my entire body. It takes far too long for my mind to clear, but when it does, I sit up straight and fix my shirt—my cheeks heating in embarrassment. I can't think straight with his hands on me like that.

Adam's white-knuckle grip on the steering wheel leaves me wondering if that affected him more than he let on, but he doesn't say a word and doesn't look my way. I turn the music back up, but neither of us sing-along.

The remaining hour is at once much too long and much too short.

I don't know why it's always there, refusing to extinguish, but a spark of hope flares in me.

Maybe this weekend will finally be different for us.

chapter two

THE DEY'S house is the epitome of a lake house. It's a two-story, log cabin-style home with plenty of land and it sits on the shore of Lake Norman, the second largest lake in North Carolina. It seamlessly merges into a modern open floor plan, with ample natural light, and the charms of a rustic cabin. Claire is a design expert.

I have many, fond, childhood memories of playing in the lake in the summertime, but it's also a reminder of everything I've lost, and all the time I spent here because my mom was sick.

It's hard to be back.

I don't realize we've parked until Adam opens my door and the sound makes me flinch. My breathing comes faster, my hands begin to shake, and my vision turns blurry. I don't need to look over to know there's nothing but understanding on Adam's face, and it gives me the courage to speak the words I couldn't face at the apartment with Caleb. "I haven't been back here since …"

The funeral. *Her* funeral.

Was it *only* six months ago?

Has it *already* been six months?

Six months since everyone was wearing black and staring at me with pity because I just lost everything. I try to shake off the memories, but they're starting to bury me. My chest is caving in. I can't breathe.

"I know," Adam whispers and grabs my hand.

That one touch starts to cut through the darkness that has begun to surround me, but it's too late. Its chokehold on me isn't relenting. I look over and am surprised to find him eye-level, squatting beside the car. His eyes widen in fear when he realizes I'm at risk of hyperventilating because, even though I'm sucking in breath after breath, none of them reach my chest, and I'm panicking.

"Look at me," he commands, so strong and compelling that I obey immediately. "Keep your eyes on me. When I breathe, you breathe, okay?"

He doesn't wait for me to attempt to answer, he just takes an over-exaggerated deep breath in. I try to copy him, but the air stops in my throat, and I cough it out. He takes another deep breath, and despite his calm demeanor, his eyes give away his terror when it doesn't work again. He tries once more, squeezing my hand tighter, and at first it seems like it's catching in my throat again, but then my airway opens and air rushes to my chest.

I breathe out in relief.

Another breath, and I get all of it this time. I move the hand he's not holding to rest against my collarbone, wanting to feel the rise and fall of my lungs as I continue to follow his lead.

I'm still alive. I'm still breathing. The darkness didn't win today.

Once my breathing is back to normal, a relieved smile spreads across his face. "Better?"

I nod, too overwhelmed by what he just did for me to be able to speak.

"You got this," he whispers, squeezing my hand, and, as I look into his eyes, all my worries fade away.

"Thank you," I say softly, trapped in his gaze. He helps me out of the car and squeezes my hand one last time before letting go to grab our bags while I stumble to the front door in a daze.

"Rylie!" The front door flies open before I can knock, and Claire pulls me into a suffocating hug. "Let me look at you." She holds me at arm's length and examines me, her face full of concern.

As my guilt grows, my gaze lowers, until I'm looking at the ground. Claire is like a second mother to me and has treated me as one of her own since the first time I met her. I know she's been worried about me these past months, and I know I haven't done a good job of staying in touch.

But honestly, anytime someone reached out I only retreated further into myself.

I realize my attempt to shelter others from my pain only worried them and hurt me, but I was never good at letting others help carry my weight.

I'm still not.

"How are you?" Claire frowns at what she finds. "Have you lost weight?"

Of course, I have. Some people stress eat, but I do the opposite and avoid food like it's the plague. My grief is filling me already, how could there be room for anything else?

"I'm good, Claire," I say with a small, forced smile, trying to reassure her. "I promise."

Her expression softens. "I'm glad you came."

"You could at least pretend you're excited to see me too," Adam says, walking up behind me with our bags.

Claire's smile falls on her oldest son and the love there is undeniable. My heart aches knowing that my mom will never get to look at me like that again. "You know I'm always excited to see you."

"Yeah, but I also know she's your favorite." Adam rolls his eyes but there's a sincere smile on his face. "And she's not even blood."

Claire just laughs and shakes her head, probably recounting all the times a version of this same conversation has taken place over the years.

"My son, you may be only a few years from graduating," she says, reaching out to pat him on the cheek. I snicker and he shoots me a glare as his cheeks redden in embarrassment. "But you still have a lot of growing up to do." With a wink at me she adds, *"That's* why she's my favorite."

I almost forgot how much I love this family.

Adam glowers at us before stomping off to go put the bags in the rooms upstairs. It only emphasizes Claire's point and we're both laughing in his wake.

"Come on, Phil made enough food to feed an army." She leads me to the dining room. "Let's get some meat on these bones."

As we head to the kitchen, I try to push the memories of my mom, and that day six months ago, out of my head and focus instead on the house, letting its coziness calm me.

The interior of the house is whiter than you'd expect. All of the dark wood is painted in here, and the light, stone fireplace in the living room is my favorite feature. Everything is open, and with most of the back wall being made up of windows, you can see out to the large backyard, and lake, from anywhere on the first floor.

"Hey, Rylie," Phil says as we get closer. "Glad you could join us."

"Dinner smells great." I smile at him.

Claire might be the heart of the Dey family, but Phil is the backbone. He's quiet and reserved, but is fiercely supportive of everything his family does. They're a perfect pairing. I aspire to have a marriage like theirs, one that's overflowing with mutual love and respect. It's the reason I rarely date. It's hard to find someone that lives up to that standard.

Adam heads straight to the kitchen to talk to his dad when he's back downstairs, and a few minutes later they walk to the table with plates in hand. Phil sets down Claire's and his own, and Adam has mine.

Okay, maybe the other reason I haven't dated much is because I feel like I've found that person in the five-foot-ten, brown-haired, brown-eyed boy sitting beside me. He's everything I've ever wanted, and everything I never knew I needed.

I just wish he saw me the same way.

I blink, trying to redirect my attention from the man sitting beside me—just close enough to feel his body heat, but just far enough away to drive me crazy, wishing he was closer—to the mouthwatering meal in front of me. The steak, potatoes, and salad taste just as good as they look.

The dinner conversation centers around work and school. Adam is taking a few classes this summer, which is why he stayed on campus. Caleb and I stayed to earn some extra cash by working—Caleb at the deli, and me at The Split Bean, a local coffee shop.

I smile to myself as he tells his parents about his finance course. He's a business major and up until now, hasn't been sure what he wanted to do post-graduation, but he's enjoying the course so much he's thinking of going the finance route.

I knew all of this already, though.

Adam likes to study at The Split Bean while I'm working, and we've been talking about this very topic a lot the past couple weeks. I can't help but grin ear-to-ear because, even now, I can see how excited he is about this, and I love anything that makes him happy.

I excuse myself soon after dinner to give Adam some time with his parents, and because it's getting harder to keep the memories out of my head. I look around and see her everywhere.

I see the chair I sat in while people lined up to give their condolences and recount memories of my mother. I see the patio chairs she always sat in with Claire while they watched us kids in the lake. I see her smiling and laughing at the dinner table with us at our regular, joint-family dinners. It's becoming too much to bear.

I head up the stairs and turn left down the hallway that leads to the guest room I've always stayed in. Across from that room is Adam's, and further down the hall is a second guest room. Caleb's room is to the right of the stairs, next to a large playroom that we frequented as kids. It's now a rec room complete with a pool table, large TV, and cloud couch.

The guest room is a decent size, with a queen bed, dresser, and a desk. It even has its own private bathroom. Claire decorated it in shades of beige, tan, and terracotta when I started using it often. "Calming earth tones" she'd called them. Objectively, it's a beautiful room, and I'm grateful to have a piece of this house that's just for me, but it doesn't feel like *mine*.

Claire always tells me that it's my room, that I've long since stopped being a guest, but the thought makes my heart heavy. Admitting that this is my room feels like admitting I truly have nowhere else to call home, which, while true, isn't something I'm ready to accept yet.

To accept it would mean that I have to accept that my mom really is gone for good. It feels like I'm replacing her, and how could I ever do that?

I don't want to hurt Claire though, so out loud it's *my room* but my heart never dropped the word "guest."

It's easier to see Phil as the father-figure in my life because I never knew my own father. He passed away in an accident before I was old enough to remember anything about him. I have nothing to compare him to, but with my mom, I remember everything. As wonderful as Claire is—as much as she treats me as one of her own—it's hard for me to think of her that way, to compare her to my mom.

Maybe it's still too soon for me to be here. Especially without Caleb.

How'd I let him talk me into this?

Needing to distract myself, I change into my pajamas—gray cotton shorts and an oversized tee I got on a trip to Hawaii with my mom the first time she was in remission. Back when we thought the worst of it was over. We were wrong. Needing something to distract me, I start sorting through the closet of clothes I brought to choose my outfits for tomorrow.

An hour later, it looks like a tornado blew through, but I'm happy with my final picks—a white bikini with a dark blue floral pattern, high waisted jean shorts, and a white tank for the day on the lake. And for the evening, I opted for a white sundress that has a design resembling something between a flower and a firework on it in pink and blue.

"Goodnight." Adam's voice carries to the second floor before I hear his footsteps on the stairs and his door shut across the hall. I've always wished the guest room was across the hall, where Adam's room is, because that side of the house overlooks the lake, and the vastness of the lake brings me peace when I'm trapped in my own head.

Knowing my mind isn't going to shut off anytime soon, especially since being here is making my thoughts louder than usual, I move around the room, cleaning up the mess I just made with excruciating slowness, gathering each piece one by one and moving it to the bed, then folding each piece to perfection before packing it away again.

The mundane tasks keep my hands busy, but my mind still roams. I don't have much hope, but it's worth a shot to try and get some sleep. After washing my face and brushing my teeth, I crawl under the covers and attempt to settle in.

After hours of tossing and turning, non-stop thoughts, and with tears beginning to flow, the walls feel like they're closing in on me. People never tell you that loss leaves behind more than just empty space. That the darkness that fills that empty space is alive, and it's greedy. It finds a way to burrow in your heart, then slowly tries to take over the rest of you.

Tonight, my darkness is at my throat—building and constricting—claiming my every breath as its own.

But I won't give in that easily.

With a shuddering breath, I regain enough control to stumble out of bed and down the stairs. This isn't the first time my darkness has come to claim me. Over the years I discovered that fresh air helps more than anything else.

As quietly and quickly as possible, I force my feet to take me outside, through the back door. The first breath of fresh air that courses through my lungs brings with it a reprieve. It's enough to quell my desperation and quiet my mind—at least for a moment.

Stumbling down the patio stairs and through the grassy yard, I head straight for the dock. Tomorrow, this yard will be full of people I knew growing up. The tables and chairs that are stored in the wooden shed on the edge of the tree line will be set up on the grass. The boat that's covered and tied up will be whipping around the lake towing tubers behind it. The spot of beach through the trees will be full of kids swimming in the lake, and the patio will be packed with adults socializing.

Tonight, there's none of that. No people, no noise. It's exactly what I need.

When I reach the end of the dock, I sink to the ground, not caring how uncomfortable the wood planks are. My knees are at my chest and I'm holding on like it's possible to physically hold myself together when I'm mentally falling apart. I sit, as still as a statue, and don't tear my eyes away from the water.

Out here, it's easier to push my problems out of my mind, to feel like I can escape reality for a little while. Out here, I can breathe.

Even though I hear the dock creaking with his approach, I don't look away from the reflection of the moon on the water.

Nor do I look up when he sits down next to me, so close the heat radiating off him warms me and his scent envelops me. He always smells of rosewood, I've never figured out if it's from his shampoo or cologne, but it's my favorite scent.

"How'd you know?" I ask so softly if there was any trace of wind the words would be swept away.

He stays quiet until I glance over at him. The intensity of his expression catches me off guard. Like he's looking through me straight to my soul—but I can't look away.

"Because I know you, Rylie," he rasps, and before I can think about it, I reach for his hand, needing the comfort of his touch right now. He doesn't hesitate, he just laces our fingers together and holds on tight, like he's trying to hold me together, too.

I smile as a silent tear slips down my cheek because he's right. He does know me, but more than that, he's the only person who intimately knows this part of me—my darkness. He knows it, he's seen it, and he still shows up, time and time again.

Originally, I wasn't planning on burdening anyone with my problems, but Adam always seemed to know when I was at my lowest and was there to help lift me up. Over time he gained my trust and my confidence. I turn my gaze back on the water and smile, thinking of the first time I truly opened up to him. It was a summer night, much like tonight, four years ago.

We laid side-by-side on the dock looking up at the stars. It must've been early morning by then, but the rest of the house was still fast asleep. My mom was in the hospital again, which meant I was barely sleeping at night. And Adam must've picked up on this habit because he seemed to always be wide-awake and ready to join me whenever I came out here.

Even if I didn't want to talk, he'd sit out here with me in complete silence. Sometimes he'd tell me stories, some about himself or his life and some completely made up—both helped. His presence had a weight that held down the darkness.

Nights like these had become solace for me.

We'd had many deep talks about life, hopes, and dreams, but I hadn't been ready to talk about my mom. I didn't want to burden anyone. But with Adam, I never felt like a burden. When talking to him I felt strong, even when being vulnerable, and for that I chose to trust him with some of the hurt in my heart.

"I'm scared," I whispered as tears rolled off my cheeks and splattered onto the wood below. It was the first time I had said those words aloud. In my peripheral vision I saw Adam rotate his head towards me. I knew if I looked over, I wouldn't be able to get this out, so I kept my eyes on the stars. "This time seems worse, like the cancer came back with a vengeance. Every time she enters that hospital, I worry that it'll be the time she doesn't walk out. I don't know what to do."

Adam stayed quiet long enough that I risked looking over at him. When our eyes locked, I couldn't look away.

He gave me a sad smile.

"Rylie, first off, you don't need to be afraid to show vulnerability. None of us expect you to be okay all of the time. What you're going through is unimaginable, and while we may not know what it's like, we are going to be here for you through it all." He took a deep breath before adding, "I'm going to be here for you through it all."

The way he emphasized the last sentence felt different, more like a vow than a comforting statement.

"But don't let your fear keep you from savoring every moment with your mom. Make sure that no matter what happens, you don't leave anything unsaid, okay? Grief will fade, but regrets . . . those last a lifetime." His eyes bore into mine and the truth of his words shook me to my bones.

I was grateful for him, for being there and for responding with understanding and truth instead of pity. I chose to trust him with this broken piece of myself, and instead of trying to smooth the sharp edges, he helped piece me back together. I was in awe of this moment—in awe of him.

His eyes shone with sincerity, and as he reached out to grab my hand, I broke down. He sat up and pulled me into his arms, holding me tight as I let out all my pent-up emotions on his shoulder. I stayed there, in Adams' arms, until my tears dried up and the first rays of light peaked above the horizon.

People always assume our friendship was born of convenience and proximity, but it's much more than that. Our friendship was born of necessity—a need to have someone who understands the darkest parts of you and still chooses to stand by your side. Against all odds, we found that in each other.

Caleb will always be my best friend and the person I go to for every other problem in my life, but Adam . . . he's the one who knows the parts of me I'm too afraid to show anyone else.

He hasn't stopped watching me since he sat down. "How are you, really?"

"I'm fi—" I stop myself before my trained response slips out. He's earned better than my lies. I look down at our still-joined hands and run my thumb across the back of his hand. With a deep breath, I tell him the truth. "It's hard being here, knowing that she won't be around tomorrow. She loved to come here for the Fourth, it was something she looked forward to each year. It was like, for this one day, we could just forget her diagnosis and live freely." I look up at him with blurry eyes. "Remember four years ago, when I first talked to you about my mom?"

"How could I forget?" I think the corners of his lips shift into a small, sad smile at the memory. "We were laying right here, looking at the stars."

"Do you remember what you said, about grief and regrets?"

His lips press together, and he nods. "Yeah, I remember."

"How long does it take—" I say shakily, getting so choked up the rest of the words stutter out. "F-for the grief to fade? Because t-this . . . this feels like it'll never end."

My tears fall fast now, the pain I usually try to hide reverberates through me in shaking sobs.

"Rylie." Adam's voice sounds pained and desperate. His free hand moves to sweep fallen hair behind my ear and lingers, resting on my cheek.

I instinctively lean into his touch—it cuts through the pain and sends a shiver down my spine. My every thought focuses on the way his thumb gently wipes my tears as they fall down my cheek. His touch comforts me more than words ever could.

With him around, I feel lighter, as if my darkness is afraid of him and hides in his presence.

When my tears slow, he finally speaks. "Rylie, your mom was everything to you, a loss like that isn't something you recover from overnight. There'll probably always be moments where her loss hits harder than usual, and that's okay, because it means you loved her—you *still* love her. I only said it would fade, not completely go away." His hand encourages my face to lift so I'm looking him in the eyes. He's looking at me like he would gladly endure pain just to take mine away. "In time, you will learn how to live in a world where she no longer exists. As unfair as it is that you have to, you will, because we have to adapt to survive."

I'm mesmerized by the look in his eyes, by the words coming out of his mouth—by him. He looks away for a second, hesitating, but takes a deep breath and looks back at me.

"And I know you will survive," he says, resolute and strong, "Because I've seen your strength and you—" His voice catches in his throat and he swallows. "You're strong enough to conquer anything."

He squeezes my hand, and I squeeze back but can't speak. I can barely remember how to breathe.

He believes in me, in my strength.

That makes me want to believe in it, too.

"I know I'm a broken record saying this, but you're not alone. We are your family and I know we could never take her place, but we want to help in any way you'll let us. We just want to see you happy."

He's smiling at me, and I try to smile back, but it's half-hearted. I hadn't even realized I'd let my hopes rise until they came crashing down with the words *"family"* and *"we."* I don't know why I keep hoping when I know it's useless. But when he's touching me, my walls come tumbling down.

No matter my disappointment at his feelings, he's here, helping hold me together.

If only that didn't make me love him more.

I laugh, forcing myself to pull my face away from his touch, even though all I want to do is never move again. But I can't find the strength to take my hand out of his. "Do you think we'll ever have a late-night conversation where I don't end up in tears?"

His responding smile shines brighter than any star. "I hope not."

My eyes narrow in question, and he quickly amends his statement with, "Wait, that's not what I meant. I don't want you to cry. I hate seeing you cry. I hate to see you hurt at all. I just hope to always be the person you come to when you need a shoulder to cry on."

Why does he always have to say things that turn my heart to mush? This is why, no matter how hard I've tried, my feelings for him won't go away.

I smile. "I hope you're always that person, too."

"What do you mean you hope so, too?" He bumps his shoulder into mine playfully. "Aren't you the one that gets to decide that?"

"I mean, yeah, I'll always choose you," I say, cheeks heating. Those words feel like too deep of an admission, so to lighten the mood I shrug and add jokingly, "But I can't help it if you do something stupid that forces you out of the position."

"You're right," he says, smirking, "That's definitely the most likely scenario."

We both laugh and I'm at ease for the first time tonight. Everything with Adam is easy, even silence. It's not awkward or waiting like most, instead it's peaceful and content. It's always been that way with him.

As we lay back to look up at the stars, a revelation rings through my head.

I'm glad I chose to come here this weekend.

chapter three

THE FIRST RAYS of morning light fall across my face, causing me to stir. I mentally curse myself for not closing the curtains last night as I squeeze my eyes shut tighter. I don't remember what time I went to bed after talking to Adam, but I'm exhausted. I'm tempted to believe that last night was all a dream, but my eyes are still swollen and stinging from all the tears.

I nuzzle my head into the pillow, hoping to be pulled back under for a little while longer.

Well, that was the plan until something brushes against my waist. My eyes shoot open and dart around, trying to figure out what's going on. A smile slowly creeps onto my face when I realize I'm not in the guest room.

In fact, I'm not inside of the house at all.

My head isn't laying on a pillow, it's on Adam's chest and the brush against my waist is from Adam's arm that's wrapped around me. Moving as slowly as possible, I rotate just enough to look up at his face.

In sleep it's gentle, peaceful, and handsome—so handsome. My breath catches in my chest as if my body is trying to hold onto this moment for as long as possible. It's already the best morning I've had in a long time, and it's only just begun.

In the quiet of the morning, without any eyes on me, it's much easier to admit that I want this man more than I want anything else. I force my eyes shut before I get too caught up in him and do something stupid—like run my fingers through his hair, or wake him with a kiss to his temple . . . or cheek or chin or neck or li—

My hands shake with restraint. It's time to shut down that train of thought. Fantasy time is over.

With a steadying breath, I open my eyes and shake him gently with the hand that's laying on his chest. "Adam."

He grumbles something inaudible and it's so adorable that I can't stop myself from smiling like an idiot.

I laugh softly as I shake him again. "Adam, wake up."

He groans and the vibration spreads through me, melting my body further into his and making it exponentially harder to not do one of those stupid things I want to do. To make matters worse, his arm tightens around me, pulling me closer, and his head turns to nuzzle into my hair.

"Ten more minutes," his sleepy voice grumbles, and I don't know if I'm just shaking or about to cry from happiness.

The number of times I've dreamed of something just like this happening is, well, embarrassing, if I'm being honest. Now it's finally happening, but Adam is asleep and doesn't mean it in the way I wish he would. This is too much to handle, but it's also not even close to enough. I need to get a hold of myself before I start wondering who is in my place in his dreams.

That just might be the thing that breaks me.

"Adam, wake up." I shake him harder this time. "We fell asleep on the dock."

His eyes flutter open and take in our surroundings. Somehow, this is the first time we've fallen asleep out here. We've stayed out all night talking before, but have never fallen asleep together like this.

"So that's why my back hurts so much," he groans.

I prop myself up on my elbow, so I'm still close enough to be touching him but I'm no longer laying on top of him. My mind clears with the small distance, but my heart screams for me to move closer again.

Looking up at him, I say, "Good morning to you too."

His full attention shifts over to me, and his face lights up, brighter than the sun that's just peeking out above the horizon. "Good morning, Rylie."

The way he emphasizes my name in his husky morning voice causes me to shiver even in the rising summer heat. And that smile . . . I want to wake up to that smile for the rest of my life.

The ease with which that thought slips through my mind rattles me to my core. I sit up, too fast, needing to put any semblance of distance between us. I'm sure my cool and collected mask is nowhere to be found in the aftermath of that thought.

What game am I playing with my heart, and what's the cost of losing?

I'm scared to find out.

"Are you okay?" he asks, following me up into a sitting position. There's a tentative look in his eyes that wasn't there before.

I do my best to put the mask back on, but I can't look at him.

"I think I'll have a bruise on my hip," I say, but we both know that isn't what he's asking. "We should probably head in and either try to get some more sleep, or put on a pot of coffee. If you're as exhausted as I am, then we're going to need one of the two."

He stands and reaches back to help me up. I take his hand but pull away the second I'm solid on my feet. Even those few seconds of contact send a shiver rocketing through me. Last night he was holding me together, and this morning I'm in ruins because of him.

As we walk towards the house, I feel his scrutinizing gaze on me. I know it's wrong of me to avoid him because of my own inability to repress my feelings, but it's hard to remember that when I'm falling apart.

Luckily, I've had a lot of practice burying my emotions.

I take another second to fully compose myself before I turn and smile at him. The last thing I want is for him to think he did something wrong.

"Thank you, for last night," I say, my voice full of sincerity. "I'm extremely grateful to have you in my life."

I look away as my cheeks flush with the admission, but I need him to know the truth of that statement.

"I'm grateful to be part of it," he responds, and my eyes flick to his, looking for any sign of the joke I'm sure is there, but I find nothing but sincerity in return.

He smiles at my dumb-founded expression. "I'll put the coffee on. See you back down here in fifteen?"

"Sounds good," I say, stepping through the door that Adam's holding open for me. He heads toward the kitchen as I head toward the stairs, but I stop to look back at him one last time, and watch until he's out of sight before bounding up to the guest room.

After locking the door, I flop face-down onto the bed and groan into the pillow. If Adam didn't know me as well as he does, I'd worry he thinks I'm psychotic after that rollercoaster display of emotions. But can you blame me?

I just woke up in Adam Dey's arms. There's no way this is real life.

My body melded into his so naturally, as if we'd been made to fuse together in that way. I don't even care that I slept on a wooden dock. I'd sleep there every night if it meant getting to wake up with him.

But Adam has never made a move, or indicated he wants anything past a friendship with me—no matter how flirty and playful that friendship gets at times. I just can't stop my thoughts from crossing that line. I know one day, when my heart inevitably shatters, this will only make it worse, but I will never regret it.

Last night was perfect, even if it wasn't real.

After freshening up and changing into the outfit I picked out last night, I start to braid my hair, as I often do for comfort. Even though she no longer stands behind me as her deft fingers work through my thick hair, seeing my hair braided brings me joy because my mom taught me how to do it. I don't need a mirror anymore, but I still like to make sure I'm not causing any weird bumps of hair to stick out. When my eyes land on my reflection, I flinch, dropping my hands from my hair to the edge of the countertop to support myself because my legs no longer are.

Just like that, all the forgotten pain from last night comes flooding back.

Because staring back at me is my mother. I see her eyes—my eyes—and for a moment I forget I'll never look into them again. For a moment, I don't see the dark brown of my hair that distinguishes me from the blonde hers was before it fell out from the chemo. I don't notice that the face in the reflection can't even begin to compare to my mom's beauty. I just see big hazel eyes and a thin oval face.

For a moment, I have all I need again, until the moment is over and I feel like I've lost it once more.

When I calm down, I have to restart, but I finish the Dutch braid running down the center of my head. It falls to my shoulder blades, and I pull out a few of my curtain bangs to frame my face. With the lake activities, there's no use doing more, because the water will ruin any further work I put into it.

After one last steadying breath, I head back downstairs to the kitchen where the smell of freshly brewed coffee is already swirling through the air.

"Smells good," I say, taking a seat at the island across from where Adam is grabbing mugs from the cabinet.

He changed into dark blue swim trunks and a white T-shirt, the latter of which is straining against his back muscles and revealing a strip of skin at his waist as he reaches for the mugs on the top shelf. My eyes greedily take in every detail his shirt gives away, roaming from his rippling arms and back muscles that have grown the past two years, and slowly lowering to the strip of skin just above the waistband of his swim trunks. It's not that I haven't seen him without a shirt on—the lake supplies many opportunities for that—it's that no matter how many times I see him, I still get butterflies. I don't think I'll ever tire of the fluttering feeling in my chest when I catch any glimpse of him.

I'm so enamored with the tease of skin at his waist, wondering what it'd feel like to run my hands across his body, that I don't notice his head turn back to look at me. The raise of his eyebrows and smirk on his lips is enough to let me know I've been caught.

Suddenly, everything else in the kitchen is more interesting than him, but I'm turning redder and redder every time I think about what just happened. I risk a glimpse back at him to find his body shaking with silent laughter.

"I guess all that time you spend at the gym isn't completely useless," I mutter, trying to diffuse some of my embarrassment.

"Mission accomplished." He shoots me a teasing grin. "I can stop going now that you've acknowledged me. That's all I've been doing it for, after all."

I glare at him for the sarcastic remark, wishing I'd never said anything, and he chuckles as he pulls a milk carton out of the fridge.

"I—" I start to say when Adam goes to pour the coffee. I'm picky about my coffee and try to tell him that, but he cuts me off.

"I know, one-fourth almond milk to three-fourths coffee and a small spoon's worth of sugar," he lists off casually.

I freeze, my eyes narrow and I scrutinize every detail on his face. "How do you know that?"

"When are you going to stop being surprised that I know you?" he teases, but his voice is tight.

"I've never told you how I like my coffee," I continue as if he hadn't asked me that.

It's not that I don't think he knows me, it's just that my coffee preferences vary greatly, depending on where it's from. Even if I had told him how I liked my coffee from his parents' house, it would've been at least a year ago, and I don't think I ever did.

"You don't have to tell me something in order for me to know it." He shrugs but won't meet my eyes anymore. "I notice things."

My eyes narrow further in suspicion and disbelief.

He noticed this about me and thought it was important enough to remember. Why?

I'm still studying him when his eyes flick to mine, only for his cheeks to turn red and him to look away again. Is he *blushing*?

He sets a mug in front of me and goes to finish pouring his own cup. I sip my coffee—perfectly made—and force myself to stop making something out of this. He could just be a lot more observant than I realized. He could notice these things about other people too.

This doesn't make me special. This doesn't mean anything.

"Good morning." Claire yawns, looking surprised to find us already awake when she turns the corner into the kitchen. "You're up early."

"Just excited for today," Adam says coolly, no hint of his earlier embarrassment remaining. "Want some coffee?"

"That'd be great, thanks."

Adam reaches to grab another mug from the cabinet, and I sneakily steal another glimpse at him as he does. This whole "feelings" issue could be resolved much easier if I wasn't also so physically attracted to him, but anytime we're in the same space I'm acutely aware of everything he does. I'm drawn to him in ways I don't even understand. It's like we're connected by a rubber band—the further apart we get, the stronger the pull back to each other is.

He's about to pour coffee into Claire's mug but hesitates. His eyes flash to me and there's a timid expression on his face that I don't understand.

He lets out a long breath and turns to his mom. "How do you like your coffee?"

I don't hear her response. I don't hear anything after that. The realization of what he just admitted swirls around me— through me—until that's the only thing that exists in the world. His hesitation earlier makes sense now. He just told me he knows how I like my coffee because he notices things, then not five minutes later he admits that he doesn't even know how his mom likes her coffee, which can only mean one thing.

He doesn't just notice things—he notices things about *me*.

I don't believe it, but he won't look at me now and his cheeks are many shades darker than they were moments before. Hurriedly, he hands his mom the mug and excuses himself to go set up for the party. Claire is still half-asleep and doesn't notice his strange behavior, while I excuse myself a second later before the coffee kicks in and she starts asking questions I don't have answers to. I leave my half-full mug next to Adam's and head outside to find him.

He's unlocking the shed door that holds the tables and chairs that need to be set up. I approach loud enough that I'm sure he can hear me coming, but he doesn't turn around. He's fumbling with the lock, trying to force it open, and cursing under his breath when it doesn't.

"So, you notice things?" I push. I should let it be, take my moment of believing he sees me as something more and leave it at that, but I can't. I'm driven by the part of me that needs to know what this means—the part of me that won't stop hoping.

He presses his forehead into the door of the shed. "Rylie." His tone is desperate, a plea for me to not ask him this.

But I don't have control anymore and I can't stop. "You knew how I liked my coffee, but my order changes depending on where I am. So, you not only knew that I like my coffee that way, but that I like it that way *only* at your parents' house." The more I speak the less believable it is. "How?"

He doesn't move but his breathing turns ragged.

"Adam," I whisper in desperation. I need to hear it from his lips.

"Dammit, Rylie." His name seems to be what snaps his control. With a deep groan he pushes off the shed door and turns toward me, stepping closer until we're almost touching, and I have to look up to see his face. He looks me right in the eyes.

"I know because I know your order everywhere, okay?" His voice is soft, like a caress sweeping across my face. I want to believe him, but it's hard. He might think he knows my order everywhere but there's no way he would—could—know them all. I don't know if I could even list them all on the spot.

He must see the skepticism on my face because he gives a frustrated groan and runs a hand through his hair. "At my parents' house it's one-fourth almond milk to three-fourths coffee and a small spoon's worth of sugar. At your apartment you do two shots of espresso with your Nespresso and add Califia french vanilla almond creamer. At Starbucks you get a sugar-free vanilla latte with almond milk and let the weather decide if it's hot or iced. At The Split Bean, you'll only do mochas because you don't like the vanilla syrup they have. If you buy packaged coffee from a grocery store you like the Califia mocha with almond milk best because you can't find an almond milk version of the packaged, Starbucks, skinny vanilla latte. And if you're trying somewhere new you always do a hot vanilla latte with almond milk and if you don't like it, you never go back."

My mouth is hanging open in pure shock. I don't know what to say, but he's not finished yet.

He takes a deep breath and continues, "Let's see, in December you only drink peppermint mochas when you're out because they taste like the holidays, and in February you must have a rose latte at least once. Even though you love them you'll only have one a year because you claim having them year-round will ruin them and your favorite is from that café next to the flower shop near campus. You love the irony of that, too. And last but not least, anytime you go to the coffee shop here in Lockney, you'll only get the lavender latte because it was your mom's favorite." He closes his eyes and takes a stuttering breath. "Do you believe me now?"

I'm speechless. My mouth moves but no words come out. Adam turns away, obviously uncomfortable with all I forced him to admit, but I reach out and grab his hand before he walks away.

"Why?" The word comes out as a breathy whisper and it's all I can manage to say right now. Why do you know this? Why do you care? I don't understand.

He doesn't turn to face me and when he finally speaks it's so soft I have to strain to hear him. "Because I can't help but notice you."

With that, he pulls his hand out of mine and steps back to the shed. I try to say something, anything, but my shock has stolen my ability to speak. He finally gets the door unlocked, grabs the first table he can find and heads to the far side of the yard, all before I've managed to move in the slightest.

I want to run over to him now, tell him I notice him too, but Phil joins us outside and the moment is gone. My mind doesn't stop racing while we set up the tables and chairs.

He notices me. Adam pays attention to *me*. I never would've believed it, but he proved it beyond a shadow of a doubt, and I just stood there like an idiot. I pushed him to admit something deeper than we ever have before, yet I didn't give him any sort of admission in return. He doesn't look at me once while we set up. I messed up, big time.

While Claire and Phil place the finishing touches outside, I head inside in search of Adam. I need to fix this, and soon. I don't want to leave him thinking I don't feel the same way, and I know I'll never make it through this evening without him.

In the back of my mind, I question if he could possibly be paying attention to me for the same reasons I pay attention to him. One half of me is saying *he wouldn't pay attention like that unless he had feelings for you* and the other half is saying *don't get your hopes up because you've only ever gotten hurt.*

Even if he doesn't think of me as more, he's my friend and I don't want him thinking that I don't care about him in the same way, when I do—and so much more.

I find Adam in the kitchen setting out snacks. His eyes flick up to me and then quickly away, the only acknowledgement that he sees me there. Nervous, I take a deep breath and walk right up to him, throwing my arms around his waist. His body tenses as I bury my face into his chest.

I had planned to say something first, but I've always been better at conveying my emotions physically than verbally.

"I can't help but notice you either," I whisper into his chest.

After a moment, his body relaxes and his arms wrap around me, holding me tight to him. We stay that way, his arms holding me, and my face buried in his chest, breathing in his calming scent until the doorbell rings, signaling the first guest and the start of the party.

chapter four

THIS IS HARDER than I expected.

After a few hours of smiling through conversations full of condolences and pity, I find myself standing near the dock, looking up at the circle of chairs on the patio where my mom loved to spend her day. Her usual group of mom friends are all there, chatting and gossiping as they always do. Everything is very much the same and I can almost forget she's not there with them.

Almost.

It's hard to see firsthand how fast the universe fills the gaps that a lost life leaves behind.

So why won't the gaps in me fill?

An arm slips across my shoulders and I look over to find Adam smiling knowingly at me. I lean into the comfort of him. We haven't talked much since this morning, but he shows up exactly when I need him, as if he knows when my heart is hurting and it's his job to heal it.

"I'd bet anything that she's here right now, enjoying the party like she always did," he says, strong and sure with a comforting air to the words.

A sad smile crosses my face. "I hope so."

"I know so." He squeezes my arm then turns to face me, his smile shifting into excitement. "Now, come on, we're up next for tubing."

Before I can say anything, he grabs my hand and pulls me toward the boat. Twenty minutes later, just as the sun is beginning to set, we're back on the dock. Adam is still mostly dry, but I'm soaking wet.

"This is one hundred percent your fault." I glare at him as we walk up the dock, back to the yard.

"How is it my fault?" He puts his hands on his chest, feigning innocence. "*You* lost your grip and fell off."

"You mean *you* lost your grip and used *me* as a handle," I counter, my voice rising with each word, "which ripped me off the tube."

"I guess I thought you were stronger than that." He shrugs and his smile is devious.

"Jerk," I grumble, moving in closer to playfully hit him in the stomach. At least that's the excuse, mostly I just want to be closer to him, and I've been dying to find an opportunity to touch his bare chest since he took his shirt off. It's such a stupid desire, but it feels like a primal instinct that I can't ignore.

He grabs my wrist, holding my hand against his stomach and I don't try to pull it away. I'm focused on the warmth of his skin beneath my hand and the way I can feel his every breath, that I don't notice the sneak attack he has planned.

His other hand is reaching around to my side, and when I finally notice, I try to pull away, but he has me shackled in place. That devilish smirk is back, and I shriek when his hand hits the bare skin on my side. A few partygoers look our way because of the noise. I'm sure I look like a convulsing fish out of water as I try to pull away but I'm stuck in the danger zone.

"Adam!" I shriek again when his assault doesn't stop.

He stops tickling me but uses the hand around my wrist to

spin me around, so my back is to his chest. "Oh no you don't," he whispers against my ear, and I shiver as his breath runs across my skin. He takes advantage of my stunned state, wrapping his arms around my waist and lifting me up.

"Adam!" My hands flail around, searching for something to hold onto as he starts to walk. "Adam, put me down!"

The commotion we're causing draws a lot of raised eyebrows. I hope they can't see how red I'm turning—more so from his hands on me than the embarrassment. He turns and starts walking back towards the dock and I realize his plan immediately. The only thing I can do to stop it is lock my arms together behind his back.

If I'm going in, he's coming with me.

"Don't. You. Dare," I threaten—breathless and overwhelmed by the whole situation. I'd never show how much I was enjoying this, but being in bathing suits leaves plenty of room for skin-to-skin contact, and I'm soaking in every second of it.

"*This* time it will be my fault," he says, putting me down on the dock—so close to the edge that I'd fall in if he wasn't holding onto me so tight. His lips are back at my ear, whispering, "But I'll let you go on one condition."

I shiver again and feel a smile stretch across his face. I try to keep my voice steady but it's still shaky as I ask, "Which is?"

"Watch the fireworks with me."

My head whips around to look at him. That is not what I was expecting. I consider giving a playful remark but the heated look in his eyes sets me ablaze. I'm an inferno under his gaze, under his touch, and all I can say is, "I wouldn't miss it."

His responding smile is brilliant, and my chest constricts until I can't breathe. I will do anything for that smile.

He steps back so I'm on solid ground and slowly releases me from his hold. With his hands off me, I regain some composure. I'm glad he brought me out here and asked me that, but I'm not going to let him get away with the stunt that easily.

He moves to stand beside me, and it only takes a couple seconds for him to drop his guard. I move my arm as if I'm going to wrap it around his waist but instead, I shove him forward. The shock of the blow is enough for him to lose his balance and go tumbling head-first into the lake.

I'm doubled over laughing before he even hits the water. The surprised look on his face as he falls is priceless.

He glares at me the second he surfaces, and it only makes me laugh harder. I have to put down a hand to steady myself as tears start to well in my eyes from laughing so hard. Sucking in deep breaths, I start to calm down but Adam is still glaring at me, unmoving in the water.

Before he can say anything, I turn to walk away and call over my shoulder, "I'm going to change before the fireworks, find me before they start!"

He calls out, "Rylie!" but I don't look back, and I laugh the entire time back to the room.

After a quick rinse to get the lake water off me, I slip on my sundress and brush out my hair, leaving it down this time. I haven't stopped smiling since walking away from the dock—remembering Adam's bright smiles, his light laughter, and the burning feel of his skin on mine. That heat is still coursing through me.

I'm aware that I'm smiling like an idiot, but I can't help it. I'm drunk on Adam's touch, addicted to his attention and I don't ever want to give him up. We're in our own little bubble this weekend, ignoring the actualities of reality, and it's perfectly fine by me.

There's only an hour until the fireworks, so it's time to rejoin the party. With a deep breath, I descend the stairs, my eyes searching the crowds for Adam, but not finding him anywhere. My smile falters, maybe he changed his mind.

I shake my head, he's the one that asked me to watch the fireworks with him. He'll find me. At least, that's what I keep telling myself, but as I get swept away in the crowd and the minutes pass in conversation, I start to doubt myself.

Lester, the elderly man who lives down the block, has been talking my ear off for almost half an hour now. He's a sweetheart but has always tended to talk and talk and talk. Discreetly, I start looking around the room for an out when I spot *him*, sipping a drink by the door, chuckling. His eyes are already on me.

He's in blue shorts, a white tee, and a red and blue plaid overshirt. His hair is freshly cleaned and pushed back out of his face. He's easily the most handsome guy here.

There's an instant relief that comes with seeing that familiar smile. He inclines his head toward the door, inviting me to join him and I nod, my smile growing.

"I'm so sorry," I excuse myself from the conversation as politely as possible, "but my friend needs me. It was nice talking to you."

"It was great to see you again, Rylie," he says, looking over at who snagged my attention and smirks at who he finds. "Don't have too much fun now," he adds with a wink.

I cough out a laugh at the insinuation he makes. "Oh no." I wave my arms around in nervous defense. "It's not like that."

He gives me a pointed look as I shuffle away to find Adam with my head down to hide my beet red cheeks.

Why would he think that?

I'm so caught up in wondering why Lester, of all people, would think Adam and I were something other than friends, that I almost miss Claire trying to get my attention.

"You've outdone yourself yet again," I say as she pulls me into a hug. "Everyone's having a great time."

"Oh, enough of that." She moves her hands like she's swatting the words out of the air. "I have an important question for you."

My eyebrows raise in curiosity.

She lowers her voice. "Did you actually push Adam into the lake?"

I bark out a laugh. "You moms sure do love your gossip."

"So, it's true?"

I laugh again and nod.

"I'm sure he deserved it." She winks at me.

Claire is always on my side. It's one of the reasons the boys have taken to calling me her favorite. I'm the daughter she never had.

"Oh, he definitely did," I assure her.

"I most definitely did not," Adam counters, stepping up behind me.

I'd almost forgotten where I'd been headed—*almost*—but I could never forget about him.

From the first time we had a true conversation in the playroom upstairs, seven years ago, I've been too aware of him. Too interested in what he's doing and how I can get closer to him. Since the first moment I saw him, I haven't been able to look away. He captivated me so completely. I never had a chance.

"Rylie," Adam says, pulling me out of my reverie. "You ready?"

I finally turn and look at him, he has something hanging over his arm. Is that a jacket? A towel? I can't tell. I smile up at him. "Yeah, let's go."

Phil walks up, excitement radiating off him. "Fireworks start in fifteen!"

He personally sets up the fireworks each year and takes pride in making them as extravagant as possible. Since he learned how much I love them, he always makes sure I get first pick of viewing spots by letting me know when they're about to start, before he announces it to the rest of the party.

"We're heading out now," Adam replies, raising his arm to show off the object I can now identify as a blanket. He nods to the back door and we quietly fall in-step as we navigate through the crowd. He heads towards a path in the trees that leads to a private little beach. It's one of my favorite spots to watch the fireworks from.

I'm still caught up in memories—in him—and forget to say anything. As we lose sight of the yard behind us, he finally speaks. "What were you thinking about back there?"

"You noticed that, huh?" I smile at the thought.

"Of course," he whispers, and there's a flutter in my chest.

"I was thinking of that summer when we both got sick and were stuck in the house." I laugh thinking about it again. "For our first real time spent together, it didn't go that well."

He laughs, obviously remembering it too. "How could I forget? I thought it'd be the ruin of my summer, trapped inside with my little brother's best friend." He shakes his head in disgust, and I swat him in the chest.

"You're being dramatic, it wasn't that bad," I say between laughs, bumping into him as we walk. "You were just in your *'too cool for us'* stage."

"And what a time that was," he reminisces with a sly smile on his face.

I bump into him again. "I still can't believe you put on super-hero movies in the playroom because you thought it'd make me leave."

"Give me a break, we were in middle school," he defends and bumps into me. "I really thought it'd work though. Who would've thought a pretty girl liked superheroes?"

"Aw, you thought I was pretty." I wrap my hand around his arm and fake pout at him.

"Way to ruin a moment." He rolls his eyes and we both laugh but I don't remove my hand from his arm. His voice turns serious. "It was the day I stopped seeing you as Rylie, my little brother's friend who I was forced to put up with, and started seeing you as Rylie, a friend I wanted to get to know more . . . even if your favorite superhero is Spider-Man."

"You're one to talk, Superman lover," I tease.

"I'm serious, though." He stops at the edge of the short beach and turns toward me. "I'll forever be thankful for that day."

I'm stuck staring at the place where he was just standing as he moves to set up the blanket. My head is spinning. *What is happening?* Those words, this whole weekend, feels more serious, more real than the light-hearted banter that frequented our friendship. For the first time I allow myself to believe there might be a flicker of what I feel reflected in him.

I must be reading this wrong. He doesn't see me that way. He never has.

Has he?

"You coming?" He smiles back at me, and my breathing picks up. "The fireworks should be starting any minute now."

My legs shake as they carry me through the sand and onto the blanket beside Adam. Something has been bugging me since the moment he asked me to watch the fireworks with him and it finally hits me.

"You don't like fireworks," I say, brows furrowed in study of him.

"I *didn't* like them, past tense." He glances over at me before settling his gaze on the still water.

"What changed?"

He pauses for so long that I don't think he's going to answer at all, but then he takes a deep breath. "You," he says, and I stop breathing. I must've heard that wrong. "It was a few years after that summer we became friends. I had . . . noticed how much you loved them."

There it is again, that small word that carries such a large meaning. There's no way he's been noticing me that long though, it must be a slip of words.

"I became curious why you loved them so much," he continues. "You were always the first to grab a viewing spot, and you talked about them as if they were magic. I wanted to understand, so one year, I watched you as you watched the fireworks."

His voice is getting smaller the longer he talks, and he pauses to swallow. He hasn't looked at me once since he started but I'm gaping at him, in complete disbelief of the words I'm hearing with my own ears.

"There was pure awe and wonder in your eyes the entire time. I've never seen someone smile as big as you did—you were glowing." He smiles at the memory as my first tear drops down my face. "You were radiant. It was like they were there to light you up instead of the sky."

How did I not know he noticed me like this? How did I not see that he looked at me this way? My heart is racing so fast I think it might rip itself out of my chest.

"I've watched them every year since then. It was hard not to see the beauty in them after seeing them through your eyes." He sighs, his voice barely a whisper. "It was hard not to love something that made you that happy."

I'm speechless. There's tears streaming down my face, my heart is pounding, and I'm probably staring at him with that same look of awe and wonder. He slowly lifts his eyes to meet mine and the moment they lock, the energy changes between us. I suck in a shaky breath, trying to breathe through the overwhelming pull I feel towards him.

With that one look, I lose hold of all the feelings I've been fighting acknowledgement of. With that one look, my heart screams the truth of my feelings.

I'm completely, utterly, wholly in love with you, Adam Dey.

Although my lips never move, I'm sure this truth is shining bright in my eyes. My hands shake, the strength of this realization terrifies me as we both gravitate slowly, instinctually, towards each other. When we're only a few inches apart, his eyes ask a question I've been waiting a lifetime to hear.

My heartbeat pounds in my ears. He's so close and I want

him closer. I want what comes next, but I'm scared this will ruin everything we've built over the years. What if his feelings aren't as strong and true as mine? I can't imagine my life without him, but I want to be with him in a way that goes deeper than what we've been. My mind is torn but my heart is sure.

It might be the wrong decision, but I shut off my brain and listen to my heart.

My eyes never leave his as I nod, hoping he understands that my answer has always been *"yes"* for him. With a nervous smile his hand lifts to brush a trail of heat across my cheek and down to my neck where it rests. He's shaking as much as I am. The gap between us closes in slow motion—the heat from his touch spreading through my whole body.

The moment our lips meet is like a private firework show just for me. Sparks fly, and the heat coursing through me combusts into an array of colors that make me feel more alive than I've ever been. He tastes like summertime—refreshing and bright—but there's an undertone of spice from the drink I saw in his hand earlier. It's a culmination of every memory I've shared with him, and every dream I've had of him. It only makes me desperate for more.

I throw all my pent-up emotions for him into the kiss, and he responds by deepening it. His hands run across my body, trying to find ways to pull me closer. Any space is too much right now. I want to feel every inch of him pressed against every inch of me.

It still isn't enough. I need more of him, and I need it now. I throw a leg over his waist so I'm straddling him. His body tenses in shock for a second before he adjusts, wrapping one arm around my waist and threading the other hand into my hair. He starts kissing me with a new desperation, like he's afraid this is all a dream and wants to take advantage of every second before he wakes.

My hands run up his chest, around his neck, and into his hair.

A thrill runs through me as I finally run my fingers through his slightly damp hair—still drying from his shower earlier. It's smoother than I expected because there's no product styling it back. I prefer it this way.

I've wanted to do this for years.

I'm so lost in the moment—lost in him—that I couldn't tell you how much time has passed. And as his lips move along my jaw and down my neck, I even forget where we are. Tightening my grip in his hair, my head drops back, eyes-closing, allowing him better access to explore my neck and collar bone with his mouth. A sigh leaves my lips, loud enough for him to hear, and he chuckles against my neck. I suck in a breath and shiver at the sensual feel of his laugh skating across my skin.

Adam's taste is in my mouth, his lips are on my skin, and his hands are all over my body. For the second time today I think, *how is this real life?* I keep expecting to wake up in the guest room disappointed, again, that it's only a dream.

As if the universe is reading my thoughts, it gives me a sign that this is real. The first fireworks go off and I jump in surprise. I forgot we were out here waiting for those. But for the first time, my attention feels better spent elsewhere, although I can't help opening my eyes and smiling at the color-filled sky.

I must've been entranced for longer than I thought, because by the time I refocus on Adam, my hands have slid down to rest on his chest and he's silently watching me.

But the way he's looking at me makes me feel like I've never truly been seen before.

His face lights up into the brightest smile I've ever seen, and I wonder why I thought the fireworks were worth my time at all. No firework could shine brighter than he is—could captivate me the way he does.

"You are radiant, Rylie," he whispers, and my stomach clenches at the way he says my name. It's more intimate than any caress. I surge forward, locking my lips to his and wishing I could throw away the key. I want to live in this moment—bathe in this feeling—forever.

Our kisses grow frenzied but it's still not enough, we're both clawing for more. I push his flannel off his shoulders roughly, needing to feel closer to him, to touch more of him. He helps me remove it and lifts his arms without a word when I move to his T-shirt.

I trace every inch of skin on his upper body, wanting to memorize every muscle on him. He was built to be a god, one that I'd gladly worship day and night. Was it only this morning I was wishing I could run my hands over his back and chest in the kitchen? This moment is worth the wait.

"I wasn't kidding when I said the gym is paying off," I whisper, breathlessly. "You look incredible."

"I wasn't kidding either," he says, and I tilt my head in confusion. "Part of the reason I started working out was to get you to notice me."

I gulp and stare at him in wonder. He did that for me?

As sweet as it is, I want to make sure he knows how I feel so I say, "I've always noticed you, Adam. Even before all of this." I run my hands all over his abdomen as I say it, and he chuckles. The movement causes friction between us that sucks all the humor out of the moment and shuts us both up.

The straps of my dress drop down my arms with a gentle sweep of his hands across my collar bone, leaving a clear path for his lips to travel. He claims every inch of bare skin on my chest with his lips as his hands slide up my thighs and under my dress. He's dangerously close to starting something that we won't be able to stop. Something I don't want to stop.

I want to get lost in him—lose touch with reality and all the problems that are waiting for me there.

He pauses, thumbs drawing circles on my inner thighs, and

pulls back to look at me. I start to complain but the look on his face stops me. He's asking for permission. As a response, I run my hands down his chest to his shorts and start to unbutton them.

His hands begin to move again, finally getting closer to where I need them to be, until a twig snaps down the path and we both freeze, eyes going wide with horror. Someone is nearly down the path to the beach we're now half-naked on. There isn't enough time to redress or even look halfway presentable, so I shift off him and we wrap the blanket around us, hiding the evidence of his bare upper body and my partly removed dress.

A couple, obviously more than a few drinks in, appear on the edge of the beach, and judging by the look in their eyes, they were hoping to use it for the same thing we were. Adam clears his throat when they start kissing, not having looked our way once.

The woman jumps back and raises a hand to her chest in surprise. "Oh, I didn't see you there," she exclaims. "I'm so sorry."

The man's eyes haven't left her, and he grabs her hand to stop her babbling. "We'll find somewhere else to go."

The woman smiles nervously at us before leading the man away, going who knows where.

I hope I don't find out.

Adam and I both laugh in relief once they've disappeared from sight. He smiles at me, and it's the emotions I see in his eyes that make me falter. My stomach drops and I don't know why but I'm suddenly second-guessing what happened between us.

His face twists into a look of concern. "What's wrong?"

"I—" I bite my lip, unsure where this feeling is coming from. I don't want to hurt him, but we need to talk honestly about this. "I'm not sure we should've done that."

"Oh." His face falls and I can tell that's not what he was expecting, or hoping, I'd say. "Do you . . . regret—"

"No," I cut him off, and place a hand on his cheek. "Absolutely not. I just . . ." I look down, conflicted. I don't understand this hesitation, this tightness in my chest, as if I was about to do something wrong.

Kissing Adam is the only thing that has felt right in a long time. So why do I feel guilty about it now?

"Hey," he says, gently lifting my chin until I'm looking at him again to find there's only care and concern for me shining back. "You don't have to hide any part of yourself around me."

My lips shake as I try to smile at his words—words that I know are true to the depths of my heart. Words that send warmth shooting through my veins.

"Would it be horrible of me to ask for the night to figure this out?"

His face softens and he moves to wipe the tears that have started falling down my cheeks. "Not at all."

"It is." I breathe. "But thank you for saying it's not."

"Now, come on." He smiles and places the straps of my dress back on my shoulders, adjusting them until it appears they were never moved in the first place. "Let's watch the rest of these fireworks."

The knots in my chest loosen.

He still wants to be around me.

"You know," I say, blushing when he moves to put his own shirt back on, "you could keep that off. Only if you want of course. Just don't feel like you have to put it back on for me. I think we pretty clearly established that I enjoy the view."

He chuckles, shaking his head, but just raises his arm and says, "Come here."

I beam and scoot closer to lean into him, wrapping an arm around him as his drops on my shoulder. I watch the rest of the fireworks with my head on his shoulder and his arm around me, holding me close. There's no sign that my confusion about our kiss has affected him, but I doubt he'd let me see if it did. I need to figure out what's going on with me, because this is—*he* is—what I've always wanted.

Now that it seems to be within my reach, why won't I let myself have it?

chapter five

I SPEND all night and the next morning running analysis after analysis in my head, hoping to find a path that leads to a different outcome, but they all end in the same conclusion. And it's not the one I want it to be.

By the time I get in the car with Adam to head back to Kasper, I'm apprehensive about how this conversation is going to go. Adam is understanding, but there's no way he'll be *this* understanding.

I haven't started talking yet and I'm already afraid of his reaction.

I hold onto the silence a while longer, since once I speak the potential of being something more will end before it's even begun. Adam breaks the tension first.

"So . . ." He trails off, the rest of his question clear even without voicing it: *Are you ready to talk?*

"So . . ." I sigh, pulling my feet onto the seat and resting my cheek against my knees so I'm looking over at him. "Were you serious yesterday when you said you started going to the gym because of me?"

He barks out a laugh and glances over at me with brows raised. "*That's* where you want to start this conversation?"

"It's just something I've been curious about since last night." I grin, cheeks flushing. It's easier to admit these things since last night, but it's not any less embarrassing to admit.

"Honestly, yes, you were part of what inspired me to finally go. This is so embarrassing," he groans, exasperated, and glares at me, "but I saw how your eyes clung to Zac Efron in *Baywatch* and I wanted you to look at me the same way."

I press my lips together, trying to hold back my laugh, but it sputters out anyway. "Adam—"

"Please, don't." He cuts me off, shaking his head, but he's laughing too—like he can't believe he actually told me that. When he stops laughing, he adds, "But I grew to really enjoy it, so I kept going for myself."

"For yourself," I echo, my smile falling away. His words remind me of the conclusion I'd come to. His light smile flattens into a stoic line, and I look out at the road in front of us as our surroundings slowly transition from congested cityscapes to wooded mountains. "I haven't done anything for myself in a long time."

"Ry—"

"Except for kissing you," I continue, and his words die in his throat. "That was just for me. Or, at least, I thought it was."

Adam's face twists in confusion, so I take a deep breath and begin. "You're the only person I've ever talked to, in-depth, about the impact my mom's sickness had on me. Did you know that? I'm sure Caleb and your parents could see some of my pain and guessed at its depth, but I've never been able to talk to them the way I've always been able to talk to you. I feel comfortable around you in a way I've never felt around anyone before. I feel safe with you."

"But . . ." Adam adds for me, and I bite my lip.

"But . . ." I breathe. "There was a moment when we were

kissing yesterday, when I thought about how good it would feel to get lost in you and forget all of my troubles. And it would've been." I look over at him and place a hand on his forearm. "I don't want you to misunderstand, so please believe me when I say, I *wanted* to kiss you, I wanted everything that happened last night. I still want it. But if we had kept going, then I would allow myself to get lost in you. I'd allow myself to bathe in the happiness I felt being around you—being with you—and I wouldn't actually deal with my grief—my pain. It would always be there, inside me, waiting for my guard to drop and I'd always be anxious that it was going to hit me harder than before."

Pain twists on his face and I start speaking again before he hurts too much.

"One day, I want to be more than just your friend. One day, I want to kiss you again. But I want to know that I'm only doing it for the right reasons, and no part of me—no matter how small— is trying to escape my pain. And assuming we'll only get one chance, as most do, I don't want to waste ours when I'm not emotionally stable enough to do it right. You deserve more than that. *We* deserve more than that."

He's silent for a while, but then lets out a breath that sounds a lot like relief. "So, your hesitancy . . . it wasn't because you didn't want to be with me."

"Oh god, no." My eyes widen in horror at the thought of him believing I didn't want him. That I regretted kissing him. "In the name of honesty, I'll admit that I've wanted to be with you for years now, Adam. I've wanted to explore these feelings for a long time, it just never felt like the right time."

"Rylie, I understand," he says with so much care in his voice a tear forms in my eye. "You don't have to justify your decisions to me."

"Your family is all I have," I explain, even though he told me I don't need to. He deserves to know my whole truth. "I'm still not comfortable in this new life without her, it feels too soon to risk the only normalcy I have left. Especially when I can't give you what you deserve—my all."

I think about how Claire hugged me when I left and whispered, *"Don't be a stranger. You're family,"* and my heart constricts. As much as I want to be part of their family, I don't feel like I deserve a place there. They've spent so much time and money helping us, and taking care of me over the years—how could I be anything other than a burden? But without any remaining family of my own, I want to be part of theirs so badly it hurts. I don't want to do anything that could ruin my relationship with them.

"Rylie, I've known you for what, ten years now? I know what you've gone through, and I've seen how it affected you. Why do you think I haven't tried to kiss you sooner?"

"Because I thought you didn't see me that way," I mumble, and his chuckle has butterflies forming in my stomach again.

"Of course, I see you that way, how could I not? In a perfect world, I would've kissed you years ago, but I didn't want to complicate your life more. All I want is to see you happy, and if that means waiting a little longer to kiss you again, I'll gladly do it."

I stare at him in awe, silent tears streaming down my face. What did I do to deserve someone who's willing to put my well-being above their own wants? The doubt creeps in and the words come out in a breath before I realize what I'm saying, "I don't deserve you."

"Don't you ever say that." The force in his voice takes me by surprise and I stop moving. "You deserve to be put first. Your mental health is too important, *you're* too important to be anything but a priority—to anyone." He gives me a pointed glance. "Including yourself."

I shrink into myself a little bit, knowing he's right. I don't put myself first, especially not when it comes to my mental health. My mom used to do her best to make sure I wasn't overwhelmed, but even then, I couldn't stop the constant stress. Since she passed, I've been trying to spoon out water when buckets of it were constantly flowing in. I'm drowning and I have been for months.

"I want to be better," I say with shaking lips. "I want to get better. For you, for . . . *us*." I smile a little at the word but then say the most important words of all. "And for myself."

"That sounds like a good start," he says, reaching for my hand and lacing our fingers together. "If you need anything, I'll always be there."

"Well, now that you have an ulterior motive," I tease, "how can I trust you'll help me actually heal, and not just rush it so you can kiss me again?"

He laughs and runs his thumb across the back of my hand. My breath stutters on the way out.

"Believe me when I say I care about you truly healing more than anyone. Maybe even more than you do. But . . ." His voice drops and I find myself leaning into him in anticipation of what he might say. "Don't, for one second, think I won't be dreaming about kissing you every moment we're together."

I stop breathing, eyes going wide, and I stare at him in shock. My hands start to shake, not in fear or anxiety, but with want. They shake from the power required to *not* kiss him again right now, because every word he's spoken since we got in this car has only made my heart swell with love for him. I know how great he is, but somehow, he still surpasses my expectations.

"But," he adds, "I don't think the world's ready for an Adam/Rylie combo. Not yet, at least."

"No? Why's that?"

"When we're together," he says, confidently, "we'll be a lot to handle."

When, not *if*.

I think I know what he means. I mean, I already feel like I'll need to tie my hands down to stop myself from reaching out to touch him, to kiss him. I don't know how I'd do anything but that if he was mine. Is he really thinking the same about me?

"That does sound like us." Is all I end up saying, a smile on my face. But the thought brings up another worry I hadn't considered much before, because I never truly believed he could feel anything for me. "So . . . what do you think the chances are of Caleb and your parents being cool about us? Whenever it happens."

"I'd put it at a conservative seventy percent chance everything will be good." He smiles, but it's the exact wrong thing to say. My heart sinks into my stomach and I bite my lip to try to keep it from shaking. He glances over and his smile fades. "I know I'm not as good at math as you, but I thought seventy percent was pretty good odds."

"Yeah, it's just . . . that's the odds they gave my mom when she went into remission the first time. *'Seventy percent of people don't have a recurrence when it's caught this early.'*" I quote the words the doctor spoke that day. The words that pushed my mom to book the Hawaii trip to celebrate. Everyone at the hospital smiled at us a lot that day. They didn't the next time we were there, less than a year later. "The logical, math part of my brain knows that the odds are in our favor. But from experience, thirty percent feels like a lot to overcome."

"I'm so sorry, Rylie," he breathes and it's devastation I hear behind the words. "I didn't know."

"It's okay, how could you?" I squeeze his hand, but the tears are flowing again. I have to focus on my breathing, or I'll have another panic attack.

I never told anyone that detail before, or that sometimes in math class I had to pinch my leg over and over, so I didn't break down because seventy percent was the answer to a problem. It was most common in my probability course last semester. What shit timing that was. It got so bad that I couldn't wear shorts because there was a constant bruise on my outer thigh. At least I had a valid excuse to hole up in my room all day every day, and could easily avoid any situation I would've had to wear them in.

He gently kisses my hand and then starts talking, as if he knows I need a distraction from my own thoughts, and tells me stories about some of his friends in his business classes. He tells me I'd like them—they're funny but don't hesitate to call him out on his shit. I smile and say he needs more people in his life that do that. That earns me a sarcastic "ha ha," but then he smiles a big, relieved smile and I know he's just happy I'm not about to fall apart again.

He's so good at helping me through my darkest moments. His warm words and bright smile cut right through the thoughts that cling to me until I'm not sure what's real and what's fueled by my fears. Admittedly, I don't know much about how to heal or else I would be much further along than I am now, which is still at the starting line. But it seems like eventually, I'll need to figure out how to help myself through the darkness.

If I can't help myself, then how can I be sure I won't use him as a crutch whenever I have a problem?

The rest of the ride is quiet, other than the music in the background, but Adam doesn't let go of my hand until we're pulling up to the bright yellow building where my apartment is. It's one of the only places in town that's missing that mountain charm, but that's probably why it was cheap enough for us to rent. Adam lives in a slightly nicer complex about ten minutes away, but he has three roommates who he doesn't see eye-to-eye with. That's why he tends to hang out at our place a lot, although after our conversation I'm wondering if there were other reasons for his visits. I smile, thinking that he might've been coming over for me this whole time.

After setting my bags on the sidewalk in front of the building, Adam pulls me into a hug. We hold each other tighter, and longer than we would've only days ago. I thought knowing his feelings would make things easier, but being here in his arms, knowing that he wants to kiss me too—it's infinitely harder to not kiss him. I press my fingers harder against his back to make sure they don't wander somewhere that'll get me in trouble . . . like into his hair. *God*, what I wouldn't give to run my fingers through his hair again. I press even harder and feel him chuckle as he tightens his arms around me.

When he eventually pulls away, I consider tugging him back against me, but I don't think I'll let him go if I do that. And staying around him, thinking about kissing him, isn't the way to deal with my real problems. And I need to deal with them so I can kiss him again. I repeat this in my head over and over. It's the only reason I let him take a step away.

"See you soon?" he asks with a sly smile that sends my heart into overdrive.

"Absolutely." I grin like an idiot despite myself.

He drives away and I already can't wait to see him again. I already can't wait to *kiss* him again.

But my brain yells, *Heal, heal, heal. You have to heal first.*

I take a deep breath and head inside to try to figure out how to do that.

chapter six

"RY!" Caleb pulls me into a hug the second he gets home from work that evening. "This place was too quiet without you."

"You're the one who does the talking around here, Cale," I tease, laughing as he lets me go.

"Yeah, but I had no one to talk to," he says in a voice that implies a *"duh"* at the end of the sentence. I can't help but smile, I've missed Caleb.

"I was just about to start dinner, and you were about to shower, hopefully. You smell like salami." I scrunch my nose for effect and he rolls his eyes at me but heads off to his room.

I throw on some noodles and say a silent hallelujah when I find leftover chicken in the fridge, because I didn't feel like cooking some. Dinner will be a simple chicken alfredo pasta, it's quick, easy, and a favorite of Caleb's. Well, anything carb-loaded is a favorite of Caleb's.

Caleb rejoins me as I'm straining the pasta and immediately pulls out the bowls and glasses. I'm plating the food while he fills our glasses with Arnold Palmer. We've been friends for so long things like this are second nature, we can execute almost any task without saying a word. It's just the normalcy I need after a weekend full of unexpected twists and turns.

As if he could read my mind, the first words he says when we sit down at the small dining table are, "So, how was your weekend with *Adam*?" He even goes as far as to raise his eyebrows suggestively at me and I flush pink, immediately becoming hyper-focused on my meal, and not on the question.

"Why do you always say it like that?" I grumble, still embarrassed and he laughs.

"Because you always look guilty when I do." He's giving me a pointed stare when I look up and my face scrunches up as I try to quickly figure out how to respond. Adam and I aren't anything, and we very clearly established that we won't be anything anytime soon, so there's no need to bring on a line of unnecessary questioning.

"Just for your teasing, you only get a one sentence summary of my weekend," I say, pausing to give him time to argue, but with a look on my face that says, *Go ahead and try but you're not winning this one*. He smartly sighs in resignation and signals for me to continue. "It was nice to see your parents again, but it was weird being back in Lockney. I wouldn't have made it through the weekend without Adam, but I missed you loads."

Caleb knows Adam and I are close—he isn't blind—but I don't know how much he's guessed about my feelings for his brother, or how he feels about it. I'm scared to find out if his jokes are in support, or a defense mechanism. But mostly, I'm worried he'll be hurt that I always talked to Adam about my mom and not him. I never told him about the late-night dock conversations, and he's never hinted that he's aware of them.

I don't want to hurt him, and it's not that I don't trust him, it's just that my heart chose Adam.

It's easier to not talk to anyone else about it and I didn't want to burden Caleb more.

He takes a sip of his drink and then grins. "That's a better sentence than I expected."

I laugh and turn the questions on him as I shove more pasta into my mouth.

His update is relatively short. The deli was busy over the weekend but managed well with Caleb leading. He even managed to join some friends of his from classes last semester and set off fireworks to celebrate the holiday.

Just that one word brings up memories of Adam's touch—his kiss. The way he whispered my name, his breath on my neck, his hands slowly inching closer t—

I take a sip of my drink just to hide my face as I try to calm down before Caleb asks about the blush creeping up my neck and blooming on my cheeks. I don't have a good response to that other than the truth, and I don't want to dive into that now.

He must not notice because he gets up to clean his plate before dropping on the couch and cuing up an episode of *Below Deck* that we didn't get to last week. He only hits play once I've joined him, and we settle in to commentate on the drama-filled love triangle currently playing out on screen. My phone buzzes sometime during the show, but I don't check it until I'm in bed that night. Caleb and I always stay off our phones when we're watching new episodes of our shows together, it's tradition.

My anticipation has been growing wondering if it's *him*, and I almost let out an audible squeal when his name is the one on my screen when I finally look.

ADAM

I've almost texted you a hundred times today, but got too nervous. I don't know what the protocol is for a situation like this, but I didn't want you to go to sleep without knowing I've been thinking about you. Sweet dreams, Rylie.

My heart is racing, he's been thinking about me. Adam Dey was thinking about *me*.

Will this feeling ever get old? I hope not.

I type back:

ME

> This bed is no dock, but it'll do. I don't think there is a protocol for this, we'll just have to figure it out together. Sweet dreams, Adam.

I'm drifting off when my phone dings again and I open my eyes just enough to see:

ADAM

> Together . . . I like the sound of that.

* * *

I GROAN as my alarm goes off. Six is too early of a wake-up call on a Monday morning when you barely slept all weekend, but I have to be at work by seven. Dragging my feet, I move around my room, throwing on my uniform of blue jeans, a plain black t-shirt, and black non-slip shoes. We have to wear tan aprons too, but it's not bad for a work uniform.

I don't even bother with my hair, throwing it up into a bun and opting for a natural, makeup-free look, mostly because I'm too lazy to commit to making it look good.

The first thing I notice when I open my door is Caleb's door is already open. Why would he be awake? He doesn't ever have to work this early, and he's not a morning person. The smells and sounds hit me then—the sizzle of bacon and the meaty aroma, the scrape of a spatula against a pan, the hiss of a pancake being flipped, and the pungent smell of freshly dripped espresso.

My eyes widen as I step out of my room to find Caleb in the kitchen cooking, focused intently on the pans in front of him.

"Need any help?" I ask half-heartedly. I had planned on only grabbing a granola bar before I left.

He startles, too focused on cooking that he hadn't noticed me here. "Just sit down, I'm about to finish up."

I slowly move to the table but feel bad that he's going through all this trouble for me and I'm not helping in any way. "What are you doing up?"

"You looked exhausted last night, so I thought you could use a pick-me-up before work," he explains, bringing two plates over before doubling back to grab the coffees.

"You did all this for me?" My voice is small, choking up with emotion and my eyes glass over.

He only smiles in response and digs into his food.

"You're the best, best friend ever," I say, biting into a crispy piece of bacon and savoring the taste. I'm not one to eat a large breakfast, but this is exactly what I need to get my week off to a good start.

I take a sip of the coffee, and while good, it isn't exactly how I'd make it. There's too much creamer and it reminds me of how perfect Adam made my coffee. Our texts last night, while sweet, made it clear that neither of us is really sure how to act right now. We know how each other feels in a general sense, but we also know we can't have that right now.

So where does that leave us? Can we be just friends again?

I hope we can figure everything out, because losing him now that I've finally admitted some of how I feel isn't something I can handle.

"I know," Caleb answers. He uses this response whenever I tell him how great of a friend he is. It's grown into a joke between us, and we both laugh.

"What's your work schedule like?" Caleb asks through a mouthful of pancake.

"I open Monday through Friday this week since I was gone yesterday, but go back to my normal Sunday through Thursday schedule for the rest of summer break." I didn't mind going to work so early when it meant I got off at two o'clock. "What about you?"

"I'm supposed to just work my usual Monday through Friday, but we will see how long George's 'emergency' lasts." The deli doesn't open until lunch time, so Caleb doesn't usually get off until right before dinner.

"You still haven't heard from him?"

Caleb shakes his head.

"Good luck with that," I say, bringing my plate to the sink once I check the time. I need to get going soon if I'm going to make it on time. I wrap my arms around Caleb's shoulders when I pass by him again. "Thank you for breakfast. See you tonight."

The walk to The Split Bean is one of my favorites—taking me through the prettiest part of campus, with brick walkways surrounded by perfectly groomed grass, and trees forming a canopy above. It's best at this time, when no one else is around and I'm able to observe the world waking around me.

A gentle, warm breeze sends fallen leaves brushing across the bricks. Rays of sunlight are just beginning to break through the trees, shrouding the area in a golden haze. Birds sing their morning melodies without interruption. The world is almost always more enjoyable, more beautiful, without others around.

Half a mile later, I walk up to the white-painted brick building that is The Split Bean. Three of the four walls are almost entirely covered in glass, giving ample natural light to the shop, and a modern, chic aesthetic that is popular amongst the university students.

And as if the windows won't bring in enough light, the interior is mostly decorated in white to brighten the place. The floor is a solid, shiny, white tile that matches the smooth countertop of the employee workstation that rests against the one non-glass wall. The outfacing part of the ordering counter is comprised of white, skinny rectangular tiles in a herringbone pattern. The non-glass wall is an accent wall of light oak planks that match the tables around the shop, and the machinery is all in shades of tan or brown to match the light brown chairs.

On the back accent wall hangs the logo, which is one of those abstract drawings that's done with a continuous line in the shape of a coffee bean. It's a mocha color and really completes the overall vibe of the shop.

Then, on each table is a small white vase—we rotate what kind of flowers are in there each season. I got to choose the flower for the summer and calla lilies were my mom's favorite, so that's what I picked. I get a strange mix of happiness and pain each time I see them, but it makes me feel like she's close to me, so the pain is worth it.

"Tell me everything!" Angie squeals the moment I step into the back room to drop off my bag and grab my apron.

Angie and I happened to request the same hours this summer and have gotten close from all the time spent together. She also happened to guess my feelings for Adam almost immediately upon him stepping into the shop the first time we worked together. Angie is obsessed with the potential of us getting together. I always roll my eyes and tell her it's never going to happen . . .

Her ego might exceed the size of the shop if she learns everything that transpired this weekend.

"Hello to you, too." I laugh.

"Stop stalling!" she says, too excited about the topic already. "What happened this weekend? Did you and Adam finally get together? Or did blondie cock-block again?"

"He has a name," I scold. Blondie is Caleb, who has the same brown eyes as Adam but whose hair is a honey-brown color like Claire, instead of a mahogany-brown like Adam and Phil. Angie has a theory that Adam and I would already be together if it wasn't for Caleb but if this weekend is any indica-tion, Caleb isn't what's holding us back. I am. "And Caleb wasn't able to go."

"What?" Her eyes bug out. "It was just you and the hottie alone together? *All weekend*?"

"Angie! We were at his parents' house, not alone."

"Oh, come on. You're really telling me that *nothing* happened?" She isn't deterred by my attempt to throw her off this line of questioning.

My cheeks burn remembering all the things that did happen and I look away, hoping she won't see, but of course, she does.

"You're totally blushing!" she screams and the color in my cheeks deepens, wishing she would drop it. "Oh my gosh, something did happen, didn't it?"

My hands try to cool the heat pooled in my cheeks and I groan. "Fine, something happened but nothing has changed. We're just friends, that's it."

Her brows furrow and lips press together in confusion. She opens her mouth to, no doubt, ask more but I cut her off. "We're about to open, we need to get ready."

I could explain more, but some part of me wants to keep this knowledge all to myself. The weekend still feels like some forbidden, fantasy land, and until we figure out where we go from here, I don't want other people involved in our relationship. Everything about this is complicated enough. If I have every person in my life pushing me towards him, I know I'll run willingly into his arms. It's already hard enough to remember why I shouldn't go now. My resolve is on thin ice, but I know I need to hold on to this resolution because without it, I'll only be hurting us.

As the week slowly ticks by, Angie's constant badgering lessens as my anxiety increases, because even though he texts me daily, Adam hasn't shown up at The Split Bean. I can't recall a week this summer where he wasn't in here at least twice. Angie notices my souring mood, and on Thursday, just before we leave, she puts a hand on my arm when she finds me staring at the door with a perplexed expression because he hasn't shown up, yet again. She knows who I'm looking for—whose absence is weighing on me—without having to say a word, and I wonder when we got to be so close this summer.

"See you tomorrow," she says, giving me a smile that only friends give each other.

I don't know if I'm just overly emotional right now, or if I'm just realizing that I'm surrounded by some pretty great people, but I say, "Angie, I'm really glad we worked together this summer."

She smiles. "Me too."

On Friday, I'm walking out of the backroom with packs of cups and lids to restock when I freeze. I lose my grip just enough for everything in my hands to go tumbling to the ground, because across the counter from Angie, ordering, is Adam. His hair is a controlled mess and he's in gym clothes. I wonder if he's already been there today, or if he's going after his class later —he likes using the school gym even though he doesn't live on campus. A picture of his biceps straining as he lifts weights, face twisted in concentration, runs through my head and I'm suddenly unsteady. I stumble forward, tripping over the cups I'd dropped and just catch myself on the counter before I face-plant. I'm mortified and try to duck back into the backroom but, at the noise, he looks over and a flicker of surprise runs through his features before he can hide it.

Why is he surprised to see me? He knows I work here.

After he orders, Angie takes the bags of cups and lids and goes to make his coffee with a pointed look that means, *Go talk to him!* Without hearing his order, I know it's a caramel macchiato. I hadn't been placating him when I said I noticed him too— my eyes cling to him anywhere he goes. I notice everything when it's about him—and *damn*, do I notice how good he looks right now.

I take a deep breath and walk toward where he's still standing at the register. "Hey," I say awkwardly, hating that I feel unsure around him. I want to know why he hasn't shown up until today.

"Hey." He gives me a hesitant smile before looking down at the strap of his backpack that's being rolled and unrolled in his hands. "I didn't expect to see you here today."

And that's when it clicks, his surprise was because I don't usually work Fridays and he knows that. My back goes ramrod straight.

"Are you . . . avoiding me?" I ask in disbelief.

He cringes, realizing the slip of words that gave him away and mumbles a small, "No."

All I can do is stare at him, unable to hide the hurt growing on my face. I know things are a little weird right now because we haven't seen each other since the car ride, but how did things fall apart so quickly?

"Adam," Angie calls, indicating his coffee is done. He opens his mouth as if he's going to say something, but ultimately closes his eyes, lets out a breath, and turns to walk away. He sits at the table farthest from the counter, but he doesn't leave. Even though it's not much, it means a lot that he didn't just walk out.

"What was that about?" Angie whispers, stepping up behind me as I'm still laser-focused on Adam and I jump. I forgot everything but him for a second there.

"Things are a little weird between us right now, it seems." She raises her eyebrows and I shake my head. "It's a long story."

Another customer walks in and I turn away from her, hoping to keep avoiding the topic but she says, "Later," before she moves to prepare to make another coffee.

For the next half-hour, I'm like a lovesick puppy, leaning against the counter and staring at him. It's almost a relief when a customer comes in because it forces me to act like a normal, not-Adam-obsessed employee, but every time he looks over and our eyes lock, my heart skips a beat. I swear there's the same longing I feel reflected in his eyes.

"Rylie," Angie sighs, and I blink away from this suffocating connection. "Why don't you take your break now."

"But," I start, face twisting in confusion. I already took my break earlier and I don't get another one. She's the one that needs to take her break.

"You have fifteen minutes." She conveys the rest with her eyes, and I smile.

I hug her. "Thank you. If it gets busy, I'll come back."

"Just go." She laughs, and I can almost feel her eyes roll on my shoulder. "You're useless when you're ogling each other across the shop."

I turn to leave, and she adds, "But I expect to hear the whole story after he leaves."

I nod, but my eyes are already on him. He's working on some assignment and is concentrating on the problem in front of him. His forehead is scrunched and the corner of his mouth pulls down. I know that look—he's frustrated, and the pencil shakes in his hand as it always has when he's stuck on a problem. I pause halfway across the store and watch as he closes his eyes, takes a few deep breaths, and then opens them with a new resolve. His pencil begins writing again, slowly, but it doesn't stop. My smile grows as his does, and only when he sets his pencil down, with pride, do I walk up and sit down across from him.

"Hi," I say, unable to dim my bright smile.

"Rylie," he breathes, and it sounds like relief. "I'm not avoiding you . . . well, not entirely. I've wanted to see you so badly it made me think I shouldn't."

I smile at his honesty, and the explanation is so true to his personality I don't have to question his sincerity. *He* wanted to see *me*. My heart is so full. "What do you mean?"

"You said you needed time to heal, and I want to give you that time. I didn't know if being around you would make that harder for you at all. I don't want things to change between us, but the truth is, it has." He's looking into my eyes and even though his words sound bad, I can see in his eyes this change might be for the better. "Now that I know how you feel, it's so hard to be near you without acting on it."

"I know how you feel." My smile turns sad as my eyes shift down to the calla lily on his table. Without thinking, I reach out and gently rub the petal between my fingers.

"Those were your mom's favorite, right?" he says, quietly and the rest of the shop fades around us as I look up at him and nod. He smiles. "She always brought them when you guys came over for dinner. I loved seeing them on the table for days after each visit."

I huff out a laugh and bite the inside of my cheek, so I won't cry. "You remember that?"

"Of course, I do." He reaches out to grab my hand. "I loved your mom, Rylie. She was family to us, too."

Now, I can't stop the tears from falling. I forget sometimes that other people have memories of my mother—that they knew her too, that they loved her. It makes me feel less alone. I squeeze his hand tight. He makes me feel less alone.

"I don't want to stay away from you, I can't," he continues. "I'm your friend, that will never change. And I know this is important, so I won't push, but I will be here."

I'm so grateful for him. I know this is hard for us both, but I also know he gets why this is so important to me, and I love him for it. "You know, we don't have to stop flirting just because we can't be more right now."

"I wouldn't dream of it." He chuckles and we're both smiling. He leans in and whispers, "I don't think we could stop even if we tried. It's who we are."

I laugh so loudly that people nearby look our way, and we only laugh more.

"I'm honored to have you as my friend, but don't for one second think I won't be dreaming about kissing you every moment we're together," I say, repeating the same words he said to me in the car and his eyes go wide. I smile, squeeze his hand one last time, and stand. "I have to get back to work, but I'll talk to you soon?"

"Absolutely." He's grinning at me like I'm all that matters.

When I get back behind the counter, I glance back and he's looking down, but that grin hasn't dimmed in the slightest.

chapter seven

SATURDAY IS a much-needed day spent enjoying the summer heat. Since both Caleb and I are off, we walk around campus, savoring the last weeks of calm before these courtyards are packed shoulder-to-shoulder with students moving between classes and trying to find a spot to rest in-between. Then, we head over to a small strip mall near campus for some shopping, mostly clothes for the year, but we check out some apartment décor, too.

I need new jeans and shorts. The not-eating thing must be worse than I realized because I've gone down a whole size in the last few months. I'm already on the thinner side, more skin and bone than muscle, and I don't want this to become a more serious issue. Which means I need to make eating a top priority. It's just so easy to work through lunch, or lose track of time and miss a meal, or two, and it's worse when I'm stressed, anxious, or sad—which I am a lot these days.

I tell myself it's just a phase because I'm too scared to think about the alternative. But I make a mental note to add it to the list I've been compiling on how to heal from loss. Google gave me a list of things to do: 1. Let yourself experience the loss fully, 2. Know that feelings may change, 3. Take care of your well-being, 4. Share memories, 5. Do something in their memory, 6. Forgive them, 7. Let others comfort you, 8. Embrace family relationships, 9. Consider support groups, and 10. Talk to a therapist if you need extra support.

Eating falls under #3, and it's probably the thing I'm worst at —along with #4, #7, and #8. Nine and ten are there if needed, although I'm focusing on the first eight for now. I don't have an issue sharing and talking to Adam about these things, but I can't do it with anyone else, and that's the problem. I don't know how to start. It's too easy to not talk about it—to have a good time and not bring anyone else down with me.

Maybe I'm not handling this as well as I thought I was.

I thought keeping everything in would be better, but everything I read says it's wrong.

Easier said than done though.

Sunday and Monday pass without major incident, although Angie has been out of control with her comments on Adam since I gave her a more complete overview of what happened during Fourth of July weekend, as promised. But I didn't know her when everything happened with my mom, so she didn't understand why I told him I wanted to wait, and I didn't want to explain. I didn't know how to. It's always been easiest to hide my pain at work, and I didn't want to make it another location I dreaded going so I just said the timing wasn't right.

I'm halfway through my shift on Tuesday when Angie clears her throat loud enough that I look up from the latte I'm making just in time to see Adam walking through the door. His eyes find mine immediately and he gives me a smile so big I ditch the coffee I'm making and walk over to meet him.

"I guess I'll take over making the drinks," Angie mumbles, and heads to the espresso machine. I shoot her a grateful smile.

"Hi." I smile when he approaches, biting my lip. How does he keep getting cuter? And when he's smiling like that, just for me . . . my legs are already shaking.

"Hi," he responds.

We stand there grinning at each other for long enough that Angie clears her throat again and I blush.

"Are you hanging around for a bit?" I ask, motioning to the backpack he's carrying.

"Yeah, I have an exam in a few hours. I have some last-minute studying to do," he says.

"Go sit down, I'll bring your drink out when it's ready."

"I'll have the—" he says while pulling out his wallet but freezes when I reach across the counter and grab his arm.

"You don't have to tell me something in order for me to know it," I repeat the words he'd spoken to me at the lake house, smirking at the shock that crosses his face. Pushing his hand with the wallet away, I add, "And this one's on the house. I owe you something for how amazing you've been."

"You owe me nothing, Rylie. You never will." He smiles and I gulp, walking away to make his drink, not trusting myself to respond appropriately to that.

As Adam takes a seat, I look behind me to find Angie insinuating a lot with her eyes. I roll my eyes at her and whisper, "No, we're just friends, now quit it with that look."

"Oh, come on," she whispers intensely, trying to make her point, but not wanting Adam to hear us from his table in the corner closest to us. "That man is perfect, and he is head-over-heels for you."

"He is perfect." I sigh. "But it isn't the right time for us, we both agreed."

Her eyebrows raise, incredulous. "Uh-huh."

I shake my head and start to make his drink. Angie is relentless, watching with a smug look as I smile like an idiot while I work. I'm just about to deliver his drink when I have an idea.

I grab a pen and write on his cup:

You're cute. Call me!;

I add my number, even though he already has it, and Angie's amused look as she watches causes me to blush. Maybe this is a stupid idea. But I stop overthinking it and bring the drink to his table. As long as he likes it, I don't care what anyone thinks.

"One caramel macchiato," I say, setting the cup down so the writing is facing away from him—he'll have to rotate it to take a sip.

"That's not what I was going to order," he challenges.

"Lie all you want." I lean in to whisper in his ear, a smirk on my face. "We both know this is the only drink you order when you're studying."

He turns to look at me and our faces are so close I can feel his breath on my skin. It sends a shiver through me, like his hands are on me all over again without ever moving. My breath catches, and a smile spreads across his face as if he knows exactly where my thoughts have gone.

"Thank you," he whispers, over-emphasizing each word and causing my blood to boil. I don't think he's just talking about the coffee either.

I take a step back before I combust and take this entire place down with me. "Anytime."

I don't look back until I'm behind the counter again but when I do, he's already looking at me with the cup in his hand and a smile on his face, trying not to laugh. I wink and we both fall into laughter.

My smile sticks around the rest of the day.

* * *

"GOOD DAY AT WORK?" Caleb asks suspiciously as we're watching some TV after dinner. I've been giddy all afternoon, hoping Adam will call, and happy that things feel right between us again.

"*Great* day." I laugh. "Thanks to you and Angie." *And Adam.*

He scrunches up his nose at her name—they're not each other's biggest fans. I don't really blame him though, she does refer to him as "Blondie," to his face, anytime he comes in. I've tried to get her to stop but she's proclaimed herself the captain of *"Team Adam"* and says it would be sacrilegious to befriend the enemy.

I'm still working on that situation.

"I'm glad to see you happy." He smiles.

I'm still up at one in the morning when my phone buzzes with an incoming call. A smile lights up my face as his name lights up my screen—Adam.

"Hello?" I answer with a question, as if I don't have Caller ID.

"Hi! Is this the beautiful barista who left her number on my coffee today?" Even through the phone his voice is like music to my ears. But I'm glad he can't see the blush on my cheeks from his use of the word "beautiful."

"That would be me," I say, playing along. "Does that make you the cute customer who was in the shop today?"

"Guilty," he says, and we both laugh. I'm so glad our carefree banter is back, I've always looked forward to it.

"How was your exam?"

"I think it went well . . . really well, actually. I'm enjoying that class but have struggled with some of the more complex concepts," he admits, and I think of his face, scrunched up in frustration last week while studying. "I think I figured them all out though."

"I'm glad to hear that." I smile thinking about how far he's come. The line stays quiet long enough that I have to check if he's still there. "Adam?"

"Remember back in high school," he says, sounding distant —like he's walking through the past. I know where he's going with this story immediately and it's uncanny how in sync we are sometimes because it's the same memory I was just recalling. "When I wanted to give up on math entirely? I couldn't understand any of it, and no one was able to help me."

"Yeah, I remember," I whisper. I'd been so mad at his teachers, who, after attempting to help, eventually made him feel stupid for not understanding. Math had always been my best subject, I was even majoring in it now, so the night he opened up to me about this, I vowed to help as my heart broke at the defeat in his voice.

He laughs bitterly. "I think even my parents had given up on me turning my grades around in the subject."

It's quiet again. I don't know if he wants me to say something now, or is just thinking, but I wait to give him a chance to say what he needs to say. Eventually he speaks again. "The only person who still believed in me was you. I never asked . . . why?"

"Adam," I sigh, my heart breaking all over again for that boy. "I guess I hated that everyone gave up on you, and worse than that, you gave up on yourself. I wanted you to know you could do it—that you were good enough." My voice lowers with the weight of the truth in my next statement. "I wanted you to see yourself the way I see you."

"You know, I never told anyone that you were the reason my grades improved. That those times your mom was sick and you had to stay at our house that year you'd sneak over to my room —once everyone was asleep—and help me with my math homework until I started to understand it." He sounds like he's getting emotional, but it's hard to tell over the phone. "When my grades started improving, I honestly think everyone assumed I was cheating. No one assumed I was grasping the concepts. I don't think I ever thanked you for it either."

"There's nothing to thank me for," I say, now getting emotional myself. I just want him to always remember how incredible—how capable—he is. "You helped me through my darkest moments, it was the least I could do."

"I still should've thanked you. There's no way I'd be where I am now without you. Today, during my exam, when I was able to work through problems that gave me trouble a few days ago, I realized that the old me never would've been able to get to this point. It's only because of you that I was able to push through until I got it." There's pride in his voice, and I'm proud of him. He was so discouraged when I started helping him, but I would never let him give up on himself.

"I wish I could take some credit, but it was all you. You're the one who didn't give up."

"Only because I wanted to be worthy of your belief in me."

I close my eyes, not trusting the 1 a.m. words coming out of his mouth, or believing that I had such a large impact on his life that long ago. But there's something about the early morning that pulls truths out of you that you'd never dare speak in the daylight.

All the same, I can't help the smile that warms my face.

As the seconds pass, I can almost feel his returning smile, the twin to my own.

"Well, I guess I just called to say . . . that. To say thank you. I'll let you get some sleep now."

I want to stay on the phone with him, I don't want to hang up, but I don't want to push it when it's already so hard to keep on the friends-only side of the line.

"I'm glad you called."

"Yeah, me too. Goodnight, Rylie."

"Goodnight, Adam. Sweet dreams."

A whisper of a breath comes through the line and forms into the words, "They will be now," before the line cuts out and I'm left staring at a dark ceiling wondering if I just woke up from a dream.

I fall asleep with a smile on my face, and with dreams of Adam that are nothing but sweet.

chapter eight

THE LAST WEEKS of summer pass as if nothing ever happened. Adam returns to his normal habit of coming to The Split Bean a couple times a week, and has developed a new habit of bringing me food on my breaks so we can sit and eat together. He's even joined Caleb and I for some nights out and dinners at the apartment.

From the outside, you wouldn't know anything changed between us, but on the inside, I relive that kiss every time he's around. Every time we accidentally touch, heat spreads across my body remembering all the places his hands have been. Every time our faces get close, I want to seal the distance between us. The worst part is I can see that he feels the same. We're getting pulled closer and closer and it's getting harder to hold back.

But every once in a while, I find that list I made of how to heal and my heart sinks because I'm no closer to checking any of them off than I was a month ago. How are we ever going to be together if I can't accomplish the one thing I need to do so that can happen? Those nights I spiral worse than I did before.

Will I ever be ready for the future I want?

Before I know it, the first day of fall semester is here and although I'm happy with my schedule, I much prefer the carefree summer days that are now past. There's no good reason to, but I still love dressing up on the first day of class. Looking good helps me feel good, so I pick out a black denim skirt with a black belt that now only notches one hole smaller than it used to—it used to be two. I pair that with an oversized, burnt orange tee, tucked in, black chelsea boots, and layer a stack of three necklaces over top. Simple, comfortable, and cute.

I pour myself a to-go cup of coffee, grab a granola bar, and begin the walk to campus. My first class is in the math building, which is on the far side of campus compared to where we live. I don't get to walk through the pretty part of campus like I do for work, but the campus is still calming. Most of the buildings are brick, and trees line the major walkways, but there's not as much open space on this side of campus.

For most students, the math building brings with it thoughts of dread, but for me it brings with it familiarity and comfort. I took to math at a young age. When my mom got sick, I couldn't control anything in my life. It was chaotic and devoid of a consistent routine. But in math class, there was a prescribed process—a way to control the chaos of the numbers on a page. I was fascinated by the way you were guaranteed to reach the correct outcome if you followed the steps correctly.

I still love that feeling of taming chaos.

Math is probably the reason I also grew to overanalyze everything. Real life isn't so formulaic, but my mind tries to process it that way. It tries to choose the appropriate next step, given the variable inputs. But my emotions are too large of a variable for me to accurately predict anything, so I'm often wrong.

I'm actually excited walking into Differential Equations because of the challenge and process, but a look around shows I'm probably the only one. It's not until attendance is taken that I remember why the first week of last semester was so hard for me. I lose the ability to breathe when my name is called—my full name. I don't use my last name anymore—ever. It only reminds me that I have no family for the name to tie me to. It reminds me how alone I am in the world. I squeak out a "here," but spend the rest of attendance trying to suck in air. The guy next to me gives me a weird look and it's enough to snap me back into reality.

I almost had a breakdown in math class. This is not progress.

The professor acts like he'll be tough but, in my experience, those professors end up being the coolest and are just trying to weed out the ones that don't need to be here. As if proving my point, he lets us go early.

On Monday and Wednesday, I have four classes, two before lunch and two after. On Tuesday and Thursday, it's just the two before lunch and then work the second half of the day. Friday, Saturday, and Sunday are solely for work.

As I search the halls of the business building for my next class, I'm glad I have the extra time. I've never been in this building before, and it shows. I'm completely lost.

I'm double-checking the room number, eyes focused on the schedule I have pulled up on my phone, when I round the corner and run smack into someone's back.

"Oh." I look up dazed and try to save my phone from clattering to the floor. "I'm so sorry."

Someone laughs but the person I ran into turns toward me. "Don't worry about it. Are yo—"

I don't hear the rest of his words because my eyes find the source of the laughter, the person who he was talking to—Adam.

"How am I just noticing you're a clumsy person?" He walks closer, still laughing.

"I am not!" I swat his arm. I try to keep an angry face on, but even pressing my lips together doesn't stop the smile that grows. "Stop laughing."

He doesn't, not for a while.

When he finally settles down, I ask, "What are you even doing here?"

"Business building," he says, waving his arms in gesture of the building, then turning the gesture on himself, "business major. I have class here. You'd think that'd be self-explanatory."

I cross my arms and glare at the stupid, handsome smirk on his face.

"I should be asking you that question." He raises his eyebrows in expectation.

I copy his earlier movements and say, in a patronizing tone, "Business building, business minor. You'd think that'd be self-explanatory."

His amusement lights up his face and he laughs again. "You're lost, aren't you?"

"What?" I become defensive. "Why would you think that?"

He gives me a knowing stare. "How about the fact that you had your face stuck in your phone, checking your schedule, when you ran into Blake."

I already completely forgot about the guy I'd run into, and that he was standing next to us, watching this exchange with curious eyes. My eyes flick to him for a second and I give him an awkward smile and wave before looking back at Adam. "Fine, I'm lost. This building is a maze."

"Come on, I'll walk you to your class," he offers, and as embarrassed as I am, I'm not about to turn down extra time with Adam. I smile and follow him down the hall. The other guy, Blake, is completely forgotten by both of us—again.

"Where do you need to go?" he asks after we've wandered aimlessly for a few minutes talking.

"Oh, right." I check my phone again. "Room 137."

"You have Campbell for finance?"

"Yeah, did you have her?"

He nods. "Yeah, she's great. You'll have no issues with the

class. You were always smarter than me, especially in subjects like this."

He's smiling when I look up at him and color floods my cheeks. "Oh stop, you always talk down on yourself. You aced the class if I remember correctly."

"And you've always been too modest." He nudges me with his elbow. "Here we are, Room 137."

Glancing around, I realize I have no idea where I am in the building, I've been too caught up in him to pay attention. I guess I'll be getting lost on the way out too.

"Down the hall, this way." He points to the left of the room. "Take a left at the end of the hall and you'll end up at the doors to the courtyard."

"Thanks." I smile, loving that he knows me so well he's started answering my thoughts before I ever get a chance to speak them. I don't want my time with him to be over yet, so I lean against the wall across the hall instead of heading in the room. "Do you have another class after this?"

"Nope, I actually gave myself a nice break for lunch this semester."

"Me too!" I exclaim.

"I'll meet you at the first column on the left in the court-yard," he says, continuing when he sees the confused expression on my face. "So we can go to lunch together after class."

"I'll be there," I assure him with a smile before checking my phone for the time. My eyes widen in alarm. "Classes are starting now. You should get going, I don't want you to get in trouble."

"It's the first day." He shrugs. "It was worth it anyways."

Before I can respond he jogs off back to his class and I stumble into mine, already feeling colder without him standing so close to me.

After class, I make it to the column with ease, using the directions that he also texted to me, just in case. It's a good thing he did too, because I forgot which way I was supposed to head down the hallway from the room.

There are five columns in a semi-circle around the courtyard. They're made of a faux, marble material and are supposed to represent the foundational pillars of success—or something along those lines. I've been told the history of it at some point, but I don't waste brainpower remembering it.

As groups of people file out the doors, I search the crowd for his face, excited to have this outing with him, and more excited that he was the one who suggested it. A smile lights up my face when I spot him. He's talking with that same guy I ran into earlier . . . is it Blake? I wonder if he's one of the business major friends from the stories Adam's told me, but it doesn't matter because once Adam spots me, he splits off from Blake and heads over to me with a huge smile on his face.

Adam pays for lunch, using the excuse that he owes me for the free coffee I often give him. I try to fight him on it, albeit half-heartedly because the other, traitorous half of my heart pretends this is a date because he asked me, and he paid.

I enjoy our lunch so much that by the time Wednesday rolls around, I've almost texted him a hundred times asking if he wants to do it again. Our classes lineup again on Wednesday, but I don't want to impose—he might have plans with Blake already and I don't want him to feel bad—so I never hit send.

But after class, I walk out into the courtyard and almost trip over my own feet when my eyes flash over to the column. I smile at the goofy grin on Adam's face as he leans back against the column. He's waiting for me.

That becomes our unspoken agreement, to wait at that column, *our* column, after class, Monday and Wednesday. And each day, without fail, we both show up.

chapter nine

ALMOST A MONTH HAS PASSED. It's the end of September and I've fallen into a normal schedule of school, work, repeat. The time with Adam and evenings with Caleb are just icing on the cake. I'm determined to find some enjoyment this semester and live the college lifestyle.

During my freshman year, fall semester, my mom was so sick, and all my free time went into visiting her, talking to her, and eventually remembering her because she died right before the start of spring semester. There wasn't any time for fun or going out, just struggling to keep up while I was constantly gone, spending as much time back home with my mom as possible.

As hard as it was, I'm glad I was able to be there for her final moments. I have very few regrets of those times, thanks to Adam's advice all those years ago. The only one is that I couldn't have done more for her.

Because of everything that happened, tonight will be my first official college party. I allowed Caleb to drag me out to some of the bars last year, but refused to go to any parties—it was too overwhelming. This isn't one of those college parties you see in the movies though, that isn't our scene. We prefer the quieter, more intimate parties held at the houses of friends.

Although even that is beginning to feel overwhelming.

After downing the drink in my hand, the heaviness of the alcohol hits me hard. I usually only have one or two drinks in a whole night, but I'm already up to five and it's only been a couple hours. My dad got hit by a drunk driver and passed away before I was old enough to know him, and it gave alcohol a bad reputation. I also much prefer to be in control of my actions and thoughts.

But tonight, my thoughts drift to Adam and I keep grabbing drinks, hoping they'll drown out the memories and give me a reprieve from the never-ending loop of his touch and kiss.

They don't help. The more I drink, the less control I have over the memories. I'm just as drunk on my feelings as I am on the alcohol swimming through my veins.

My only saving grace is that Adam isn't here—even though my eyes betray my true feelings, constantly straying to the door, hoping to see him walk through it. If he showed up right now, I don't think I could restrain myself. My self-control is the only reason I'm able to be so close to him daily, and I don't have any right now.

I stumble over to Caleb, tripping and falling into him. My clumsiness is only exacerbated by the fuzziness in my head. "Cale, please make sure I don't have another drink for a while."

If I have any more, I might push past my limit, and I'd really like to avoid that outcome.

He chuckles. "How many have you had?"

"Four . . . five . . . too many." I giggle and have just enough awareness to know this isn't a good sign.

"Oh, Ry," he says, holding back another laugh. "Just stay by me, I've got you."

"You know you're the best, best friend. Like best best best . . ." I can't shut up. Words start spewing from my mouth and if I can't stop them soon, I'll probably end up saying something I shouldn't about Adam. "I don't think I tell you enough how much I appreciate you being such a constant in my life. Sometimes I think I wouldn't have made it through . . . well the past few years, but the past months especially, if I didn't have you."

He rolls his eyes, but I can see how touched he is by the drunken words that are full of truths. "You know I've always got your back, just as you always have mine." As if accentuating the point, he loops his arm through mine and helps me stand straight. "But maybe you shouldn't talk too much until you have better control over your words."

I nod my head too fast and get dizzy—Caleb's arm through mine is the only thing that keeps me from falling.

"I've never seen you like this," he says, and his eyes narrow as he considers his own words. He stops walking and turns to look at me. "Is everything okay, Rylie?"

Everything in the room is suddenly extremely interesting, more interesting than the question. I should've known he'd see right through me. Sometimes I wish he wasn't so observant, but that's what makes him such a great friend too.

"It's nothing," I say, the words slurring together. "I'm just being haunted by the ghosts of fingers and lips." My sober self rams her head into a wall in my brain at how revealing that response was. I need to stop talking, and soon.

"Ry—" His eyes are wide in confusion and concern. Even *I* can hear how crazy I sound.

"I haven't said anything because I'm not ready to talk about it." I look him right in the eyes, the memory of what I'm trying to forget sobers me up enough to not say anything more. "I promise, I'll tell you everything once I'm ready. I promise. But for right now I need to figure things out on my own."

I'm worried he'll be upset with me, for keeping secrets, for not trusting him, but all I see is understanding and care. "Just don't forget I'm here for you whenever you need me."

"I know." I squeeze his arms and we set off toward a group of Caleb's friends from class in the back of the room.

I'm only half listening to the conversation going on around me. We've been standing here long enough for me to sober up enough that I can control the words flowing out of my mouth. But the more sober I get, the more I wish Adam was here. This group is Caleb's friends from his economics classes, and I'm bored out of my mind listening to them talk about, well, economics.

It's not that I don't enjoy the subject, but I didn't know I was signing up for a lecture when I agreed to come here tonight. Maybe that's why I sobered up so fast. My mind strays off, thinking about the person who jumbles my brain enough without the alcohol, and how I'll eventually tell Caleb about it all.

Arms slip around my waist, and my body goes cold. My reflexes are slower than usual because of the drinks still in my system, so the personal space intruder has time to put his lips to my ear before I can turn and slap him.

"Hello, beautiful," the intruder says, and I turn to liquid. I'd know that voice anywhere.

Adam.

Even though I've had time for my mind to clear up some, those two words and his hands on me have me completely unraveled. I might as well have had three more drinks. "I've been looking for you everywhere."

He's obviously had some drinks already too because our flirting isn't usually this obvious unless we're uninhibited, and I've never seen him freer than he is right now. Out of the corner of his eye, Caleb watches us, eyes narrowed at the display, and I can see the gears turning in his head, piecing together all the clues I've left him tonight.

I look up at Adam and beam. "Well, here I am."

What a stupid response, sober me comments, but there's nothing I can do to stop it.

"Yes, here you are."

With the way he's looking at me right now, I feel bright, I feel . . . radiant. His words from that night rattle through my head, *"You are radiant, Rylie,"* and I realize that it's him. I'm radiant because I'm around *him.*

"And here you are."

Sober me is having a field day with that one but I'm lost in his stare.

He chuckles. "Here I am."

I rotate in his arms, sucking in a breath when his hands skid across my back and stomach, and throw my arms around his neck, practically jumping on him. His arms tighten around me.

"I'm glad you're here," I say into his neck, sucking in an intoxicating breath of his smell that has an undertone of spice from the alcohol on his breath. "I didn't think you'd be here."

"My plans fell through, and I saw on Caleb's Instagram that you were here so thought I'd stop by."

I pull back just enough to look up at him and give him the goofiest grin, one full of happiness, love, and want. My heart speeds up at his returning smile, it's radiant too.

You've got it bad, sober me is still commentating. *Remember your resolution. Heal first, then you can have him.* That thought slips to the forefront of my mind and keeps me sobered up enough to not let this night go further than the harmless flirting that is already threatening to tear me apart.

"Want another drink?" he asks.

"I should probably lay off the drinks for a bit, you're looking far too good right now." I bite my lip and look down realizing I said that out loud. Damn my buzzed self for having no filter. "But I'll come with you and grab a water."

"As long as you're coming with me," he says, leaning in until we're cheek to cheek, his breath on my ear. "But just so you know, I think you look this good all of the time."

My breath catches, heart racing, and I almost break my vow

to not let this night go too far right then. I can feel the smile growing on his face, scraping his jaw against mine and sending chills through me. I use all my control to hold back a moan, but a noise still escapes. I'm breathing heavily when he pulls away, a smug look on his face. He *likes* that a reaction was pulled from me.

Oh god, if he keeps looking at me like that, I won't be able to control what happens tonight.

His arm stays around my waist as he guides us off to the drinks and my fingers drift beneath his shirt to the skin just above his waistband. I glance back at an intrigued Caleb and flash him a smile before we disappear into the crowd.

Adam doesn't break contact with me all night. If his arm isn't around my waist, then his hand is holding mine. If he's not holding my hand, then it's his arms wrapped around me as we dance. I bask in his attention while trying not to let things go too far. We've both been drinking, and even though we both want this, we agreed not to when we were sober.

Caleb has been watching us all night with a smug look on his face. By now, he's probably guessed that my comment has something to do with Adam, I'm just hoping he's dumber than I know he is, so he doesn't understand what I was saying. But I'm pretty sure, just from the glint in his eyes, that he knows.

It's well past midnight and I find myself sitting on the dewy grass of the front yard with Adam on my right. He sits close enough that our legs touch from the hip down, and our hands touch when we lean back. It's been long enough that we're both sober enough to realize what a spectacle we made of ourselves tonight and have toned it down—a lot. But we still won't stop touching.

All I can think of is his lips, and how I want them on me again. But the time for mistakes has passed, and I won't be making any now. Instead, I sigh and lay down on my back to look up at the stars.

"You know," I whisper, already hating the words I'm about to say, but he deserves for me to say them. He deserves for me to not be selfish when I'm the one who isn't ready to commit. "I don't know how long it'll take for me to heal, for me to be ready for this. I . . . I don't expect you to wait. If you find another girl you want to be with, I won't be mad that you moved on."

"Rylie." Adam looks down at me and his lips are twisted with tension, his eyes tight with thoughts that I can't decipher. His mouth opens, beginning to form words I'll never hear because our attention moves to two guys approaching up the lawn.

"Adam, there you are," one of them calls out. Adam's expression changes, like flipping a switch, and he looks more relaxed as he spots them and stands, helping me up after him.

When they're closer they speak again. "This is what you ditched us for?"

With raised brows, I look at Adam and catch the tension shift in his jaw. He said his plans fell through, but that wasn't true. He skipped them to come here, and he didn't want me to know it.

"Blake, Ryan, this is Rylie." He gestures to each of us with each name. "Rylie, this is Blake and Ryan." He laughs before adding, "You might remember Blake as the guy you almost mowed over on the first day of classes."

My face heats in embarrassment. "I never did apologize for that, did I?"

Blake's smile grows. "Don't worry about it. Glad to officially meet you, *Rylie.*"

There's something in his voice, something I can't quite identify when he says my name. I don't understand why.

Adam cuts in. "They're business majors too. We met freshman year in our intro courses."

So, they're probably the friends I've heard stories about.

Blake is still grinning ear-to-ear, and Ryan has been looking at me wide-eyed since the introductions. Confused, I give them a smile. "Nice to meet you."

"You're Rylie?" Ryan looks amazed, or surprised—maybe both.

"I told you, dude," Blake answers.

"I thought you were lying, but you're so right."

I have absolutely no idea what they're talking about and look at Adam for some help. He's shaking his head and muttering under his breath, "Lord help me."

I look between the three of them—Blake and Ryan, who are amused and chatting between themselves about something, and Adam, who looks embarrassed. What am I missing?

"Please ignore them," Adam says through gritted teeth, shooting each a hard glare that only causes their smirks to grow bigger.

My phone vibrates in my pocket, a text from Caleb asking if I'm ready to go. I glance at the stare down happening around me and text back.

Me: I'm out front. Grab me on your way out.

"I hate to interrupt whatever is happening here," I say, gesturing to the group before turning to Adam, "but Caleb is on his way out. We're going to head home."

His face drops in resignation, because he knows that this is as far as our night goes. Truthfully, we both know it, but sometimes I wish he could be a stranger, one that I meet at this party and bring home with me because even in a few hours he made me smile brighter than I ever have. I could bask in his attention, his touch, his kiss, and not be weighed down by our history.

But our history is what makes me love him so much, so no, I don't wish that.

I smile at Blake and Ryan. "It was nice to meet you."

"Glad we *finally* got to meet you, Rylie," Ryan says.

"Hopefully we'll see you again soon," Blake says, and I'm still left wondering what they think they know.

Feeling their eyes drilled on us, Adam pulls me in for a side hug.

"I'll see you later," I say, squeezing his arm.

"Yeah, see ya." Adam forces a smile that isn't the least bit convincing.

Just before I turn away, his face shifts from guarded hesitancy to painful defeat as he watches me before he turns a glare back on his friends. That look feels like a knife in my heart.

When they think I'm far enough away, Ryan says, "Dude! You didn't tell me Rylie looked like *that*."

Adam grumbles back, "Just drop it guys, please."

"What about Olivia?" Ryan says, and I miss a step, almost tripping from the shock of another girl's name. Maybe my speech earlier was for nothing because he's already moved on. *Oh my God, what if he's already moved on?*

The thought is too much to bear so I shut out everything as I walk home with Caleb in silence, trying to stop my hands from shaking.

"Rylie," Caleb says once we walk through the doors.

"Please," I beg, my voice already cracking and tears threatening to spill over. "Yes, something is going on with your brother, and no, I don't know what happened tonight, but it only made things more complicated."

Caleb's face tightens, he wants to ask more but the tears spilling over soften him. He sighs. "I just hate seeing you hurting like this."

"Do you . . ." I bite my lip, shaking as I prepare for the potential to hear an answer that will break me. "Have you heard anything about someone named Olivia?"

"Olivia?" He's taken aback. "No, I don't know any Olivia's."

"If you do, could you let me know?"

"Of course," he says, still looking worried for me. I just nod, then shut myself in my room as the tears start to flow.

chapter ten

BY THE TIME I wake in the morning, Caleb is already gone, and I groan with each movement. My head is pounding so hard I can't think.

I squint at the bright light of my phone and see a text from Angie. That's when it hits, I was supposed to work today, and—*shit*—I was supposed to be there four hours ago. I curse under my breath and groan again from the pain associated with speaking.

ANGIE

Blondie called and said you were "under the weather." That's not like you. I need details next time I see you! Feel better, I've got you covered today.

I smile. Caleb went through the trouble of calling Angie, someone he hates talking to, for me. Even after I shut him out yesterday, he still did this. How did I end up surrounded by the most caring people? I would've been miserable if I had gone to work today, and Angie probably would've sent me home for being useless anyways. I'll be useless at home too, but at least I can lay down. First, I need to find something to help this pulsing headache.

As I trudge into the kitchen, I notice my favorite mug—a blush pink mug with gold painted lilies that belonged to my mom—out on the countertop. Confused, I walk over to it. Beside the mug, on a napkin, lay two Tylenol and inside the mug is a folded-up piece of paper.

> Ry,
> I'm sorry if I overstepped last night. I'm not trying to pry, but you're my best friend and seeing you hurt, hurts me, too. I respect that you're not ready to talk about it, but I want you to know, I will support you through anything (even if that thing involves my brother).
> I work til 8, but movie night tonight after? I could use a quiet night in.
> Your forever best friend,
> Cale
> P.S. Your favorite vanilla iced coffee from the shop on the corner is in the fridge, and take the Tylenol, it'll help with the headache!

With tears in my eyes, I take the Tylenol and grab the coffee from the fridge. My eyes close as I take the first sip. The creaminess hits first, then the undertones of the bitter coffee and sweetness from the vanilla. It's just what I needed. I'm already feeling better.

I haven't been a good friend lately—I can see that. I've been keeping him at arm's length, and taking out my frustrations on him.

He deserves better than that. He'll write it all off because of what I've been through, but to me, it's not a valid excuse. Caleb is the one person that's been there for me since day one—he deserves my best. I need to be better for my best friend, and that starts tonight.

I shoot him a text.

ME

I don't deserve you. Seriously, you're a lifesaver. Movie night sounds perfect. I'll make dinner, lasagna, your fav<3

Ever since I shared my mom's lasagna with him on the first day of fourth grade, it's been his favorite. I should've made it weeks ago—for the first day of classes like she always did—but it was another reminder of what I lost. Because of my pain, I took away something he loved too. I need to be more mindful of that.

After chugging my coffee, I head for the shower. Now that I have something to look forward to tonight, my mood is brighter and it's easier to force myself to stay out of bed. But first, I need to cleanse myself of the memory of last night.

Last night.

I groan, remembering how handsy we got last night, how we didn't care who watched as we danced and laughed and talked as if it was just us in that room. The things we said, the way we acted—it doesn't help the "we can only be friends right now" pact. What does this mean for our friendship? And why can't we be around each other without taking it too far anymore? If he hadn't put his hands on me like that, I wouldn't have forgotten myself. But, if I hadn't had so much to drink, trying to drown out the dream that he'd show up and do just that, I wouldn't have let things go on as long as they did.

Dreams don't have consequences, this will though.

Like the mention of Olivia. Who is she and why were his

friends asking about her? I could drive myself insane just trying to decipher that one moment.

As I step under the hot water, I try to let it all go. Today will be Adam free. I can read into what he's thinking when I see him tomorrow after class, but until then, there's nothing I can do. So I stay in the shower long enough for the heat to release the tension in my shoulders, and with it, my thoughts of Adam.

* * *

I ROAM the aisles of the grocery store, checking off my list as I go.

> ~~Ground Beef~~
> ~~Marinara Sauce~~
> ~~Mozzarella~~
> ~~Lasagna Noodles~~
> ~~Garlic Bread~~
> ~~Salad~~

Add to that a cheap bottle of wine and brownie mix—because desserts on a movie night are a must—and I have everything I need. I've always felt oddly at peace in grocery stores, like an artist picking out paints for her next masterpiece. The calm before the storm. I consider myself to be an average cook, but the kitchen does tend to look like a disaster zone after I finish.

There are some perks to officially being twenty-one though, like not having to use a fake-ID at checkout. My birthday was in May, but I hadn't been in the mood to celebrate this year. It's hard to experience everything for the first time—the first time without my mom. My birthday was one of the hardest ones yet.

But my spirits today are higher than they've been in a while. I didn't realize the weight I'd been carrying around until it was temporarily lifted. From my mom to Adam, things have been hard lately. And I'm starting to see how much I've pushed people away because of it.

It's five o'clock in the evening when I get home—perfect timing. I use my mom's original recipe which means hand-making the filing, but it's worth it for the rich flavor.

I love cooking home alone, with the music blasting and no one around to see my horrible dance moves. I'm transported to another world—hips swaying as I stir the meat sauce and head bobbing as I fill the pan with layers of sauce, noodles, and cheese. I use the whisk as a microphone while mixing the brownies—twirling as I move items in and out of the oven. Spinning a turntable as I scrub the dishes.

A throat clears behind me, shocking me enough that the pan I was scrubbing goes clattering into the sink and I whip around with a hand on my chest. Caleb is leaning against the entryway, lips curled up into an amused smirk.

"How long have you been there?" I ask, still breathless even after taking the time to turn off the music.

"Long enough," he says, and I can hear the stifled laugh in his voice.

I groan, cheeks reddening, and turn back to the dishes. I look back, unsure if he's left or not, and find him mocking my dance moves.

"There's no way I looked that dumb doing that move."

His eyes fly open, eyebrows shooting sky-high. He's been caught red-handed and he knows it, but he laughs anyway, hand flying to his mouth to try to cover it, but it's too late.

"Hey!" My faux anger is cracking, but to make my point I chuck the wet dish towel at him before he can run off. The slopping sound it makes as it nails him in the cheek breaks the last of my façade. I'm laughing so hard I collapse to the ground.

With tears of laughter clouding my vision, I can only hear Caleb's suppressed laughter as he walks toward me. I realize too late what his plan is, shrieking as the towel I threw at him is wrung out over my head, soaking my hair with lukewarm, sudsy water that drips down my back, But I'm laughing too much to care.

"Caleb!" I try to grab his hand to stop him but he's already dropping to the ground too.

We sit there for at least ten minutes trying to stop ourselves from laughing, only to start back up again. My cheeks hurt, stomach cramps, and tears stream down my face. I haven't felt so free in ages. I can't remember the last time I laughed this much, or felt so buoyant.

"Go get changed, I'm about to pull everything out," I say after we finally settle down. "You can pick the movie tonight."

"It smells great." He smiles before heading off to his room. By the time he's back I have the table set and plates portioned.

"Movie now, or after dinner?"

"After?" His eyes narrow in question, and I nod in agreement.

As we catch up on work and school, I feel guilty realizing how little I know about his semester. He tells me how one of his professors has taken an interest in him and is considering bringing him on for a research project that will start in the new year. He's excited that it's a paid position because that means he could quit the deli. And this professor notoriously has high standards, so it means a lot that he was singled out.

I don't have many updates on my side, just that classes are going well, and I've been enjoying my programming class so much I'm considering adding computer science as a second minor.

"Would that affect your graduation timeline?" he asks, intrigued. He'd taken the class last year and hadn't enjoyed it at all.

"I don't think so," I say, getting excited, "I looked at the requirements and I think I can overlap most of them with my required electives. It should only end up being two or three extra classes in total."

"Well, if it makes you this happy, I say go for it."

I smile, heart soaring at the genuine joy in his voice. "Thanks, Cale."

I bring our plates to the sink and refill our wine glasses. The smell of chocolate pulls my attention to the brownies, so I grab those too.

"You seem different today," Caleb says, watching me as I walk over and sit down on the couch next to him. "I think I'm only really starting to understand how much you've been carrying with you all these years. We were so young when everything happened, I didn't understand how it changed you, and then it just became normal. Seeing you today, dancing and laughing, you seemed lighter, like you'd finally shed some of that weight."

He's getting choked up, and each word rips deeper into me. I tried to shield everyone from the depths of my pain. I could handle it without bringing anyone else down, or so I thought. I can't look away from the sadness in his eyes as we both shed tears.

"I guess what I'm trying to say is I'm excited to see you finding some happiness again. I know it won't be this easy every day, but I'm glad you're able to begin that healing process. If you ever want to talk, I'm here, and I want to help you carry and shed that weight." He reaches his hand out to me, and I squeeze it before pulling him into a hug. "We may have been too young to know better back then, but I don't want us to go on pretending it's normal when it's not. You deserve to be happy, Ry. You deserve to be free."

I'm speechless. All I can do is hold him tighter as I cry on his shoulder.

I always thought I spared Caleb from the worst of my pain, but it shouldn't surprise me that he's known all along—he is my best friend after all. I've just never felt worthy of the compassion given to me by anyone, especially the Dey family because of how much extra work they had because of me. They helped raise me, took me on family vacations when my mom was too sick to take me anywhere, and made sure I was never alone through the process. Everything they did meant the world to me, but it couldn't have been easy. Adam was always my go to for talks like this because he shared his darkness with me too, so I felt like we were sharing each other's load instead of being a burden. But I think of that list buried in my desk somewhere, and #4, #7, and #8 comes to mind. Sharing feelings, sharing memories, and embracing relationships are things I need to do to heal. I know, without a doubt, that Caleb is the person I want to share with and embrace. It's time to start trying harder to heal—to be happy again.

"I think I'd like that." I pull back to smile at him, and as much as I know I'm ready to share with him, tonight I just want to enjoy this movie like old times. Tomorrow, I begin my true journey. "I'm not sure if I'm quite ready just yet though."

"Whenever you are, I'm here."

As we set up for the movie, I can't help thinking how right this feels, this night with Caleb. I needed it, needed him. With overwhelming joy, I cozy up into my fuzzy blanket, feeling more content than I have in a while.

The theme music for Harry Potter starts playing, my first indication of what movie he picked.

"A man after my own heart." I shoot a faux fawning look at Caleb, and he laughs.

"This was always our favorite as kids. Seems like a good choice for the night."

And it is perfect. The night is full of intense laughing and yelling at the decisions the characters make. It's just like we're kids again.

chapter eleven

MY SPIRITS ARE high when I wake up, feeling refreshed after my movie night with Caleb and excited to tell Adam about being ready to take the next big step in my healing . . . and try to figure out what that look was about, but I try to keep that out of my head. I bounce around my room, searching for a sage green, v-cut, long sleeve top that I've caught Adam checking me out in before. Taking a step further in my healing also means taking a step closer to him—to us—and right now being closer to him is all I can think about.

I throw on gray jeans and white high-tops, and quickly straighten my hair but leave it down. Practically skipping, I grab my bag and head out into the kitchen to grab my coffee—to-go as always—and a granola bar. Caleb sits at the table, looking like a zombie with bags under his eyes and robotic movements as he sips his coffee. I silently chuckle at his disheveled appearance.

"Morning," I chirp but the only response I get is a grunt. My smile grows as I pour coffee into my thermos, I want to laugh but that usually only worsens his mood, so I restrain myself. Before I'm out the door, I look back. "Thanks for yesterday, Cale. I needed that. Have a good day."

The brisk morning air washes over me like it knows today will be a new beginning. Fall is on its way and I'm excited for the change. The clean smell of cool air, the greens that will morph into beautiful shades of red, orange, and yellow. Nature explodes with life—especially up here in the mountains.

I search every tree on my walk for the signs of fall, but it's too early to see them.

There is one, singular leaf, hanging low on a tree, that is already sporting the season. I reach out to touch it and smile at the first sign of the beauty to come. I don't dare remove it—it's a good omen, a good luck charm for the day ahead. There's much more beauty to come.

My calm façade holds up through Differential Equations. It's easy to focus on the complex problems on paper instead of the ones in my head. I only hope the ones in my head can be worked out as easily. But when I enter the business building, my nerves take hold of me. His pained look, and another girl's name, are all I can think about and I'm bouncing with the anticipation of seeing him.

My mind runs through all of the directions this conversation could go, and it does nothing to relax me. I've always been too good at dreaming up the worst-case scenario. Before I know it, class is dismissed, and I don't think I can recall a single word the professor said if my life depended on it. My every thought, every ounce of attention is directed towards Adam.

Slowly, I make my way to our column. He's not here yet, which isn't unusual. Oftentimes, his professor keeps them a few minutes longer than scheduled. I attempt to look as casual as possible while I wait, checking my phone and leaning against the column, but I'm a mess on the inside. Shifting my weight from foot to foot, eyes searching each face that exits the building.

Five minutes pass and I start forming the words I want to speak.

Ten minutes and the first tendrils of doubt start to creep in.

Fifteen and the sinking feeling in my stomach intensifies as the stream of students slows.

After twenty minutes, when the trickle of students leaving the building has finally concluded, I'm forced to admit it.

He's not coming.

This isn't just bad, this is the worst case, outlandish scenario that I never dreamed was an actual possibility. We have never missed a meetup without a heads-up, yet here he is, completely blowing me off. The worst part is I don't understand why.

Did I do something to cause the pain on his face? Something I don't know I did? Is he done waiting for me? Does he not want me anymore?

Is this because of Olivia, whoever she is?

My mind spirals, down, down, until my back is sliding down the column and I'm sitting on the ground, knees pulled into my chest, trying to hold myself together again. My mom is gone, and Adam holds such an important space in my life, but here he is, ghosting me. A new hole joins the gaping space in my heart that my mom left. How much more can it take before it refuses to keep going?

How much more can I lose before I have nothing left to give?

The darkness expands, filling the new empty space. This time, when it comes for me, it's stronger, and I no longer have a light to cast it away with. The pain of this betrayal pulls out all the pain of the past, clinging to each other like newfound lovers, morphing together until I don't even know what it is that's tearing me apart.

This pain, that I deny the existence of because I don't want to be more of a burden than I already am, has become an undeniable force, dragging me down with it.

This pain, that's been slowly tearing me apart from the inside because I refuse to release it, has left fractures I can no longer ignore, because I've finally shattered.

I'm broken, and I have been for a while. Only now, the one person who knows how to put me back together is gone.

No wonder Adam doesn't want to be around me anymore. Who would?

I sit there and cry, not caring who sees me, wishing that I could call my mom right now. She'd know what to do, what to say. I miss her every second, but in moments like this, the reminder of her loss is the final, crushing blow.

I pull my phone out, needing someone to stop me from free-falling. If I don't stop soon, I'm sure to hit rock bottom . . . if I'm not already there.

The name at the top of my contact list is Adam Dey and a sob rips through me as I scroll past his name as fast as I can. Angie and I are close at work but haven't talked much outside that. I stop at Caleb's contact. After last night I know he's the person I can trust with this, even if I have to explain here and now why this is affecting me so much.

How it hurts that he can just walk away when I can still feel the echoes of every touch we ever shared. How the memory of every place his lips have been is tattooed on my skin.

My heart belongs to him, always has and always will.

"You've reached Caleb, sorry I missed yo—"

I groan and hang up, finally noticing the time. Caleb will be in class for another hour, and mine starts in thirty minutes. Looks like I'm on my own for this, but that's the way I know best.

All I can do is let the tears flow until I have nothing left to give.

When I finally find the strength to stand, I'm sure I look as bad as I feel. My thoughts swim freely through me, weighing me down, refusing to be ignored. I huff out a laugh at the irony, yesterday I felt buoyant, while today, I'm drowning.

I sluggishly move toward my next class. If there's one thing I can't do, it's let this affect my academics. If I could keep my grades up even while my mom was spiraling, I can do it when *I'm* spiraling. No one's dying.

Except a piece of you.

I ignore my heart's protests.

This isn't half as bad as what I had to go through last year. *But it's still bad.*

I don't want to admit that it's true.

If there's one thing I know I can pour myself into, it's math. Control the chaos. I could use some of that right about now. I can do this. I can pull myself together and lock away my feelings—go on with life as if everything is fine. I'm good at that, pretending everything's fine.

On the walk, I internally pull together all my thoughts and feelings about Adam and shove them back into the box they'd been in before July 4th. Cramming feelings that have only grown into a box that has remained the same is a struggle. My subconscious jumps on the lid, trying to force it shut, like an over-packed suitcase.

It takes the whole walk, but I lock the box and throw away the key, convincing myself this is all it'll take to move on. I know I won't stop loving him overnight—I'm not sure I'll *ever* stop loving him—but if he's moving on then I'll have to keep this locked away and hope the feelings will shrink in time.

I force a smile to my face. *Everything is okay, everything is okay, everything is okay* . . . I repeat over and over until there's nothing else but those words.

Everything is okay. This isn't the worst thing that's happened to me.

But it's still bad.

I'm lying to myself, I know it, but I'm so desperate to believe in something that I grasp on tight and walk into class with a new resilience. By the time I get home I have my emotions in check and a plan in place. Focus on my studies—my future. Study hard and don't let anything, or anyone, hold me back.

I'm still working on the sincerity of these claims but have adjusted to this new plan over the course of the day. I don't need anyone who doesn't want me.

No matter how much I want them.

Every time I renounce my want for Adam, the locked away feelings beat against the lid of the box, trying to escape. They want to bring truth back to my thoughts, cleanse me of these lies. But the lock holds tight, for now, and I bathe in a river of lies of my own making.

I'm eating leftover lasagna and watching *Friends* reruns when Caleb gets home, looking pale-faced and more serious than I've ever seen him look. The lasagna turns sour in my stomach and some piece of me already knows what he's about to say. What I've known since the moment he didn't show up today.

"What's wrong?" I squeak.

"You asked about Olivia the other day . . ."

I close my eyes, now completely sure I know the next words he's going to say.

"Olivia is Adam's new girlfriend," he says, and I bite my lip, keeping my eyes shut in hopes it'll be enough to stop the tears. "My mom called today."

He didn't show up to meet me because he was with *her*. Is that what the pained look was about? Did he want to tell me himself, but his friends interrupted?

All the work I did today to lock my feelings away is undone in seconds. I think I'm crying because Caleb's arms close around me, but all I can see is Adam. As Caleb soothes me, I realize that I don't want to keep pretending everything is okay when it's clearly not. I don't want to keep holding things back from Caleb. I want to talk, I'm ready to talk.

So, I do.

I talk about how I felt when my mom first got her diagnosis, how I didn't fully understand it, but how happy I was when the doctors told me it was going to be okay. They said she was better, and I could breathe again. Then when it came back, and I was old enough to see on the doctor's faces that it wasn't good. They tried to comfort me, but I knew then that it was much worse than I'd been led to believe.

Once I start talking, I find it hard to stop. I talk about how much his family means to me, and how I could never repay them for everything they've done for me. But I've also been so scared I was a burden so I didn't ever talk about my feelings with them. I tell him how hard it's been since my mom died. How often I have panic attacks—like when I hear my last name, sometimes when I look in the mirror, and many times at his parents' house.

He stays quiet to listen but when I look over, he's frowning, his emotions spilling over and dripping down his cheeks. "Is that why you always change the conversation whenever something good is said about you?"

I nod, looking down with embarrassment.

"Rylie," he says, tipping my chin up so I'm forced to look at him. "You are, and always have been, deserving of every compliment anyone's ever given you. Why don't you believe that?"

"Because I don't . . . I don't deserve them," I whisper, any tears remaining in me come to the surface now as I prepare to say the words I'd hidden in my heart long ago. Words that have taken root and grown into an undeniable truth. "Because I come with more baggage than I'm worth. I'm a burden to everyone, especially you and your family. You got stuck with me and all I've ever brought is hurt and suffering to your lives."

"Rylie," he squeaks, voice cracking with pain. "We don't see you as a burden, not a single one of us. And I'd bet not a single person that's ever met you has felt that way."

I shake my head at the lies, it's not true.

"You're the daughter my mom always wanted but never got," he continues, undeterred by my refusal to accept the words. "She loves you as one of her own and sees you as nothing but a light in her life. My dad, he doesn't say much, but I see the pride clear as day on his face. He cares about you and wants the best for you because even to him, you're family. And Adam, I've never seen Adam care about anyone the way he cares about you. Even if there's something complicated going on between you guys, I know that hasn't changed.

"And to me, you're my role model, my hero. You have such strength and resilience. You were going through your own hell so young, and you never stopped being kind, caring, compassionate, and thoughtful. You never stopped being my best friend. You've always put others' needs before your own. I thought that only proved your strength, and it does, but I now see it was also your way of avoiding what you thought of yourself. I only wish I saw it sooner—"

I look up at him then, entranced by these words he's using to describe me. I want to be that girl he's describing. I need to know what he's going to say.

"—because if I had, maybe I could've helped you see that you're not a burden, you're a bright, shining light. None of us, especially me, would ever wish for a life without you. We love you, Rylie. *I* love you. And I think it's time you finally start loving yourself too."

I lose control—tears streaming, body shaking. I don't know where all the tears come from, but they come and come. Caleb's arms wrap around me, steady me. I cry until the well dries up again and all the while Caleb is whispering reassurances to me. Like he knows if I have a second alone with my thoughts, I'll convince myself everything he said is a lie.

"I wish you could see yourself through my eyes," he says gently, trying to soothe my shaking body. "Then you could see how truly incredible you are. How strong and kind and brilliant. How you make others better just by being you. How I've looked up to you all our lives. How grateful I am every day to have you in my life and by my side as my best friend."

I slowly start to calm down, allowing his words to sink in and trying to believe them.

"Thank you, Rylie," he says, looking me in the eyes. His face looks as puffy and red as mine feels. "For talking to me now, for trusting me with this. I want you to know you're not weighing me down, Ry. But I do want to help lift you up, you just have to let me."

A stuttering laugh comes out. "I'm going to try, Cale. I promise."

As I lay in bed, I think back to my walk home after class earlier. I passed that tree again, the one with the leaf starting to change colors, the sign of beauty to come. It lays in pieces scattered across the ground, because at the time, I didn't think there was any beauty left for me. But now I see there's beauty all around me.

Caleb's friendship, his love, is beautiful. I took my first real step forward, and that's beautiful. Adam is with another girl, and yet I'm lying here with a smile on my face—*that* is beautiful.

I still want him, still love him, but getting closer to him only kept me further from my goal. It's time to focus on me and what I need. How can I be mad he's moving on when I wasn't any closer to being ready to be with him?

I believe we'll find our way back to each other.

I believe that one day, we will be beautiful too.

chapter twelve

I HADN'T REALIZED I'd gotten back up to my normal size over the past few months until I put my jeans on one October morning to find they're too big, again. I frown as I dig out the smaller-sized jeans I bought at the beginning of the school year. When I try to pinpoint the change, I realize how often Adam was bringing me food to work, or how we'd always go out to lunch together. Was he actively making sure I ate? Or was it just a coincidence?

Either way, I make it my goal to tackle this issue this month. I enlist Caleb to keep me accountable and I text him every time I eat the first two weeks until it becomes normal again and I don't need someone to remind me.

Now that I've opened up to Caleb, I don't know why I didn't do it years ago. He's just as compassionate as I've always known him to be, and there's so much about his life that I didn't know either. Like how he'd been scared to burden me while my mom was sick. We talk almost daily about everything. Well, everything except Adam. I'm pretty sure he generally understands that we have some sort of feelings for each other, and that the Olivia thing is complicated, but he also seems to understand that's not where I need my focus to be right now.

I will talk to him about it, though.

October flies by and Halloween is here in the blink of an eye. Earlier in the month, Caleb and I ran into a guy we met at orientation. He invited us to a costume party at a house just off campus. It's a different crowd than we usually hang around, but I'm excited to have some fun.

That is, until I'm looking in the mirror. The self-proclaimed "sexy" Hogwarts uniform—Ravenclaw, of course—is way too revealing. The blue plaid schoolgirl-style skirt is quite a bit short for comfort, but at least the black robe is long enough to cover the parts of my butt that the skirt doesn't. What's harder to hide is the low-cut top meant to show off more cleavage than is cute. At least it's long enough to cover most of my midriff.

I'm all for dressing up, and I'm not opposed to showing off my body, but I prefer to do it in ways much more subtle than this.

"Damn girl, you look hot!"

I whip around to glare at Caleb who's leaning against my door frame in his Gryffindor outfit.

"Why do you get to wear pants and a sweater vest, and I'm stuck in fabric leftovers?" I ask, exasperated.

Caleb's laughing now, he knows how I feel about this outfit, but we didn't have time to find a new costume. "You were there, Ry. You know this is not what it looked like in the listing."

"Stupid, lying, online listing," I say bitterly. "If I didn't love you so much, I'd break my promise to go in a heartbeat."

Caleb gives me a warm smile. "I know. We can leave whenever you're ready, deal?"

I cross my arms, only to uncross them when they, impossibly, make the cleavage situation worse.

I groan. "Deal."

* * *

"WHAT'S a bombshell like you doing in the cor—"

"Keep walking," I say to the newest idiot approaching me. I might've spoken to one of them if they hadn't had their eyes glued to my chest as they approached. I try to pull the robe around to cover me, but it's not made for that.

I look around again for Caleb, we've been here for half an hour, and I've already lost him. With every pair of unwanted eyes on me, I shrink further towards the edge of the room, hoping to become invisible. I can't find a familiar face here, and the only friendly faces are too friendly, intoxicated guys.

Where did Caleb go?

I pour myself a drink, non-alcoholic—I learned my lesson after last time—and go in search of him. After circling the room, there's no sign of him. The only other place I've seen people go is through a hallway off the back of the small front room. That seems to be where the music is coming from too.

The hallway leads to a larger living space where all the furniture has been cleared away to create a makeshift dance floor, and off to the left is the kitchen. I'm weaving my way through the crowd looking for Caleb when a flash of white catches my attention and I stop dead in my tracks. I'd recognize him, anywhere, from any angle.

Adam is here.

His back is to me, but I can tell his costume is supposed to be a toga, like a Greek God. I smile, heart racing. He looks incredible. The costume suits him, but I always thought he was built to be a God. I can try to lock away my feelings all I want, but they're still here.

Seeing him reminds me that we haven't spoken to or seen each other since that party in September, and it exposes the gaping hole in my life that is his friendship. I miss him like crazy. From our late-night talks, to little texts, to seeing him at

The Split Bean, and school meet-ups. We used to talk all the time. Just because it's easier to focus on healing when he's not around, doesn't mean I don't want him in my life still.

Just as I work up the courage to step toward him, a gorgeous, blonde-haired girl walks up to him and snakes a possessive arm around his waist. I stop breathing and watch in horror as Adam smiles one of *my* smiles at her before pulling her into a kiss. She's dressed as a Greek Goddess—*his* Goddess.

That must be Olivia.

All the blood drains from my face. I feel lightheaded. I might as well call my costume Moaning Myrtle now since I'm sure I look like a ghost.

She's everything I'm not—glamorous, drop-dead gorgeous, and born to be the center of someone like Adam's world. She's my opposite in looks, with blonde hair, brown eyes, curvy in all the right places, and modelesque in height. Honestly, even *I'd* drop me if I could choose her.

I close my eyes and take a few deep, shaking breaths. This hurts. This hurts a lot. I try to remember that I told him he doesn't have to wait for me. I told him I wasn't ready. I'm still not ready. But that doesn't make it easier to see the person I want with another girl.

I *am* mad at Adam, but not about this.

Even so, I'd rather not subject myself to watching it all night.

I keep looking for Caleb, pushing through the thick crowd of people in every variety of costume imaginable, until I finally spot him in the kitchen chatting with a gorgeous brunette who's also dressed in Hogwarts attire. He looks so happy, smiling and laughing, blushing and flirting, and she appears to be just as into it.

My grin is over the top when he glances over and meets my eyes, blushing at the look there. He says something to her then heads over to me.

"I am *so* sorry," he starts, pleading, and I just laugh. "I was on my way back to find you when I started talking to Jess, and I guess I got carried away. You okay?"

"I think I'm going to head home," I say, and he immediately flips into protective friend mode.

"What happened? Do I have to kick someone's ass?"

I laugh but my smile fades as I say, "Adam is here with Olivia."

His face turns to stone. "I had no idea. Oh my god. Are you okay?"

"Surprisingly, yes." I smile but a tear drops down my cheek. "I thought seeing them together would hurt a lot more than this. It hurts, but it doesn't feel like it's tearing me apart. It would've a few months ago, though."

His brows rise like he knows there's more to the story, but he doesn't push. "I'll come with you."

"No, Cale. She's cute and she's into you. Stay."

"Are you sure?"

I reach out to grab his hand. "Because of you, and how you've helped me, I know I'll be okay. I'm not going to go home and spiral, I swear. I just think it'll be healthier for me to not watch them all night. I promise I'll text you if I need anything, but I won't. Now, go. You deserve to be happy too." I wink at him, and he grins.

"I'm proud of you, you know. You're putting yourself first, taking care of you." He squeezes my hand. "You're amazing," he adds in a whisper, leaning in to hug me. "And thank you."

"Go get the girl." I smile at him and raise my eyebrows suggestively. "And tell me all about her . . . tomorrow."

He laughs and says one last goodbye before heading back over to her. She's looking over at me with tight eyes, sizing me up. I don't know if he notices, but I do.

I turn and leave, hoping I haven't done anything to ruin his chances.

When I get home, I rinse off the smell of smoke and alcohol, and throw on my faded Hawaii shirt that I wear every night to feel closer to my mom, cotton shorts, and fuzzy socks. I sit on my bed, crisscross, and hug one of my pillows into my chest.

I'm not sure exactly what I'm doing, but I look up and start talking.

"Hi, Mom. It's me. I'm sorry it's taken me so long to talk to you, I just—" A tear slips down my cheek. "I just didn't know how to do this before. I still don't, but I'm going to try."

I squeeze the pillow tighter as tears flow steadily. My voice is a squeaky mess, but I just keep going. "I miss you. So much. I wish you were here, every day. I wish I could call you and talk to you when I do well in my classes—I am doing well by the way. Sometimes I overhear funny conversations on campus that I know you'd have loved to hear. You moms always loved your gossip in Lockney. You'd be so proud of how amazing a friend Caleb still is. I think he met someone special tonight. Don't worry, I'll make sure she treats him right.

"I miss you when I want to talk about boys, I've been having some troubles lately. I never told you, but I fell in love with Adam years ago. Yes, Adam Dey." I smile through the tears and huff out a laugh. It's like I can hear her talking back. "I know, how cliché. Falling in love with your best friend's older brother. He likes me too, though. Or at least, he did. He's seeing another girl right now and they look happy together.

"Don't roll your eyes, but I think I told him to date her. How stupid am I? I've just been so lost without you, mom. It's like every day something new happens that I want you to know about and it just reminds me you're gone. I'm scared that I'm going to change into someone you didn't know. I'm scared that one day I'm not going to remember your gentle eyes and bright smile, and the way you felt next to me when I'd curl up beside you on your hospital bed. Until recently, I haven't been handling things well. I'm still figuring out what it means to live without you. It still hurts so much, like a huge piece of me is gone.

"That's why I told Adam I couldn't be with him right now. Was I wrong? What if he ends up with Olivia all because I didn't think I was ready? But I can't deny that I've only come as far as I have because I told him we had to wait. I was too obsessed with him to accomplish anything when he was around. I think you'd be proud. You always told me we were strong enough to accomplish anything without a man, but you also told me good men were worth the risk. Adam is one of the good ones, Mom. I know he is, but I had to do this without him first. Do you think we'll end up together in the end? God, I wish I knew what you thought of all this."

I flop back on the bed and close my eyes.

"I hope you're watching from up there with a smile on your face. I love you, Mom."

I curl into a ball and fall asleep on a tear-soaked pillow. In my dreams, she talks back. She's happy, she's pain-free, and she's proud of who I've become.

chapter thirteen

THE WEEKS before Thanksgiving break pass quickly. Between classes, exams, and work, I haven't had much time for going out. When I told Angie what I saw at the Halloween party, her jaw dropped, and she threatened to drop-kick Adam next time he came in. Considering she takes karate classes for fun once a week, I don't think she was joking. But Adam hasn't stopped by in over a month.

Caleb spends most of his free time now with Jess. He came home the morning after the Halloween party with the biggest smile on his face and woke me up to tell me how amazing she is. She's in nursing school, and from the few times I've met her, I think she's perfect for Caleb. She's intelligent and kind, and has one of those sweet, innocent, southern personalities that's infectious. Claire is over-the-moon excited to meet her at Thanksgiving—her family lives in Oklahoma and it wasn't convenient to go home for the shorter break so Caleb invited her to go home with him.

After Caleb told me about Jess, I told him about my talk with my mom and he just hugged me and said, *"I bet she loved hearing from you.*" I cried again, but more from happiness than sadness.

With him out most evenings lately, I've been focusing on myself. I've been making good progress, but one thing I still need to learn is how to be happy on my own. I'd realized that I look for happiness in others—my mom, Adam, Caleb—and when I don't have them, I lose my happiness. I feel empty.

I want to be whole on my own so that when I have other people, it's just the icing on the cake, not the foundation of who I am. Part of that is discovering activities that bring me joy. Things I do just for me.

I've started reading more, they're advanced coding books, but it's still fun—to me. Sometimes I'll read them in the bath with Epsom salts and candles, so it doesn't just feel like studying. I watch a lot of rom-coms and chick flicks. I used to love doing this with my mom and stopped after she passed—it's nice to be able to enjoy it again. And with the holidays coming up there's a lot of new ones coming out so it keeps me busy.

But as the holidays approach, so does my dread. No amount of healing could save me from the pain of the first holiday season without my mom. Even though last year she wasn't doing well, she was still around. She was even able to leave the hospital for Thanksgiving to come to the Dey's. But by Christmas she couldn't get out of bed at all, so I spent it at the hospital. There are so many bittersweet feelings that come with these traditions, these memories.

I haven't thought much about Adam since Halloween, except the time Claire called us one night and gushed about how Adam's girlfriend is coming to Thanksgiving too and I felt sick. Spending multiple days in the same house as them is different than running into them at a party—I can't just walk away this time. But there's nowhere else I could imagine being for Thanksgiving than with the Dey's, so I'll just use it as a test to see how far I've really come.

I think I'm starting to figure out who I am again, and it feels good, but it doesn't make the loss hurt any less. The few times I have let my mind drift to Adam—usually when it's late at night and I've just watched a rom-com that reminded me of us—it's to wonder if he cares about me anymore. Adam always used to know when I was having a hard time and would be there for me. Either he doesn't realize how hard this is for me, or he does and doesn't care enough to reach out.

I'm not sure which one I prefer, but neither sounds like the Adam I love.

The Sunday morning before Thanksgiving break, which starts Wednesday, I'm opening the shop alone. Angie is supposed to be here, but I woke to a text that she caught the flu and can't come in. It's too late to find someone to cover and she's always stepped up for me, so I'm solo until lunchtime.

It's going to be a long day.

I've just unlocked the door and am walking back to the counter when the bell rings, signaling a customer walking in. My eyes close and I let out a quiet sigh, it's never a good sign when someone is waiting for the shop to open. It usually means we're going to be extremely busy.

"Good morning," I say, putting on my best customer service voice—cheery and bright. "Welcome to The Split B—" My voice dies in my throat when I turn around and see who's lingering a step inside the door.

My bright and cheery demeanor drops into surprise, hurt, and jealousy. He still looks as good as ever. "What do you want, Adam?" I ask, trying not to get blinded by my emotions shifting into overdrive seeing him again.

He recoils at my tone. "Rylie, I—"

I don't have the time or patience for this today.

I cut him off with a bitter laugh. "I swear if the words *I'm sorry* come out of your mouth I might hit you. Now please, get to the point. Why are you here?"

He looks like each word I speak physically hurts him, and underneath the anger my heart breaks for his pain. But this is the guy that stood me up, made me look an idiot for waiting for him, and hasn't talked to me in two months when he knows what I'm going through. Anger is definitely winning.

Exasperated, I sigh, already exhausted by this encounter. "Shouldn't you be with your girlfriend?"

He stares wide-eyed at me, face draining of color. "Who told you?"

"First, I overheard Ryan ask about Olivia at the party in September," I say, trying not to raise my voice or let my pain slip through but it cracks as I continue. "Second, I was at that stupid Halloween party and saw you, and third, your mom called, practically jumping for joy that your girlfriend was coming to Thanksgiving."

"I'm so sorry, Rylie. I wanted to be the one to tell you." His face twists in pain and I want to spit back that he's had two months to tell me, but I don't trust that I won't scream at him right now. But then he says, "Let me explain," and I lose it.

"Explain? Explain what? You've made it glaringly obvious where we stand and how you feel about me. You don't have to explain anything, your actions have done all the talking for you." I turn and continue to move behind the counter so there's something solid between us. It gives me security so I won't do something stupid like run into his arms, which is all I've wanted to do since the second I saw him standing there. I hope he understands that I'm so mad because I care so much—too much.

"Ry—"

"No, Adam. I don't want to hear it," I say, forcefully and the rest of the words come tumbling out of my mouth even though I wish I'd just shut up. "Do you know how long I waited for you at the column that Monday after the party? I looked like an idiot, waiting for someone who never showed, who didn't even have the decency to send a heads-up. And what's worse is I still look every time, hoping to see you there."

Tears start to form, and I hate that I'm admitting all this to him, but I can't stop. "You knew what I was going through, you knew how I felt about you, and you still just walked out of my life with no explanation. So please, don't give me some excuse about how we're still friends or how you still care, because if that's how you treat your friends, then I don't want any part of it. And thanks for asking, but I've been doing just fine without you."

"Rylie, I never meant—"

"No," I cut him off again, shaking my head. My day is already going to be too long, I don't need to start it out with some sob story. "I think you should leave."

Pain washes over his face as he realizes I'm not going to hear him out. He turns to leave but stops after a few steps. "I know I've been a bad friend lately, and I'm sorry . . . ." He turns to look at me and for a moment our eyes lock and that connection is still there. We lose ourselves in it for as long as we dare before he looks away and continues. "I just didn't want you to be blindsided if you didn't know, you don't deserve that." As an afterthought, he adds, "I never wanted to hurt you."

A tear drops down my cheek and I wish he'd ignore the words coming out of my mouth and come wipe it away like he's always done before. "It's too late for that."

I regret saying it the moment it hits him, and he actually staggers back a step. He turns to leave but stops with his hand on the door. "You deserve better than how I've been treating you."

With that, he walks out leaving me stunned into silence. It felt like he still cared during that conversation, but the past two months tell a different story. Why aren't things ever simple for us? I'm more confused than ever.

How many times will I let him break my heart before I stop

laying it in his hands? The issue is that my heart is only his to break. Even after all this time it still belongs wholly to him.

* * *

I TRY to forget about Adam as I climb into the back seat of Jess's car, she's driving Caleb and I to the lake house. Luckily, she offered before I had to come up with an excuse of why I didn't want to ride with Adam . . . and his girlfriend.

I haven't stopped replaying our conversation since that day. We're both hurt, but all we seemed to do was hurt each other more. I only made things worse, that's for sure, but I don't know how much better that conversation could've gone. What did he expect when he showed up?

But enough about him. I want to use this long drive to learn more about Jess.

Caleb was right, she's kind and caring, intelligent and outgoing, and beautiful. Most of all, she seems to like Caleb as much as he likes her. She's always leaning toward him, or finding excuses to touch his arm throughout the ride.

They make a great couple.

It's enough to distract me from the couple I've been dreading seeing, until we pull up to the house to find Adam's car is already here. It's one thing to know that he's with her, but it's a whole other thing to have to witness it with my own two eyes. It's easier to say I'm fine with it when I'm not watching them hold hands or share secrets. Is it wrong of me to hope that he doesn't look at her the way I've seen him look at me before? Because I *really* hope he doesn't.

Caleb picks up on my robotic motions and fake smile hiding the hurt and hesitation and stops me before we get inside. "Are you sure you're ready for this?"

I'm almost positive if I say no, Caleb will put us back in the car and drive somewhere until I am, or drive me all the way back to campus if I'm never ready. The knowledge that he's on my side even against his brother makes me smile and I say softly, "As ready as I'll ever be."

Claire is happy as ever to see us and starts doting over Jess immediately. From the warm smiles and fond eyes, it's obvious Claire loves her already. Caleb leads Jess to the living room, and I follow a few steps back. Caleb awkwardly stops as he steps into the living room and I take a deep breath, preparing myself for what I know he's now seeing. I step forward and my eyes lock with Adam, who's already watching me as he pulls his arm quickly off the blonde from the party, Olivia. Not quick enough.

Caleb reaches for my hand, and I squeeze it in reassurance. It doesn't hurt as much as I expected, as much as it did the last time I saw them together. Adam's eyes stay on me as he walks towards us, but I keep mine on Olivia, surprised by how little anger I feel towards her.

"Caleb, Rylie, this is Olivia." Adam looks uncomfortable as he makes these introductions. His eyes flash to me and he's about to say something, but I'm still not wanting to talk to him.

I walk right past him and approach Olivia with a genuine, warm smile. "Hi, Olivia, it's nice to finally meet you."

Adam's eyes are locked on us, probably wondering if I'll be as rude to her as I've been to him, but he doesn't need to worry, I don't have anything against her—except that she's with him, which isn't a good enough reason to hate her. *He's* the one who hurt me so it's unfair to take out my frustration on her. I'm going to try, really try, to give her a fair chance.

I hate to admit it, but by the end of the night, I really do like her. She's kind-hearted and has a good sense of humor. We have a lot more in common than I'd ever have guessed. But as much as I like her, it's still hard to be around her knowing she has everything I want—Adam.

He's been hesitantly watching me all night, particularly when I'm talking to her, but even when I'm not, he's trying to get my attention, to talk to me. It's a lot harder to ignore him when I'm still so aware of everything he's doing, but I'm doing an outstanding job if I do say so myself.

It doesn't go unnoticed by the rest of the house that I'm blatantly ignoring him, although Caleb is the only one who has any idea why and he steps in, pulling me aside if a situation ever comes up where I might have to talk to him. Jess catches on fast too and I adore her for it, for not knowing anything about what's going on but stepping up to help me all the same.

I'm in the kitchen grabbing a glass of water, trying not to think about what was revealed in this room only months ago, before heading to bed when Caleb walks in and leans against the counter across from me. "You okay?"

"Yeah, I'm fine." My smile is sadder than I want it to be. It's still hard being in this house, although I haven't gotten close to a panic attack yet which is progress from the last time I was here.

He raises his eyebrows. "You seemed friendly with Olivia."

I sigh. "I don't have anything against her. I actually think, under different circumstances, we could be friends."

"Do you want to talk about what happened?" he asks, always quick to cut straight to the topics I'd rather avoid. "I think this is the one topic you haven't opened up about yet."

I planned to tell him eventually, might as well be now. "Adam and I kissed on the Fourth of July."

I pause to gauge his reaction, hoping he won't be mad but instead he appears to be holding back a smile.

I continue. "On the way home we ended up admitting we have feelings for each other." My eyes narrow when he doesn't react to the words. "You're not mad?"

"Rylie, I'm your best friend." He smiles, not a single drop of betrayal or anger can be found in his expression. "I'm more insulted you think I wouldn't realize you have feelings for my brother. Why do you think I tease you about him so often? I've been waiting for you to say something first."

Color creeps onto my cheeks. "I mean I figured you'd guessed close enough to the truth, but I wasn't sure if the jokes were a deflection or in support."

He laughs and there's such warmth in the sound I feel silly for ever thinking he'd be mad. "When I first noticed it, it was a little weird. But then I started paying attention to how you two interacted and I wondered how I didn't notice sooner. It's obvious how much you care about each other, support each other, and how happy you make each other. It's all I could ever want for my best friend, or my brother, so I got past the weirdness quickly."

"How did I get so lucky to find a friend like you?" My eyes are glassy but I blink the tears away.

"I got pretty damn lucky too." He smiles and reaches across the counter to squeeze my hand. "But what happened next, I want to hear this story."

I laugh and remember where I left off. "Right, so after we admitted our feelings, I told him I wasn't ready for anything because of my mom."

His brows furrow. "What do you mean?"

"Well, when we kissed"—I blush, still feeling weird talking to Caleb about kissing his brother—"there was a piece of me that wanted it because it was a distraction from my problems. I told you how I hyperventilated when we pulled up to the house, but I also had a breakdown the first night too. I was in such an emotionally unstable state, I didn't want to jump into something that I wasn't ready to give my all to. I didn't think it would've been healthy for me to dive into a relationship if any part of me was in it for the wrong reasons. So I told him, I needed to heal more first so that when we were together we'd have a real chance."

"Wow, Ry . . ." He pauses for so long I'm convinced he thinks I'm psycho now, but he surprises me. "That's really mature of you."

"For a while after that, we couldn't stay away from each other. We were texting constantly and every time we were near each other it was so hard to know what we knew and act normal. And then that party in September happened."

His eyes widened. "When you guys were all over each other? Yeah I remember that."

I smile sheepishly, ears and neck turning red. "Well, I felt selfish for asking him to wait for me when I didn't know how long it'd take me to heal, so I told him he didn't have to wait for me if he found someone new. But I overheard his friends at the end of night ask him about Olivia, which is why I asked you."

He's nodding. "This all makes so much sense now."

"And you know we always met after class on Monday and went to lunch together. The Monday after the party he never showed up. He hasn't talked to me at all since, except earlier this week he showed up at The Split Bean to warn me he was bringing Olivia. But obviously I already knew everything by then, and I kinda blew up at him for ghosting me like that."

"Why didn't you say any—" His voice cuts out and his eyes widen. "That's the Monday you tried to call me when I was in class."

I look down and nod, still trying to hide how deeply hurt I am. "I didn't know he was officially with her then, but you came home and told me. I realized I hadn't done any true healing since July and panicked that I was going to lose him. I'd already decided I was going to tell you everything, but that pushed me to do it all right then." I shrug. "At the end of the day, I've only come this far because he left, but I'm still mad at him, and on top of that still care for him so much. The holidays are already a hard time so I've just ignored him because I couldn't handle it all."

Caleb moves around the island and pulls me into a hug. "I'm sorry this happened and that I didn't know to be there for you through it. You have every right to be mad at Adam, I'm even mad at him for what he did. He hurt you. I'm not excusing his actions in any way, but I know my brother enough to know he still really cares about you. He was watching you tonight, everyone could see that, but it wasn't to see what you'd say to Olivia. He was watching to see how hurt you were. He's hurting too."

I hold him tighter. "I know, that's what makes it even harder. I just think I need to take care of myself first right now."

"I hope you can see how much you've grown, because you really have—a lot," he says, pulling back to look at me and I'm taken aback. "You've always been too kind, putting others' happiness before your own, and even at your expense. But right now, you're handling this with a new strength. You're still being kind, but you're putting yourself first and I'm proud of you for that."

"You know a wise man once told me it's about time I learned to love myself." My smile is warm in remembrance of everything Caleb has done to help me. "So, I'm learning."

He beams back. "He sounds very wise indeed."

We laugh together, letting the bonds of friendship strengthen between us.

"You ready for bed, Caleb?" We look over to find Jess in the doorway, looking extremely uncomfortable to have found me and Caleb still half-embracing.

I grimace, the last thing I want is for them to have issues because of me. Judging by Caleb's half-smile as he starts to walk away, he's worried too. He just helped me and now, it's time for me to help him.

"Hey Jess, can I talk to you for a minute?"

Her eyes flash to Caleb in confusion but he only shrugs, not knowing what I'm up to either.

"Sure," she says hesitantly. Caleb gives her a kiss on the cheek before heading up stairs.

When we're alone, I smile at her. "I wanted to say thanks, for earlier, for helping me when you didn't know the situation."

Her face softens. "You don't have to thank me. I figured there was a reason Caleb was acting that way so the least I could do was help."

"How much has Caleb told you about our friendship?"

She blinks a few times in quick succession, my questions catching her off-guard, but she recovers quickly. "Just that you're his best friend and you've known each other since fourth grade."

"He never was one to tell other people's stories." I smile.

"I don't understand."

"I've never seen Caleb as happy as he is with you," I say, and her small smile and the blush on her cheeks conveys how much she cares. "I'm sure it can be hard dating someone who's best friend is another girl and I'd never be able to forgive myself if I got in the way of Caleb's happiness."

Jess looks down, cheeks flushing in embarrassment this time as she gets where I'm headed. "I don't think negatively of you, Rylie."

I give her a soft smile. "I know, but I also don't blame you for being uncomfortable at times." Her cheeks redden further and it's a silent acknowledgement that it's the truth. "I really like you Jess, I think we could become good friends—if you wanted that too. Regardless, I'd like to help you understand me and my relationship with Caleb better."

"I'd like that too . . . to be friends."

I smile and take a deep breath. "Growing up, it was just me and my mom. My dad died when I was young, and I never knew any other family. A year after I met Caleb, my mom was diagnosed with breast cancer and as soon as Claire found out, she did everything she could to help. When my mom was in the hospital, I'd stay here. The Dey family became my second family and Caleb and I only got closer because he was there for me through all this.

"In January, my mom passed away," I say, my voice down to

a whisper and Jess's eyes snap up to mine. There's an understanding there that I didn't expect. "It's been a tough year and the Dey's . . . they're the only family I have left now. Caleb's been by my side as I've gone through hell and back. He's family, and I've never seen him as anything other than that."

To make sure she truly understands, I take a deep breath and tell her the truth. "And between us, my heart belongs to the other Dey brother, which is what that whole mess was about today."

She nods but there's tears in her eyes and she takes a step toward me. "I lost my dad to cancer a few years back. While my situation is different, I understand more than you know."

The feeling of being fully understood is overwhelming and without realizing what we're doing, Jess and I both move in for a hug. We hold each other as tears stream down both of our faces. Two hearts bonding over the same dark pain.

"Thank you for sharing your story with me," she whispers. "I know how hard it can be to talk about. I'm so glad you had Caleb to lean on all those years. No one should have to go through that alone."

"I'm so glad you and Caleb found each other. He deserves happiness and I can see you make him so happy."

"I'm grateful he has a friend who cares about him as much as you do."

We release each other and I have a feeling she'll quickly become a valued friend.

"And Rylie," she says before we head upstairs, "I know how hard first holidays can be without a parent, so please don't hesitate to reach out if you need someone to talk to."

"Thank you, Jess." I smile at her and the same happiness I feel is reflected back in her. At the top of the stairs I head left to my guest room and she heads right, to Caleb's.

* * *

I SLOWLY CREEP down the stairs and into the kitchen. It's almost two in the morning and I can't sleep. I'm not struggling to catch my breath, but I needed to get out of that room. I head to the Keurig machine to get a cup of hot water and the pantry to grab a bag of chamomile tea.

Mug in hand, I'm about to head back upstairs when a silhouette in the living room catches my attention. Is someone else up?

I walk in the direction of the stone fireplace and find it on, with Claire sitting on the couch. Her usually perfectly done hair is a messy slop on top of her head, and her feet are pulled up underneath her. She's staring at the flames, seemingly lost in memory. An empty mug sits on the table beside her.

"Couldn't sleep either?" I whisper and her head whips around in surprise, eyes widening as if she's seeing a ghost. She blinks a few times as if adjusting to the light and her face relaxes again.

"Oh, Rylie. I didn't hear you coming."

"Can I sit?" I ask, unsure if she wants to be left alone.

"Please." Her easy smile is back, and I sink into one of the chairs perpendicular to the couch, facing the fireplace.

We're both quiet for a while, the soft crackle of the fire and howling of the wind are the only sounds around us. Claire is staring into the fire again and she looks sad. I'm about to give her some space when she speaks.

"Is it hard for you to be here?"

I lower the mug from my lips before I take a sip and look at the fire too. "Yes, and no. It's not as hard as when I came in July, but I can still see her all over this place."

She lets out a long breath. "Me too."

The words feel like a punch to my chest, stealing all my air. How did I never think about the fact that Claire lost a friend when I lost my mom? I'm a little ashamed that I never said anything to her.

"At first I only saw the bad days," I say. "After the funeral, the time she felt pain at dinner that led to the diagnosis of her third relapse, the New Years she was throwing up because of her treatment. But then I realized that this house holds so many more good memories of her. All the holidays and dinners that she couldn't stop smiling—she smiled so much when she was here. The times you guys would sit out on the patio and watch us on the lake. The movie night we had when we forced the boys to watch all our favorite chick flicks. Now, I remember those and it's like she's alive in the memories of this place."

I didn't realize how true that was until the words were out of my mouth. It's hard to be here, but that's because I remember her best here and I wouldn't trade that for the world.

Claire looks up at me, the fire reflecting in her glassy eyes. "You're so much like her. When you first walked up, all I saw were your eyes and I thought I was dreaming of her."

"The same thing happens to me with mirrors," I admit and pain flickers across her face.

"You know I lost my mom when I was about your age."

"I didn't know that," I breathe.

"I knew what it felt like to go through what you were going through, that's why I did everything I could to make things easier for you. I just wish I could've done more."

"Claire," I squeak, tears in my eyes. "What you did was everything. I know it meant so much to her, and it's meant so much to me. I don't know what I'd do without your family."

"It's your family too, Rylie." She looks directly in my eyes, leaning towards me. "You are part of my family."

I only nod because I can't speak through this feeling building in me. I've spent so much time fighting against this, telling myself I'm not their family. Being scared that admitting that would feel like replacing my mom. But right now, I see that the Dey's have always been part of my family. They were my mom's family too.

I set my mug down, move to the couch next to Claire, and

hug her. "I'm so sorry, Claire. I've been so selfish. You lost your friend, your family, too, and instead of being there, I pushed you all away as if you couldn't understand."

"Oh, honey." She squeezes me tighter. "You lost your mom, nothing you do has to make sense."

"I'm so sorry," I cry into her shoulder as she strokes my hair and soothes me.

After we've both calmed down, we head to bed but we're both lighter after the conversation. Something just permanently changed between us, and it changed for the better. I can picture my mom smiling down on us, having waited for this moment when the two people she cared for most finally connected.

It's as if she planned it this way.

chapter fourteen

THE SMELL of bacon and sound of laughter wakes me Thanksgiving morning. With a smile on my face as I remember the conversation I had with Claire last night, I open the door to head downstairs, not bothering to change out of my gray sweats and Hawaii shirt. A creek at the end of the hall snags my attention and Olivia emerges from the second guest room at the end of the hall.

"Good morning," I say, trying to keep the surprise and intrigue off my face. I assumed she spent the night in Adam's room, as Jess had with Caleb. The thought had sent a pang of jealousy through me but for some reason, I never thought about going out onto the dock. Maybe because I always did that with him and he isn't part of my life right now, or maybe because I always went out there to breathe and I wasn't suffocating. I'm surviving, healing, without him.

"Good morning." Her smile is genuine and kind. Even though I like her, I don't see how we can be friends. Just because I won't hold it against her that she's with Adam doesn't mean I want to subject myself to the pain and jealousy I feel when I look at her.

"Grab some food and join us," Claire says when she spots us entering the room. Claire, Phil, Caleb, and Jess are around the dining table laughing and talking. I grab some eggs, bacon, and fruit before taking a seat next to Phil and across from Jess.

We all fall into easy conversation, that is, until Adam finally comes down and the only seat left is between me and Olivia. The rest of us are done eating and as Adam sits, the conversation dies down and unease clouds the table. I don't look up from my plate even when I feel his eyes on me and he's sitting close enough to touch.

Jess stands, her chair scraping against the floor and my eyes lift to her. "I'm going to go get ready, if you'll excuse me." Her eyes lock onto mine. "Rylie, could I bother you for some help with my hair, I love the way you do your braids."

My fondness for Jess grows exponentially. "Of course, as long as you'll show me how you always get your eyeliner to be so perfect."

Smiling at each other, we head upstairs, arm in arm. Caleb and Claire watch us, both looking extremely happy that we're getting along. Adam's eyes follow me out of the room even though he keeps his head down, trying to pretend he's not watching.

Why does his gaze still set me on fire?

Thirty minutes later, we're both ready and sitting on my bed, gossiping. Some of Caleb's extended family, close friends, and neighbors are coming over in an hour. These are people I grew up around so I'm giving her a rundown on everyone coming when there's a knock at the door.

"Everyone decent?" Caleb calls through the door.

"Come on in!"

He looks us over and smiles. "You're both looking lovely today."

Jess is in a beige sweater dress with her hair pulled back into one of my mom's signature braids, and I'm in gray jeans with a rust-colored sweater. My eye makeup is immaculately done by Jess.

"Thanks babe." Jess beams at him. "Rylie was just giving me the lowdown on everyone coming. It's quite an . . . interesting group."

His eyes widen. "It would take years to explain it all."

We all laugh, and Caleb's face softens, taking in how friendly Jess and I are. He says softly, "I'm glad to see you guys getting along."

"I think we're going to be fast friends." I smile at Jess.

She smiles back. "I think we already are."

And she's right—we are.

* * *

THE PARTY'S in full swing. The smell of a turkey roasting fills the air, and the sounds of laughter are all around. Drinks have been flowing freely for hours, and most are nursing their second or third drink while some are already hammered. For Caleb's Uncle Sal, who I've been stuck talking to for too long, it's the latter. I zoned out of the conversation a while ago and have been looking for an out since.

"Thank goodness that one woman isn't here this year," Sal slurs, and I start paying attention again.

"Who?" I ask, hoping that I will end this conversation soon.

"The bald one," he says, and every muscle in my body hardens in place. There's only one person he could be referring to with that description. My mom. "Why couldn't she have worn a wig or something. It was so rude of her to not be considerate to us who had to look at her."

The more he talks the less I can breathe.

"She might've even been attractive if she just wore a wig."

My legs are weak, I might fall over at any second. There's no way this is really happening, he's not actually being this disrespectful to my face. Does he not realize he's talking about *my* mom? He's still talking but I'm no longer listening, I can't.

My blood is boiling with rage, and I'm seeing red. I'm not one to make a scene but there's nothing else but my sadness and anger right now.

I don't know if I'm interrupting him or not, but I ground out, "I'm sorry that *my mother's cancer* was such an inconvenience to *you*."

My anger is so overwhelming it brings tears to my eyes. He must snap into reality for a moment because his eyes widen in horror as he realizes who he's talking to and realizes what he just said.

"Why don't I just bring her back from the dead to tell her to wear a wig, so she'll be more attractive to you." I scoff. "As if looking attractive to you mattered to a woman fighting for her damn life."

I try to keep my voice down but I'm sure anyone in the vicinity can hear me now.

"Ryl—"

"Don't you *dare* say my name," I snap, my whole body shaking. Tears start to fall but I don't care who sees. "And learn some goddamn respect before you ever try to talk to me again."

I turn and head straight up the stairs, not caring who heard or saw, just wanting to get away from everything and the dock is too public with everyone around. I sit on the edge of the bed, teetering between flopping back onto the bed and collapsing down to the ground, caught between rage and overwhelming sadness. If I missed my mom before, her absence is a black hole now, pulling me into the darkness.

"Rylie," a voice says softly, and there's a blip of light cutting through the darkness. A muted click of the door closing again registers, but through the pounding in my ears I can't distinguish who the voice belongs to. But who else could it be other than Caleb.

I look up, desperate for Caleb to comfort me, to help save me from myself, and I freeze because it's not Caleb in the room. Adam's here and he looks just as pained and enraged as I am. But I'm also angry with him, so I spit out the same words I said earlier this week. "Shouldn't you be with your girlfriend?"

Hurt flashes across his face but his lips press together as he shakes his head and confidently says, "No, I'm exactly where I should be."

I collapse back onto the bed, not wanting to sort through his hot and cold treatment right now. He takes a step toward me, but I halt him with a look. His face drops.

"I kicked him out," he says softly.

My head snaps up. "What?"

"I was close enough to hear what he said." His breathing turns ragged with rage. "The *horrible* things he said. I told him to get out and not come back until he's sober." He takes a small step toward me, and I watch timidly, wanting him to come closer still but not sure I should let him. "I'm so sorry, Rylie. For today, for the past two months, for . . . god, for so many things. I'd convinced myself that being around you wasn't giving you the time to heal, and then I started to worry that maybe things hadn't worked out with us because we weren't right for each other. But staying away from you is the hardest thing I've ever done."

We lock eyes and I can't look away. I don't know if that's a tear falling down his cheek or just the blur of my own tears.

"But hearing what was just said . . . I don't know, I just lost sight of everything. Seeing you hurt like that, I didn't think, I just ran after you. You were the only thing that mattered."

Those are definitely tears in his eyes. Part of me hates myself for being ready to forgive him so easily, but the other part is ready to kiss him right now. There's one thing I need to know before I decide which side will win. "And Olivia?"

He flinches as if just realizing he left her downstairs somewhere. He looks away. "Things weren't going to work out between us anyways. I think we both realized it. I knew the second I saw you on Sunday that it was over. I shouldn't have brought her, but she didn't have anywhere else to go and mom had already invited her"—*Claire invited her?*—"and I panicked, and you wouldn't talk to me. I fucked up, Rylie. I stopped seeing you because part of me knew that the second I did, it would be over between Olivia and me. I convinced myself I just needed time to settle into the relationship, but I knew, of course, I knew. She could never be what I wanted because she could never be you."

His voice breaks on the last word and tears come streaming from his eyes. My heart reaches for him, wanting to soothe his pain the way he's always done for mine. It doesn't excuse what he did, but I can at least understand part of why he did it.

"I know I have no right to ask for your forgiveness, to ask for space back in your life, but I am anyway, because selfishly, I'm the one who needs you." He's pleading. He takes a step closer, and I sit up, my attention fully focused on him as he continues. "I hate that I only hurt you by leaving, and I hate that I told you I'd be your shoulder to cry on and then wasn't there when I knew you needed me. But I'm here now, and I'll wait forever for you to be ready if that's what it takes. I promise, I'm not walking away again." His voice grows more desperate with every word spoken. "Please tell me there's still room for me in your life. I want to help you heal, not leave you on your own. Please forgive me for being such an idiot. Please give me another chance."

"I've been so mad at you," I say, already knowing I will give him a second chance but needing him to know how he hurt me.

"I know." His voice is small, and his head drops.

"I thought that you didn't care anymore," I whisper, a solo, traitorous tear drops down my cheek as I remember the feeling of loneliness that washed over me that September day. "You knew better than anyone how much I was struggling, and you weren't there."

"I swear, it'll never happen again," he says, voice cracking with pain. He drops to his knees before me. His eyes are full of agony, his face twisted in pain as if he'd just been stabbed in the chest. All I want is to fall into his arms and never leave, but there's one more thing he needs to hear.

"But I wasn't joking when I said I was doing fine without you. I've been healing, truly healing. For the first time in a long time, I'm happy with who I am. I barely have panic attacks anymore; my mom's memory doesn't suffocate me. I'm getting better." And my friendship with Caleb is stronger than ever because of this. I wouldn't have become this strong unless I was forced to be. Sometimes you need to get rid of your crutch to learn how to stand on your own two feet. But just because I can carry my own weight doesn't mean I don't want someone to help hold me up occasionally. I reach down and grab his hand. He looks up at me with so much hope my heart skips a beat. "I want you in my life, Adam, and my feelings haven't changed, but I won't let this stunt my progress. I'm closer than ever to being ready, but I need to be able to trust you and right now, that trust is broken."

"I *will* earn your trust back." He looks up at me and I see how seriously he's taking my words.

That's all I need. I drop off the bed and fall into his arms, the one place I've wanted to be every day these past months.

His arms immediately close around me, pulling me in closer, and his cheek buries into my neck until I can feel the dampness of his tears. My heart shatters that these tears are for me, but I needed him to know that just because I'm forgiving him doesn't mean I've forgotten. It'll take more than this to get things back to normal but at least we're on that path.

"I believe you." I smile. "Now enough with the sad and serious." I nuzzle my head into his chest, letting his smell overwhelm me and calm me like it always has. I tried to forget it, but it's just as good as I remember. "I've missed you."

He sighs in relief, his whole body relaxing until it's melding further into mine and he's still pulling me, impossibly, closer. "I've missed you, too. So much."

I don't know how long we stay just like that, holding each other like we can make up for the time apart, but it's a long time. I can't let myself get lost in him again though.

For that reason alone, I pull back just enough to look up at him, it'd be too painful to pull away completely right now. "You've got a lot of work to do to make it up to me," I tease.

He chuckles and flashes a smile that makes my heart stop beating momentarily. That smile. I've missed that smile. I tried to not think about it before, but damn, I missed him like crazy.

My breath catches when his thumbs move to my face, wiping the streaks of tears that are drying up. "I will make it up to you. I promise you that."

He doesn't seem to be joking like I was though.

"How are you holding up?"

I shrug and look down. "The holidays are hard already and then your uncle . . ." I shiver and his hand rubs my back in comforting strokes. "I just lost it when he spoke. All the pain I was already feeling . . . I took it out on him."

"Rylie," he says, tilting my head up so I'm looking at him again. "You didn't do anything wrong. He's the one who was out of line."

Adam can always read between the lines of my words, and he's always right. It's a strange comfort to have someone who can know what you're really thinking by just looking at you. Someone who knows you're lying when you say, *"I'm fine,"* and is there to listen to your truth. No one has ever known me the way Adam does, and it's scary to think that it's possible no one else will.

"I just didn't have to be so . . . I don't know . . . cruel."

"Neither did he. I think you handled yourself beautifully," he says, and I can see it in his eyes that he truly believes it. "He's always been a drunk, you know that as well as I do. It's about time someone called him out for the shit he spews." He hesitates before continuing. "You know, I kept checking to see if you were out on the dock last night."

"I ended up in the living room with your mom, actually," I say, and smile. "I wasn't bad enough that I needed the lake, but I went down to grab some tea and she was there. It was really nice."

I feel him swallow and I pull back to look at him. There's regret in his eyes, regret that I think stems from not being there for me, for not being the one comforting me. "I'm glad you're doing better. You deserve to be happy."

With every word, emotion, tear, and action of this conversation, I know he'd take it all back if he could. While it doesn't erase the mistakes, it makes me confident that he truly cares for me and that each word he speaks is the truth.

After a while longer we head back downstairs, and almost immediately run into Caleb and Jess who must've seen us coming down the stairs and bee-lined over.

"Do you know what happened wit—" Caleb's eyes narrow, taking in my puffy, post crying face and then flash between me and Adam. We're standing close enough that my hand grazes against his leg and his hand rests on my back, every-so-often casually moving up and down making me fight full-body shivers even though there's a thick sweater covering my skin. "What happened?"

"Have you seen Olivia?" Adam asks before we can launch into the story.

"Last I saw her was maybe a half hour ago, she was heading out front," Caleb answers, confused by the direction of the conversation.

We were up there longer than a half hour?

Adam pulls out his phone with the hand not on me. His lips press together, and I know there's something there, from her.

I look up at him. "Is everything okay?"

He just hands me his phone to read for myself.

OLIVIA

> A friend who lives nearby picked me up. I'll be spending the rest of break there. I think we both know that this is over. I have no resentment towards you, or the situation. I see now that I never stood a chance with your unresolved history. I hope you find what you've been looking for.

I reread it three times. Unresolved history? Does she mean me? I look up at Adam and his expression is unreadable.

"Are you okay?" I ask, hesitantly. He did just get broken up with over a text on Thanksgiving after all.

"Like I said, we both knew it was coming." He shrugs but there's tension in his shoulders. "I just wish it hadn't happened this way."

I wrap my arm around his waist and squeeze. He surprises me by pulling me into a full hug and lowering his lips to my ear. "It's better like this," he whispers.

Confused, I look up at him, wanting to ask what he means but Caleb clears his throat and I grimace. I'd forgotten they were still standing there. I step away from Adam, but he keeps an arm around me, so I don't move far and give Caleb a small smile. "I have a story for you."

Caleb's jaw drops as I recount what transpired with his uncle.

"He really said that?!" he practically shouts, almost as mad as Adam was.

I can only nod, not wanting to talk about it more.

His eyes flash to Adam, conflicted. "And Olivia?"

I let Adam tell this part of the story and look away, blushing, when Caleb looks at me with an expression I don't think I want to understand when he gets to the part about ditching her.

When he's done, everyone's just looking around at each other, unsure what to say.

"So, you guys are . . . okay again?" Caleb asks, breaking the silence.

Adam gives me a *"you can take this one"* look and I take advantage of the opportunity.

"Well, when you have a man groveling at your feet about how sorry he is, it's only fair to give him a second chance." I smirk up at him.

His lips twitch up into an amused smile. "There's that famous Rylie sass I missed so much." Of course, he knew I'd tease him like that, but he let me do it anyway. "But I don't recall it happening quite like that."

"Then let's hear your side." I bump my shoulder into him as we grin at each other.

Caleb's watching our exchange with that face he always gives to tease me about Adam, only now, I know he's sincere in his interest in us as a couple. Jess is smiling like she knows what's happening here too.

"What really happened is I apologized and promised I'd make it up to you, and you forgave me."

I shrug. "Sounds like the same thing I said."

"You're impossible." He rolls his eyes, but his laugh is joyous and I'm sure my returning smile is brighter than it's been in a while.

Jess meets my gaze. "Come on, I think dinner's ready."

I begrudgingly leave Adam's side to walk with Jess, the boys a few steps behind.

"You two seem . . . happy together." She gives a suggestive glance and I laugh.

"We're just working on our friendship," I say but after a second add, "for now."

"For now?"

"We will see what happens in the future." I smile at the idea of something more that I hope is waiting for us.

The rest of the time at the Dey's felt normal, no more awkwardness or tension, just smiles, laughter, and the four of us enjoying the time together. Claire and Phil were confused about what happened with Olivia because we didn't tell them the full story, but they were horrified to hear what Sal had said. They promised not to let him back until he's cleaned up his act. They wouldn't hear it when I try to say that's not necessary.

But Thanksgiving's a time to be thankful and through it all I'm thankful that I do have a family to come home to still. Thankful that I have incredible friends, old and new, that are by my side through it all. And I'm thankful to have Adam back.

Even though the holidays are bringing up painful memories, and I'm missing my mom more than ever, I'm still surrounded by love, and I vow to never forget how lucky I am. To never take this for granted.

My family.

chapter fifteen

"CAN I ASK YOU SOMETHING?" I say to Adam on the ride back to campus. I decided to give Jess and Caleb their space and ride with Adam. We needed to talk anyway. Things are healing between us, but we still need time to be comfortable again in this friendship—relearn the boundaries.

"Anything," he says. "Always."

"Why did Olivia sleep in the other guest room the night she was there?" It's embarrassing but I really want to know, and I know I can talk to Adam about anything.

He laughs nervously. "Seriously?"

"I'm just curious," I mumble and smile at the window.

He sighs but smiles at me. "Even if things were serious between us, I would've asked her to sleep in there out of respect for you. I think it would've been classless of me to share a room with her, right across from you, especially with how things went down between us. But we never got that serious and she suggested separate rooms before I even could."

"Have you talked to her?" Adam's too nice of a guy to be okay with leaving things that way. He wouldn't be the man I loved if he hadn't tried to reach out to her.

"I sent her a message, but she never responded. I'm going to try to talk to her on Monday. I just don't want to leave things off that way. I did like her, and I never wanted to hurt her. I don't regret running after you, but I should've ended things sooner." He groans. "We only lasted as long as we did because I didn't see you. Because the first time I did, all I wanted to do was run across that shop and kiss you. I really am sorry for putting you through all of that."

"Adam, I'm not mad that you were with Olivia. Hell, I even told you to be with other people if you wanted—although I didn't expect it to happen so fast." I give him a half-sarcastic glare and his face shifts into an *I'm sorry* puppy-dog look that makes me laugh. "But seriously, the only thing I've been mad at you about is that after everything we've been through, you cut me out of your life with no explanation. Everything else, regardless of how I felt, were decisions you had every right to make, and I have no right to blame you for." I put my hand on his arm to make sure he's listening, but I shift my tone to be playful. "And I was serious when I said you had some making up to do."

I smile when that receives a laugh from him, and I feel him start to relax.

"But seriously, you haven't done anything else wrong, okay?"

He releases a breath, one hand drifting off the wheel to meet mine and interlace our fingers together. "Okay."

Neither one of us stops smiling the rest of the ride back.

"HAPPY PEPPERMINT MOCHA SEASON!" I burst out of my room on Monday half-skipping, half-dancing with excitement. Even though they started selling peppermint mochas weeks ago, I always wait until December first to drink one. It signals the start of my favorite time of year, and I never miss it.

I'm hoping I have time to run to the Starbucks on campus before class, or else I'll have to wait for later in the day.

Caleb's awake enough to laugh and roll his eyes at me. "Have a good day, Ry."

"See you later, Cale." I bound out the front door, stopping to close my eyes and inhale the crisp, clean winter air before zipping up my jacket and pulling my beanie over my ears. The sky is clear and bright, a beautiful light blue color and the sun doesn't give off any heat, but its presence lifts my mood anyways. It's like the universe gave me this perfect day, today, on purpose.

I'm halfway down the walkway before my eyes shift to the street ahead and I smile, because somehow this day is already getting better.

"I thought you might like a ride to campus today." Adam's leaning against his car, smiling at me with the sweetest smile and softest eyes I've ever seen on him.

For some reason, with him looking at me like that, I feel shy and look down as a smile that gives away the flips my stomach is doing grows.

"And those?" I look up, arching an eyebrow in question at the two coffees he's holding.

His grin widens like he was hoping I'd ask. "I thought we could have our first peppermint mochas of the season together."

I almost trip down the stairs to the street at his words, my breath getting heavy instantly. The smug look on his face says he wanted to remind me of that conversation we had five months ago, the conversation that started everything. What is he playing at? And why can't I stop myself from moving closer?

I only stop when I'm standing a foot in front of him, an answer to the challenge hidden in his words. "You know, when I said you needed to make it up to me, I didn't mean you should try to buy my friendship back," I tease, playing along. I'll always play along when he's the one challenging me.

His responding laughter shakes me, even without touching him. I reach for one of the cups, now close enough to smell the chocolatey-minty goodness, but he moves it out of my reach. "Oh, so you don't want it? I guess I'll just find another way to get rid of it then."

Fine then, two can play at this game.

"I never said I wouldn't take it," I say, closing the last foot of distance between us and reaching for the cup in a way that presses us together from hips to chest. His chest shudders when he sucks in a breath, and I can't even remember to be smug about it. My hand shakes as it reaches the cup and closes around it and his hand.

My fingers are cold in comparison to his, which have been heated by the cup he's holding, but instead of pulling away, his fingers shift. It's a small shift, but it's enough that his fingers are now covering mine. Heat blooms not just in my fingers, but in my gut, causing me to lean into him more, craving any semblance of the closeness we had that night.

A cool breeze hits my cheek and it's enough to remind me that this was supposed to be playful, not consuming. I hope that one day soon I can do something like this and let myself fall into the feelings that have always been there, but that time isn't now. As much as I love the holiday season, it's the wrong time to try to start anything, and I still need to make sure I can trust him fully again.

Because I want the time we finally try to be the start of something that'll last, not a moment we got lost in, and not a distraction. I need to be careful though, it's still too easy to get lost in him and lose my resolve.

I allow myself one more perfect second of his body against mine and lean in so my lips brush against his cheek on the way to his ear. "Thank you," I say, so softly it's no more than air fluttering across his skin and he shivers.

When I pull away, he lets me take the cup but grazes his

fingers across the back of my hand as I pull away. My eyes shoot to his, wondering what he's thinking, but his eyes are closed as if he too is trying to savor one last perfect moment.

"I didn't get it for that reason anyway," he says, eyes snapping open and locking onto me. "I had some extra time and thought this would make you happy. That's all."

How do I respond to that? He's going out of his way to do things that make me happy, but without any strings attached. I have to look away from the sparkle in his eyes that I know is his true feelings shining through. It's in my eyes too.

I just take a sip of the drink, close my eyes, and let the feeling run through me. It's fresh and light but also heavy and bitter, add the sweetness of the chocolate and it's a seemingly perfect drink. It makes me feel more alive than I did before, but that might also be because he's the one that gave it to me. This drink feels like the holidays in a cup to me.

I open my eyes with a giant smile on my face. "Well, you succeeded. I'm overflowing with happiness."

And love. For him. Always for him.

His smile is brilliant as he steps aside and opens the passenger door for me. As I watch him wrap around the front of the car, he looks buoyant, alive, and . . . radiant. Maybe I forgot how things were before this mess, or he's just as happy as I am that we're good again, but things feel different somehow.

Good different.

We fall back into our old habits as if no time has passed. Monday and Wednesday lunches are back, and he's back to hanging out at The Split Bean often. Angie's been berating me with questions and insinuating looks since he showed up all smiles after break. He continues this trend of showing up in the mornings to drive me to campus when he can and stops by in the evenings sometimes, particularly when he knows Caleb and Jess are out on a date. He'll show up with dinner and we'll spend the evening watching shows or playing video games together.

Caleb watches us a lot, I think he's trying to gauge if anything has changed in our relationship, like if we're together yet, but he doesn't say anything. He knows what my hesitancies are. He knows I'll tell him when something happens too. But he's *excited* for us to be together and that alone confirms that fourth grade Rylie chose the right best friend.

chapter sixteen

I'M ON MY BACK. Adam's face hovers over me with a smirk and he asks, "Are you sure you want to do this?"

If I didn't know better, I'd have told you it's the start of a sexy dream.

Yet, it's the least sexy thing that's ever happened to me.

My arms are shaking, and dread fills me as my eyes shift back to the silver bar above me. There aren't even any plates on the bar, and I could barely do five reps earlier. To be fair, this is the last exercise on Adam's starter list for me. My arms were shaking before I even got to this contraption that looks more like a torture device than a workout machine.

I set my lips in a hard line and nod. I can do one last set.

As I raise my arms to the bar, Adam moves to spot me.

And thank god he does.

Arms trembling, I get the bar off the hooks holding it up with a grunt, but my arms give out the second they're supporting its full weight, and the bar comes crashing down toward my neck. My eyes widen in fear, there's not enough time to move out of the way and I'm not strong enough to stop it. It moves in slow-motion but all I can do is watch as gravity does what it does best.

The bar freezes a foot above me and I'm heaving in breaths as his face comes into view above me again.

"And that's why you should never do this without a spotter." He racks the bar and steps around to help me sit up. "You good?"

"Yeah." The word is almost lost in my heavy breathing. "Thanks."

"I think that's enough weights for today." He smiles like he's proud of me and it gets even harder to breathe. "You did great."

I laugh because I'm pretty sure I sucked and could barely do the minimum weight on each machine he brought me to. But I got through his whole list, even though I thought I couldn't go on half-way into the workout. He's a great teacher and motivator.

"Adam." A guy walks up from behind me and claps him on the shoulder.

"Rylie," Adam says, nodding at the guy before turning to me. "You remember Blake and Ryan. We usually workout together."

I look up and see Blake's blond hair, only then seeing the black buzzcut Ryan's sporting behind him. They look like they just got here, yet I'm a disgusting, sweaty mess. But I'm too winded to attempt to look presentable.

"What are you guys up to?" Blake says, as Ryan grins at us. I wonder if they knew we'd be here together and showed up on purpose.

"I'm pretty sure this one"—I point back at Adam and smile —"is trying to kill me. Why the hell do you guys choose to do this every day?"

They chuckle and Adam steps up behind my back, so I'm forced to tilt my head all the way back to see him, the top of my head presses into his abdomen. I can't help feeling self-conscious of my sweaty back, but he presses against me like it's no big deal.

"Did I not just save you?" he says, staring down at me. The corner of his mouth pulls up into a sly smile.

"Good point." I grin up at him before looking forward again

at Blake and Ryan who are both watching us with curious eyes. I stand up and say, "Okay, maybe not kill, but this is definitely a torture device."

Their smiles soften—I think I'm winning them over. I get the feeling Adam was right when he told me months ago that I'd like them.

Adam snakes an arm around my waist and puts his lips to my ear. In a soft voice he says, "Don't get me started on torture. You show up here looking like an athletic-wear model and I have to watch every guy here stare at you, all the while knowing I have no claim to you whatsoever. That's torture."

I suck in a breath, hoping my earlier exertion covers any signs of the heat flushing across my body, and turn to look at him. "It feels like you're laying claim to me right now."

A wicked smile grows on his face as his arm tightens around me. He knows exactly what he's doing, and I can't say I hate it in the slightest.

"Should we clear out the gym? Seems like you two are having a moment here and I'd hate for you to be interrupted by people who actually came here to workout."

That comes from Blake, he seems to be the snarky one who isn't afraid to speak his mind. He's my favorite because of that. Ryan's looking around like he's embarrassed to look at us in this position.

"Are you offering to make yourself useful?" I counter, but step away from Adam.

Blake's eyes widen. "Holy. Shit." He slowly turns to look at Adam, a grin spreading across his face. "If you don't marry her, I will."

I feel Adam stiffen behind me, but I bark out a laugh. It's confirmed, I love Adam's friends.

"I'm going to head up to the elliptical now." I turn to Adam. "How long do you need?"

"I'll just do thirty. I'll come grab you when I'm done."

"Sounds good." I wave to Blake and Ryan. "It was nice to see you again."

I head upstairs to the second floor where it's a cardio-lovers paradise. Treadmills, bikes, rowing machines, stair climbers, and ellipticals circle the room. The center of this floor is open so you can see the weight machines below. I grab an elliptical right next to the railing so I can look for Adam and hit "quickstart" on the machine.

The air conditioning up here isn't as good as down below and in a few minutes I'm so hot I decide to strip off my top, leaving me in just my blush pink biker shorts and sports bra matching set. My whole body is on fire. I haven't worked this hard in a long time, but it feels good. When I asked Adam to be my trainer, I wasn't sure what I'd think of it. I only thought it was a way to spend more time with him while also working on my self-care—a win-win.

But I can see why he likes coming here so much. There's a specific satisfaction that comes with testing your body's limits and pushing past them. I feel strong and capable.

My eyes slowly scan the area below me. I can't see people's faces well from here, but it ends up not mattering because when I find him, he's frozen and is staring at me with a look that almost makes me fall off my machine. His eyes move over my body and my previously steady movements stutter. While I was being a good student earlier, I tried not to get distracted by his arms that are on full display in a shirt with cut-off sleeves, but now I let my eyes roam over his muscles, hoping that the distance hides the hunger in my eyes. We stare at each other until Ryan snags his attention. As I look away, my gaze meets Blake's momentarily and he crosses his arms, looking at me with pouty lips and raised brows that make me feel like I've done something wrong.

Adam said it was torture to have me here and know we weren't together. Is it torture for him every time we're together? I'm not trying to hurt him, but am I unintentionally being cruel?

I don't even know where I'm at with being ready. So much of my history with Adam is tied up with my mom, and with the holidays tangling my feelings even more, it's hard to separate what I feel for him, for us, from the loss I'm feeling for her.

When Adam's done, he comes to find me. On the walk out, he stays closer to me than he usually does, and I look up at him with a questioning expression. His answering smile has me believing this is, again, a way for him to deter the eyes he claimed were on me earlier. I haven't seen anyone looking my way, but I also haven't been able to tear my eyes away from him.

I take in every up-close detail of his arms as we walk and *holy shit* he's really been working hard. A statue should be erected in his name because he *is* a God. I'd gladly volunteer to make sure the sculptor captured every rise and fall of his muscles to perfection.

In the car, I can't stop staring at him. Thinking about how those strong arms have held me before, about how I want them to hold me again. About how, *and where*, I want them to touch me. I'm more breathless now than I was at the gym.

"Rylie," he says, voice tight, when we're about halfway back to my apartment. "Put your shirt on and look out the window."

"What?"

"Please, put your shirt on and look . . . anywhere but at me." He sounds desperate and it makes me extremely curious. I should listen, but I'm a hot mess from what he said earlier, from how he looked at me, and from how I'm feeling about him right now.

"It's too hot for a shirt," I counter and I'm sure he has no idea that it's him who's making me sweat now.

He takes a slow, deep breath. "I'm trying my best to respect your wishes to wait until you've had time to figure everything out, and I don't mind waiting." We stop at a red light, and he closes his eyes as he continues, "But you're sitting in my car with very little clothing on, and you're looking at me like . . ."

He gulps before opening his eyes just as the light changes. "Like . . . *that* and all I can think about is how much I want to pull you over the center console, strip off those last pieces of clothing and . . ."

He doesn't need to finish that statement because my mind already is, and *holy hell* I want that so badly I start shaking. My lips are trembling as unsteady breaths pass between them.

"*Rylie.*"

"And what if I want that too." My voice sounds desperate even to my own ears.

"Then I have to ask if you're ready for everything that comes with it." His arm muscles strain as his grip tightens on the steering wheel and I never thought the sight of a tricep could make me feel the things I'm feeling right now. "Because just kissing you now won't be enough. I want days, months, years of kissing you, so if you're not ready for that yet then look away because I swear, Rylie, I only have a few seconds left in me before I pull this car over."

Years. He wants years with me.

I close my eyes and try to remember what I was thinking about earlier—that it's too much right now. I need to make it through the holidays first before I can be sure I'm ready for this. In order to have our years, we can't have what we want right now.

"Fuck," I curse out of frustration. With my eyes still closed, I rotate to face forward, pull my shirt above my head, and try to hold back tears. My voice is small when I ask, "Is this really torture for you?"

"I didn't mean it like that," he says immediately.

I open my eyes and glance over at him. "But is it cruel of me to do this to you?"

"Cruel? Rylie, you could never be cruel." He reaches over to grab my hand and I'm craving the warmth of his touch too much to pull away. "Is it hard to stop myself when I see you and I *know* you're thinking about me the way I'm thinking about you because it's all there in your eyes? Of course. It's so hard to not kiss you every time I see you."

My head lowers in shame.

"But Rylie"—he squeezes my hand and I look up at him—"I know how hard this is for you. I know what you've gone through, how confusing this is for you, and I could never be mad at you for taking care of yourself. I'll gladly wait however long it takes, because even the hard times with you are better than easy times with anyone else."

My stomach is doing somersaults, and my brain is trying to commit each word to memory. "Thank you." I smile and squeeze his hand so hard my tired arms start shaking. "Earlier, you said you have no claim to me, but just so you know, you're the only person that does. It's still healing and guarded, but every bit of my heart is yours, and yours alone."

"That's all I could ever need," he says, and I don't second guess my instincts. I just lean over and kiss his shoulder and then kiss his hand that's still gripping onto mine.

I don't speak them, but the words sit in my chest, heavier than any dumbbell in the gym: *You're all I could ever need.*

chapter seventeen

FINALS WEEK IS HERE before I know it. By Wednesday night, all my finals are done except one, finance, which is on Friday morning. Tomorrow is for studying, which is why I'm already in bed and falling asleep when my phone rings just past midnight.

"Hello?" I murmur, still half-asleep. I didn't open my eyes to check the caller-ID, but I know who I want it to be.

There's a low chuckle that comes through and I smile, imagining I can not only hear, but feel it. On the verge of dreaming, I can recall, in painstaking detail, exactly how it feels to be pressed against his chest when he laughs. I wish he was here now. I almost groan with the thought and my eyes shoot open.

"Did I wake you? I'm sorry, I can let you go back to sleep." That voice, *his* voice, rings through the speaker.

"No!" I say much too fast and smile sheepishly when he laughs again. It never fails to quicken my pulse when he calls. "It's fine, I'm glad you called."

"How have your finals gone?"

"I think they've gone well." I haven't stopped smiling since I picked up. "I had my differential equations final today, and it was kind of . . . fun."

His laugh sputters through the line. "Okay, none of those words are fun on their own, but the fact that you described the combination of them as fun is scary."

That makes me laugh. "Shut up."

"No, seriously. We might have to commit you, you're certifiably insane."

When I stop laughing, I say, "Ha ha. Make fun of the math lover. I seem to recall you're also in a math intensive major."

"Having to do some math in my classes is different than saying differential equations is fun." I can see his raised brows and pointed expression as clear as if he's standing right in front of me. The corner of his mouth would probably be pulled up into one of those sexy smirks that would make it so hard not to kiss him.

"What about you?" I close my eyes to force myself to move on. Even though he's not here he affects me as strongly as if his hands were on me.

"Pretty good, just have one left on Friday morning. That's when your finance one is too, right?"

"Yeah, I'm all done except for that."

"Want to study together tomorrow?"

I'm glad he's not here in person to hear how loud my heart is beating right now, although it wouldn't surprise me if he could hear it through the phone at this volume. "I'd love that."

"I'll pick you up at ten?"

"Sounds great."

"Want me to let you get back to sleep now?"

What's sleep compared to time talking to him? We only just started talking, I don't want him to go so soon. "Not really."

"Good," he says, and I can hear the smile in his voice.

We talk as long as we can stay awake, so long that I don't even remember falling asleep at all.

* * *

"RYLIE?"

My eyes flutter open for a moment before closing again.

"Rylie? Are you awake yet?"

I groan and sit up, searching for the source of the voice that pulled me from dreams I didn't ever want to wake from. A familiar laugh fills the room and for a second, I'm back in July, on the dock, waking up in his arms. All the air leaves my lungs, the memory feels like a punch to the gut. The longing for that to be my reality tramples me as I finally find my phone, I never unplugged it from my charger so it's still connected on the call with Adam.

"Good morning, sleepy head," he chimes when I finally pick up the phone.

"What time is it?" I groan, not able to pull off grumpy because I'm smiling too much.

"Nine," he says. "I'll be there in an hour, if that still works?"

"Yeah, that's fine." I yawn. "I just have to wake up a little bit more before then."

He laughs again and the last thing I want to do is wake up. I want to slip back into a dream world where I can be in his arms right now, feeling the rumble of his laugh against my back while I'm tucked into his chest.

My voice is suddenly dry and unsteady. "What time did I fall asleep? I don't remember."

"I don't even know. We must've fallen asleep around the same time. It was late, I know that for sure."

"You've always been a bad influence on my sleep," I say, teasing, now that I'm waking up.

"Hey," he defends, "I asked if you wanted to sleep, and you chose to stay up."

I laugh. As if that was a fair choice, I can't think of anything

I'd choose over him. "That's because I enjoy talking to you too much."

"Can't say I'm mad about that." Sometimes just from the tone of his voice, I can picture exactly what his face looks like as he says it. This is one of those times. It's soft and shy. If he was here, he'd have looked down and probably blushed a little as he spoke through a reserved smile that would give away every thought he was trying to hide. I love that look.

"Alright, well if you want me looking half-way decent for our study date," I cringe at the casual use of the word, the morning bliss of waking to his voice is causing me to say more than I should. "I'd better let you go and start getting ready."

"You'll look more than decent no matter what. See you soon." He hangs up before I can form a reply. Oh god, it's getting harder and harder to spend time with him without anything more happening. Especially when he says things like that so casually.

* * *

I RUN out the door at ten, dressed in leggings, an oversized tee, no makeup, and hair thrown into a messy bun. Pieces fall out and drop into my face with each step I take.

He doesn't move to drive when I get in the car and after a second, I look over, wondering why, only to find his eyes on me. By the time I turn to fully face him, his hand is reaching towards me, inches away from my face. I stop breathing when he catches a loose strand of hair and tucks it behind my ear.

"See, I told you," he whispers. "You always look better than decent."

His hand slowly lowers but our eyes stay locked on each other with a building intensity that's overwhelming the small quarters we're in. He closes his eyes first and looks away, shattering the moment but leaving us suffocating in the tension that never seems to be able to leave us alone. He begins to drive and I spend the time recomposing myself.

I can never figure out how he's able to rattle me in seconds, no matter how much I prepare myself for his presence. The second we're in the same space all my sensibility leaves me. He occupies my every thought, and every fiber of my being focuses solely on him. Every feeling and emotion I feel is heightened exponentially and there's no pushing it away.

Why am I not ready for this? Why won't I let myself be happy with him?

What is wrong with me?

After two hours at The Split Bean, there's very little studying to show for it. Between laughing and talking with Adam, and the looks Angie keeps giving me—of course she just happened to be working today—it's hard to stay focused on the practice problems in front of me.

"Can you help me with this problem?" I ask Adam, throwing down my pencil.

I know how to solve the problem, I'm just not in the mood to actually write the steps down. As he walks through the problem, face serious, like he's being paid to tutor me, my smile grows and my mind wanders back to a few years ago.

* * *

"MOM'S MAD AT ME," Adam *sighed one night on the dock, after being quieter than he's ever been. I didn't want to pry, he'd never pushed me to talk, but I was worried about him.*

"What happened?"

"I failed my math test."

When I looked over at him, I saw a boy more broken than I'd ever seen him before. His head hung low and his body slouched like he had no reason to stand tall, no reason to look ahead.

He kept talking. "I didn't understand it, and I tried to get help from my teacher but nothing she said helped it make sense. I even tried one of those tutoring services, but nothing. I think Mom feels like I wasted the money, she thinks I'm not trying to learn it. But I'm trying so hard it's driving me insane. I don't know what else to do."

He tried to hide it, but I could hear how hurt he was. He idolizes Claire, everything both those boys do is to make her proud, but he felt like he let her down. My heart broke seeing someone who was usually so confident and positive feel so hopeless.

I couldn't stand by and let him keep feeling that way. I needed him to see how capable and brilliant he was. I had to do something to help.

I stood up and held out my hand. "Come on."

He looked up slowly, confused and questioning. "Where are we going?"

"I'm going to help you," I said, confidently. Math was always my best subject, I'd been in every advanced math class possible and even though he was a year older, I took the class last year. My heart couldn't stand letting him continue to feel worthless. "If you'll let me."

"It's no use," he grumbled, defeated. "Don't waste your time."

"Look at me," I said, forceful enough that he listened and our eyes locked. "You are not a waste of time. I know you can do this. They're all idiots for giving up on you. Please don't give up on yourself too. I'll never give up on you."

There was still apprehension in his eyes, but he nodded and took my hand, letting me lead him back to his room.

Fifteen minutes later he threw his pencil down in frustration and avoided my gaze in embarrassment. "I just don't get it."

He'd taken one look at the problem and froze. He didn't move for minutes until he finally threw down the pencil, like he was too afraid to even attempt it.

"Adam," I said calmly but he shook his head. "Adam, look at me."

He looked anywhere but at me.

"Please," I begged, reaching out a hand to touch his shoulder. I needed him to look at me, to see the sincerity in my eyes when I spoke.

Slowly, he stilled and his eyes lifted to mine. There was a frenzied and frantic look that made me squeeze his shoulder in encouragement.

"Take a deep breath." I was relieved when he actually followed my instructions. "You know more than you think you do. Let's take this one step at a time, okay? What's the first step you'd take to solve this problem?"

We worked our way through the problem that way, step by step. With each step he did correctly, his fear lessened, and he started gaining some confidence back. It wasn't until we got eighty percent through the problem that he truly didn't know what to do next.

His anxiety was beginning to creep back so I spoke before he could retreat again. "Look at everything you knew how to do."

He looked at me, conflicted between the positive words and his negative thoughts. "But I don't know how to finish it."

"And that's the part I can help you with, but first, look at everything you do *know. You did all of that on your own. Regardless of if you finished or not, eighty percent is much better than never starting at all. Don't give up so soon, take a deep breath and believe in yourself because you've got this. Even if you don't believe it yet, just remember that I do."*

He wasn't bad at math, he'd just been put down so much that he'd grown afraid to even try. Anytime I had to stay at the Dey's over the next months, our late-night talks moved to study sessions and soon he'd caught up on the course material. Slowly, the frequency of those tutoring sessions decreased until we only met in his room when there'd been a particularly difficult lesson for him.

My heart soared as his confidence slowly came back. Claire suspected something was up, but I don't think anyone ever figured out how he turned his grades around.

I didn't care, I wasn't doing it for the recognition, I did it for him.

And seeing a smile back on his face was reward enough for me.

* * *

IT'S A FULL-CIRCLE MOMENT, watching him explain this problem to me, and I couldn't be prouder of him. He deserves all the credit for working hard to get to where he is now.

He looks up at me after he's done, and his eyes narrow in suspicion at the expression on my face. "You already knew how to solve it, didn't you?"

I smile innocently at him.

"Rylie," he says, pretending to be annoyed but he's holding back a smile.

"Is this how you felt when I tutored you?" I ask, feeling bold. "Because if so, I don't know how you learned a thing." I lean across the table until our faces are only a foot apart, eyes locked, and whisper, "That was incredibly hot."

His eyes flare and a laugh bursts out before he can stop it, but he presses his lips together, trying to play along. "Was it? Do you want me to do another one?"

My eyebrows raise in emphasis. "Absolutely."

Both of our mask's crack and we fall into laughter. Looking at him now, I know I never want to live without him. The sound of his laughter fills the room with life and the world looks brighter in his eyes.

chapter eighteen

CLAIRE AND PHIL surprised us all with a five-day family ski trip around Christmas, and then Caleb's heading out right after that to spend New Year's with Jess's family.

The Dey's are kind enough to invite Jess and me along too. Claire wasn't happy that when she said, "Family Trip," I assumed I wasn't going, but it's a habit. I know I'm family to them, but I still hate that they spent extra money on me, especially because with me tagging along, we need a fourth hotel room.

Not that I'd mind if I had to share a room with Adam, but I keep that thought to myself because it doesn't help the not-right-now thing.

"Are you sure you don't want me to stay with you?" Caleb asks Jess and I as we head out on the slopes for the day.

Both Caleb and Adam are skilled snowboarders, but Jess and I learned quickly on the first day that we don't have any skill on skis. We stick to the bunny hills while the boys are running black diamonds, but we have each other. Mostly we just laugh about how bad we are the whole way down.

"We're good, seriously." Jess smiles at him and gives him a

peck on the check that turns his face rosy before the wind has a chance to.

"Yeah, go get your money's worth," I add.

He's kissing Jess bye before I'm done talking, too excited to get back out there to need convincing to ditch us. He's off toward the lift, but Adam hangs back, watching me.

His expression asks if I want him to hang back. I do, but I only smile and motion with my head that he should go with Caleb. He'll just be bored with me. He gives a small smile, but I swear that's disappointment I see in his eyes. With a pointed look he's telling me to be careful and I shoot back an annoyed, defensive glare that says, *"I'm not that bad."* He just smirks and I roll my eyes and start to walk with Jess, but I can't help but look back, watching him go and wishing he was walking towards me.

He glances back, and when our eyes lock, we both look away. My cheeks are heating even in the snow, but I risk one more glimpse. He's looking again too but this time we both just smile. I might have been caught looking at him, but he was caught looking at me too.

"He seems worried about you," Jess says, pulling my attention away from Adam.

I smile back sheepishly. "He just knows I'm not the most coordinated person on a normal day, and it's very likely I'll fall."

"No, it's not that." She shakes her head. "He cares a lot about you, anyone can see that."

I look down, blushing, hoping the rosiness can be written off because of the gust of wind passing through.

"Why don't you make a move?" she pushes.

"It's complicated." I sigh, thinking of stopping the conversation there but then I remember our conversation at Thanksgiving, and I decide to tell her more. "So much of my history with him is interwoven with memories of my mom. The situations we had that allowed us to get so close only happened because my mom was sick. It's been a little hard to separate the two, especially with everything being so fresh with her loss. I don't want to start anything if there's any chance I'm only doing it because he's always been there. It's not fair to him, and for both of our sake, I need to make sure I'm ready for this before we try because I don't want to mess us up."

Jess has gotten quiet and apologetic eyes look up at me as we get in line for the ski-lift. "I'm sorry. I should've realized it was related to that."

"It's getting easier, but with the holidays . . . it's just not a good time right now."

"I get it." She squeezes my hand. "The holidays are still hard for me. It's always when I notice his absence most. When I'm at school I can almost pretend he's still at home waiting for me, but every time I go back, which is mostly just holidays now, I feel that loss again because he's everywhere in that house."

"I know exactly what you mean." I squeeze her hand back. I might not have my childhood house to go back to, but the Dey's house is the place that still holds so much of her. If I don't stop thinking about it though, my impending tears might freeze on my cheeks. "Now, come on, let's go embarrass ourselves on the bunny hill surrounded by five-year-olds."

She laughs, but that's exactly what happens. We carefully zig-zag our way down the hill on shaky legs, going as slow as possible. If I let myself gain any speed at all, I'll lose control. It's a slow process but we make it down safely a handful of times, slowly gaining confidence.

I swear I've seen Adam going down the bunny hill every now and again, checking up on me, but it's probably just wishful thinking. I mean, it's hard to tell who's who in full-gear, but the body-shape, the way he moves, the way his eyes are only on me —how can it not be him?

We're on what we decided is our last run before meeting back up with everyone at the lodge for lunch. I'm starting to feel good about this whole skiing thing, until, on my next zig-zag down, my skis lock together when I try to stop. Instead of slowing down to wait for Jess, as intended, I find myself heading straight down the hill, picking up speed with each second.

I forget everything I've learned—how to stop, how to slow down, how to do anything other than panic. All I see is blurs of white snow, black blobs of the people I'm flying past, and the ominous approach of the bottom of the hill and the crowd of people there. Not thinking about anything but needing to stop, I squat down and sit back on the snow between my ski's.

Wrong decision.

The forward momentum of my legs is too strong and I shoot forward, tumbling down the hill instead of stopping. There's nothing but dizzying flashes of white then blue, over and over, until I slow enough to stop with a flop in the snow. Lying flat on my back, staring up at the sky, heart racing, and breathing rapidly, I'm frozen in shock and cold from the snow melting inside my jacket and soaking through my shirt.

I vaguely register that my skis and poles are no longer attached to me—abandoned somewhere up the hill in the midst of tumbling. But I'm too shocked to look around for them.

A face pops into view above me, lips moving frantically but the only sound I can hear is my heart trying to rip itself out of my chest from the adrenaline. I take a deep breath, blinking as I find my way back to my body and into the present moment.

"Rylie!" the voice shouts, still muffled. "Rylie, are you okay?"

The person attached to the voice rips off their goggles and beanie. I blink again as I try to comprehend what my eyes are seeing. His eyes are panicked, and he won't stop asking if I'm okay.

"Aren't you supposed to be doing something badass on the big boy hills?" I ask, sitting up and groaning when my muscles protest and my snow-soaked shirt sends a chill through me.

Adam laughs, relief coursing through him and his eyes soften as some of the panic resides. He's looking intently at me, scanning for any sign of pain. "Are you sure you're okay?"

"I'm fine," I reassure him, placing a hand on his shoulder. "I promise."

Jess reaches us then, my tumble probably making her take her own trip slowly. I look up at her as she approaches but Adam's eyes never leave me.

"You okay?" she asks, short of breath.

I smile. "Perfectly fine."

Her eyes flash to Adam, who's staring at me like he's scared I'll disappear if he looks away, and she just grins. "I'm going to meet Caleb for lunch, but I see I'm leaving you in *very* capable hands," she implies and my cheeks heat thinking about those hands and wanting to know how capable they really are. I shoot her a glare before she continues down the hill.

"So, why are you here?" I turn back to Adam after thanking the man that dropped off my equipment—he was nice enough to gather on his way down.

He looks a little embarrassed, but he's unwilling to tear his eyes from me to look away. "I was . . ." He sighs. "I was admittedly worried about you. I know how easily you trip while on solid ground and I couldn't stop thinking about the possibility of you falling, so I thought I'd check in on you. And good thing I did."

I raise my eyebrows at him, remembering what I'd seen throughout the day. "But this wasn't the first time you checked in. I've seen you many times this morning."

His eyes narrow skeptically. "You're telling me, that of the hundreds of people here, you think you'd be able to pick me out of the crowd in full gear?"

I lean in and whisper, "I would recognize you anywhere, and in anything."

I stand and start walking down the hill, smirking at the open-mouthed look I'm leaving him with. I make it a few steps before he catches up to me on his snowboard.

"Come on, I'll give you a ride down." His grin is mischievous, but it sends my heart into a frenzy, and I can't refuse.

It takes some maneuvering, determining who's going to hold the skis and how, and where's the best place for me to stand. I end up with my feet together in the middle of his board, arms wrapped tight around his waist and face buried into his chest. I'm holding the skis and poles against his back so that his hands are free to help with balance and control.

We get many strange looks on the rest of the ride down, but I don't care. I'm holding on tighter than I need to and pressing into him more than I should, and I'm loving every second of this. As we put up our gear for the morning, and the adrenaline wears off, I start to shiver. The wet shirt chills my body and renders my thick jacket useless.

The lobby of the ski resort is decorated to maximize the feeling of comfort and warmth. The lighting fixtures are all circular chandeliers with the lights standing up looking like a ring of candles and bathing the room in a warm golden light, even during the day. It's all dark wood, everywhere, to emulate being in a log cabin, and the furniture and decorations are all in shades of brown, red, and orange. There are a few stone fireplaces scattered around the large room too.

Adam leads me toward one of the fireplaces in the back corner, where there's no one around, instead of to the restaurant where we're supposed to be meeting everyone for lunch. I try to hide how cold I truly am from the shirt, but he must notice that walking into the air conditioning sent my teeth chattering.

"We're going to be late for lunch," I say, trying to keep my words steady but they shake more than I'd like because of the shivering.

"I don't care." He shoots me a look that says, *You won't get out of this no matter how much you protest, and if you don't sit*

on the bench in front of the fire willingly, I'll make you sit.
"You're freezing, they can wait a few minutes for us to show up."

Part of me wants to see how he plans to make me sit, but before I can do something stupid, I sit down. He's looking at me with such concern and care, I think I'd do anything he asks.

"Take off your jacket," he says, and I comply immediately. That's an easy one.

As soon as the jacket is draped over the bench to dry out, he lays a thick blanket over my shoulders, and I immediately pull it tighter around me. The warmth starts seeping into my bones, slowing the shaking and I almost groan.

"Thank you," I whisper, looking up at him with a smile.

His concern shifts into relief and a sweet, gentle smile is what's left. "I'll be right back."

Now that's something I won't comply with, my hand flies out to grab his before I even realize what I'm doing. My eyes are begging him not to go.

"I'll be back so fast you won't even have time to miss me," he reassures me. "I promise."

I let him go, but his promise is already broken. I miss him before he even starts to walk, and if I'm honest with myself, I've missed his touch and kiss every second since I first felt them that night. As I watch him walk away, I can't help wishing he wasn't in those loose ski pants. I could really enjoy the view if he was in those jeans that fit him just righ—

The air comes whooshing out of me. I must be colder than I realized because there's no filter on my thoughts anymore and that's a problem when I'm around him. Self-control is the only reason I'm able to be around him without giving into everything I want, and right now that control is slipping.

The only thing that stops me is remembering that my goal is to make this as easy for him as possible until we can be together, and saying everything that comes to my mind about him will only make this harder. I stare into the flickering fire and try to let it lull me out of my thoughts, but I only find visions of us dancing in the flames. Color floods my cheeks at just how far this vision, this *want*, goes, and I have to start deep breathing before I lose it.

I'm still trying to calm down when he returns, and at least hope he attributes the red in my face to the heat of the fire. He's carrying a cup in each hand, the kind of cups meant for hot drinks so I can't tell what's in them, but when he walks past me to take a seat on my other side, the smell of cocoa hits me.

"Thanks," I say, trying not to cringe as he hands me a cup. I don't like hot chocolate, but it's still a thoughtful gesture.

I prepare myself to take a sip, not wanting to show any signs of displeasure at the taste, since he won't stop watching me with a smile on his face. I close my eyes and tilt the cup back, but when the liquid hits my tongue, my eyes shoot open and I take a bigger sip. My eyes narrow on Adam, who's now smirking, because this isn't hot chocolate, it's apple cider, and it's exactly what I would've chosen for myself.

My heart skips a beat as his smirk grows into a taunt, he's challenging me to ask and this time I have to. This time I know for absolute certain there's no way he could know this about me. No one knows that I don't like hot chocolate, and definitely not that I'd choose apple cider. It's never come up and I've never brought it up.

"Why didn't you get me a hot chocolate?" I ask, hoping the wording of the question will make him second guess what he thinks he knows, but he doesn't miss a beat.

"Because you don't like hot chocolate, and much prefer apple cider on a cold day."

My eyes are still narrowed, and he smirks again, knowing exactly what I want to hear but he's going to make me ask.

"How do you know that?" I ask through gritted teeth.

"Remember the winter festival?" he says, and I have no clue what he's talking about.

I pause and think, eventually something comes to mind, but it can't be that because . . . "Are you talking about the one we went to in middle school?"

He smiles, seeming pleased I remembered, and my eyes go wide. I feel unsteady, I remember that night for a completely different reason, but I have no recollection of having apple cider that night.

"My mom got us all drinks and when she asked, you were the only one that asked for apple cider. They didn't have any, so she got you a hot chocolate instead. You took a few sips, fighting a grimace each time but you were too polite to say anything. You poured out a little bit at a time throughout the night, pretending to drink it."

My mouth is hanging open in shock. Why would he have noticed that back then, and why would he hold onto that information for eight years?

I compose myself when I see the smirk of delight on his face, he likes surprising me like this.

But two can play this game.

"That's the night Caleb and I really wanted funnel cakes, but you said you didn't like them and got kettle corn instead," I say, making a face because funnel cakes are obviously superior.

His smirk is gone instantly and is now residing on my face as his mouth drops open. "But you've ordered kettle corn when we've gone to the county fairs and other events."

"Because I knew you liked it better," I admit, and something changes in the way we're looking at each other, the way we see each other.

Could we truly both have been noticing each other for that long and never realized? Have we both been *that* preoccupied with each other for that long and neither of us said anything or acted on it until recently?

His face melts into a warmth I want to bask in for an eternity before he clears his throat. "Warm enough?"

Any chill that remained vanishes the second he looks at me like that.

"Burning."

* * *

THE NEXT DAY is Christmas Eve and I decide it's safer to keep off the snow. I choose a seat by one of the fires in the lobby and read. Caleb and Adam both made fun of me this morning because it's a coding book I'm reading in preparation for an advanced coding course I'm taking next semester. But it's a lot more interesting than they give it credit for.

I'm at one of the fireplaces on the opposite side of the one we sat at yesterday, but I chose this one for a reason. From this seat, I have the best view of the sliding glass doors that you enter when coming back from the slopes. There are no specific plans to meet for lunch, but I'm hoping to catch Adam on his way in.

It's just after noon when I finally see him walking up to the door. I put my book down and watch. Everyone else just walks right through the doors, tracking in snow on their shoes and shaking out their jackets on the lobby carpet, but Adam stops. He wipes all the snow off his jacket and pants and stomps out his shoes before entering. He even tries to smooth his hair as much as possible.

I can't help but smile as I watch, he's just a genuinely good human being—kind, caring, and considerate. It's the reason I never believed he could have feelings for me before. How could someone as good as him want to be with someone as messy as me? I've never felt like I was good enough for him, but when I'm around him, I feel like I'm enough, *he* makes me feel good enough.

In fact, sometimes it feels like he feels the same way towards me. It's absurd. How could he ever be the one that's not good enough? He's incredible and he doesn't see it. It's always been my goal to make sure he does.

He walks in the door and his eyes immediately drift to where we were sitting yesterday. I think he's just reminiscing but when his face falls, I realize he was looking for me there. I give him a "caught you" face until he finally looks my way and freezes, cheeks reddening but he recovers quickly and nods toward the restaurant in invitation. I smile and walk over to him, falling in step as we head to lunch in silence.

I bump into him and can't even force my smile to be sly because I'm too high on happiness just being around him. "So, you were looking for me."

"And you were waiting for me." He bumps back.

"I've been there all morning."

"Oh, so you've been waiting for me for a while then." He smirks and I shove him.

"Jerk," I grumble, but we're both laughing as we walk into the restaurant and take a seat.

* * *

I FEEL his eyes on me the second I step out of the elevator to meet everyone for Christmas Eve dinner, taking in the emerald green dress I'm wearing to highlight my eyes. It's modest in cut, a straight neckline with inch-wide straps, and falls a few inches above my knee, but it's skin-tight. It hugs me in all the right places and leaves little to the imagination, shape-wise, and I paired it with soft curls, white heels, and gold accents. I was worried it'd be overkill, even with the formal setting of this dinner. Now, I'm glad I wore it, if only for the reaction it pulls from Adam.

He's in a dark gray suit with a sage green tie, we're only a few shades away from matching and from the light in his eyes, I wonder if he wore that color on purpose. He looks so handsome my mouth dries up and I can't speak. The suit fits him perfectly, and with his hair pushed back, he's breathtaking. I have butter-flies in my stomach, as if I don't know him well enough to feel confident talking to him. I'm *nervous*.

Before I work up the nerve to say something to him, we're being seated, and the moment is gone.

His eyes drift over to me often throughout dinner, although we still haven't spoken a word to each other, and I'm glowing in his attention. My smile is bigger and brighter and I can't make it go away even if I try. It's hard to ignore the weight of his gaze, but I think I do an admirable job of carrying on as if he's not devouring me with his eyes, even while I'm sneakily devouring him with mine.

I try to keep up with the conversation at the table, but Adam barely says a word unless he's directly addressed. From the smirk on his face, I can tell Caleb sees the way we're looking at each other. I've kept him mostly updated on everything that happens between Adam and I, although I cut out details that feel weird to share with his brother—like the conversation after the first gym session that still sends heat coursing through my body when I think about it. I keep my shirt on in the gym now, to be considerate, although all I want is for him to strip off each piece of clothing like he promised. Was it a promise? I like to think it was, because one day I will wear that matching set again just to fulfill that fantasy.

It's an interesting dinner to say the least. Adam isn't trying to hide that he's staring at me, and Caleb isn't trying to hide that he notices Adam staring. Jess is trying to play it cool but every time our eyes meet, we end up grinning because we both know what's happening, and all the while Claire and Phil carry the conversa-tion as if none of this is happening. Although I think I catch Claire smiling at us from time to time and I wonder if they also know exactly what's happening. No one says anything about it though.

After dinner, we all head up to the rooms and after "good-nights," everyone heads in, except for Adam. He stays back and pulls me aside before I head for my door.

"Rylie," he says, sounding breathless, "you look beautiful."

"Thanks." I blush and run my hand across the lapel of his suit jacket. "You clean up nice yourself."

He's quiet again and it's so unlike him that I have to ask. "You haven't said much tonight. Everything okay?"

His mouth moves like he's trying to speak but can't find the words. He takes a deep breath. "How can I . . ." He pauses, shaking his head. "I don't know how to speak when . . . You're breathtaking," he finally stammers out.

My eyes lock on him, and it's my turn to be speechless. It's still so hard to truly believe that I have that strong of an effect on him. I reach for his hand and lace our fingers together like it's muscle memory; like they've spent their entire lives together and will spend forevermore doing the same.

We stand like that, staring at each other, for who knows how long. Staring like it'd be physically painful to look away, and it would've been. I want to live in this moment with him, getting lost in each other's presence, forever.

But moments never last.

He snaps out of it and looks away as the clock chimes, signaling midnight.

"Merry Christmas, Rylie," he whispers, looking conflicted as his hand starts to reach towards me. I want to reach out and meet him, encourage him. Maybe if I did, I wouldn't have to go to bed alone tonight.

But I'm conflicted, too. It's Christmas and I'm not sitting in front of the tree watching Christmas movies with my mom. I want to be happy, enjoy the holidays, but how can I do that fully when I know I'm missing out on my favorite traditions. That I'll never get to do those traditions again because they were traditions *because* of her.

Halfway to me, he huffs out a breath, losing his nerve, or thinking better of it, and disappears into his room.

I stand there staring at the space he just occupied and whisper, "Merry Christmas, Adam."

In a daze, I stumble into my room, and I spend the whole night talking to my mom.

chapter nineteen

I WAKE up on New Year's Eve feeling apprehensive about the day ahead. Adam and I are back at the Dey's house and Caleb and Jess are at her family's place. The rest of the ski trip went smoothly. We celebrated Christmas together, although no gifts were actually exchanged. The ski trip was Claire and Phil's gift to us all, and the four of us decided to pool our money to plan a spring break trip together.

I avoided the slopes the rest of the trip, opting to stay by the fire most days. Jess joined me some days and Caleb would stop by when he needed a break. Adam found me for lunch each day, and on the last day he spent the entire day with me. It was the best day of the trip. We ran around like we were little kids again, having a snowball fight and playing in the snow. We laughed so hard we cried and smiled until our faces hurt. And when we walked hand in hand into a cafe near the resort for lunch, I could see our future in those little moments.

But the high I was riding from that feeling has dulled in the face of this day I've been dreading for a long time.

This evening friends and family are coming over again for a

New Year's party. I stayed in my room most of the morning, trying to work through the dark thoughts clouding me before others get here, but all I manage to do is spiral.

It's the last day of the last year my mom was alive.

The changing of years feels more significant this year, more permanent. I'm not ready to move on yet. I'm not ready to live in a year she hasn't seen. Even though I didn't have her for long this year, she was still there to listen to my hopes and dreams. We could still wish for better days ahead. It feels wrong to wish for better days when I know all my days with her are behind me.

I keep to myself throughout the evening, not in the mood to celebrate or converse. Claire checks in with me and gives me a big hug, and I can feel her keeping an eye on me. I don't blame her, I probably look as sad as I feel. But as I catch the pitying glances of more and more people, I can't even try to pretend anymore.

Adam is nowhere to be found so I head to the one place I'll be able to breathe, the one place that's always made me feel better. The dock.

There's a clear sky, showcasing an almost full moon and my dark thoughts are already starting to lighten up as I sit on the wood planks. Closing my eyes, I take a deep breath, and let the fresh air course through me. Slowly, my body starts to relax into the familiarity of this spot.

The more I relax the more the cold seeps in. I was in such a rush to get away that I didn't bring a jacket and the brisk winter air cuts right through the thin, black, long sleeve I'm wearing that shimmers in the light. The black, faux-leather pants don't do much to keep me warm either, but I'm not ready to head back inside.

The cold is a welcome distraction from the thoughts that have been burrowing in my head throughout the day. I plan on toughing it out for as long as I can before the cold forces me back inside, but I'm not putting up much of a fight.

I'm so focused on trying to stay put for another few minutes that I don't hear him approach until he's standing over me.

"I thought I'd find you here," Adam says, out of breath as he takes a seat beside me. "You look like you could use a drink." He hands me a glass of champagne. "And a blanket." When the thick fuzzy blanket hits my shoulders, I groan at the immediate warmth it provides. He wraps it around us both, forcing us to sit shoulder to shoulder. "And a friend." He gestures to himself, and I laugh.

"You read my mind."

My shivering starts to ease up but I'm still shaking when Adam slips his arm around me and starts rubbing up and down on my shoulders and arms, trying to warm me up faster.

"What were you thinking coming out here in freezing temperatures without even a jacket?" He's doing as much as he can to stop my shivering. "You're still shaking."

I lean into him, savoring the warmth of his body. "I'm good, I'm almost warm."

"You could've frozen out here or got sick or something."

It's sweet how genuine his concern is. "I was about to head in before you got here."

"Why didn't you have a jacket?"

"I wasn't thinking, I just had to get away from everyone. I needed to . . ." I pause searching for the right word and settle on one I know he'll understand. "Breathe."

He huffs out a breath. "I was in my room grabbing something and was about to come look for you when I saw you out here through my window. I could see you shivering from up there. I ran a few people over trying to get out here as fast as I could."

So that's why he was out of breath when he first got here.

"I couldn't find you so this was the only other place I could think to go," I say softly. I take a sip of the champagne now that I've finally stopped shaking.

He removes his arm from around me and I try to hide the

disappointment on my face. He starts shifting for long enough that I look over at him curiously. He finally settles and looks up at me.

"I got this for you," he says, looking away nervously. "It was supposed to be for Christmas, but it wasn't ready in time."

He holds out a small light gray box with a white bow. I can only stare at it, overwhelmed with emotions. He grabs my hand and places the box in it because I'm too frozen to reach for it myself.

"Go on, open it," he urges and there's a hint of excitement in his words.

"I didn't . . . You shouldn't . . . You didn't have to get me anything," I stammer out.

He just smiles and nudges me. "I know, just open it."

My hand shakes as I pull off the lid of the box. Inside lies a gold necklace with an oval locket. A tear springs to my eye and I run my thumb over the intricate etching on the locket. Wispy vines wrap around the edges of the oval, creating a border that surrounds a calla lily. It's beautiful, and delicate, and has my mom's favorite flower on it—I love it already.

But when I look up at him, he's shaking with excitement. "Open it."

I snap open the locket and gasp, tears immediately spilling over, because inside the locket there's a picture of me and my mom—my favorite picture of us. It's from two and a half years ago, her last good summer. We went on a picnic, with all of our favorite foods and just sat in the park, soaking in the sun. It's one of the last times I remember feeling carefree.

We took so many selfies that day, and in this one she has her arms wrapped around me, we're cheek to cheek, and we both are smiling our biggest smiles—so big that our eyes are closed. But even through the photo you can feel the happiness and love radiating between us.

On the back of the lid, there's one word etched into the smooth gold. One word that steals all the breath from my lungs and sends a shock through me. It's a word I've avoided as much as possible since she passed, my last name. Lewis.

I let out a strangled, stuttering laugh as tears fall freely from my face.

"I know today is hard for you. I know you're worried about leaving her memory behind as time moves on without her. I know you're dreading midnight, dreading the start of a year without her," he says, and each word brings on a new wave of tears. "I've also noticed that you don't use your last name anymore, and that it brings you pain anytime you hear it."

I've never felt as seen as I do right now, never felt so understood. How does he know these things when I've done my best to hide them from the world?

"But that name, right there?" He points at the locket. "You are who you are today because of that name, and I think that's a lot to be thankful for. It's worth remembering, worth celebrating, because the Rylie Lewis I know is intelligent, kind, strong, caring, beautiful, and she lights up every room she walks into. She's incredible."

When he talks about me like that, when he says my name like that, how can I not love it?

He always has a way of reminding me what's important and helping me push past the pain to find the love that's worth remembering.

"No matter how much time passes, she will always be with you. Do you see how happy that girl in the photo is? I haven't seen you allow yourself to be that happy in a long time. Every time you look at that photo, I want you to remember that you deserve to be that happy. You still deserve happiness, Rylie."

Through my tears, I look up at him and there's a tear running down his face too. When I look at the photo, I think the only time I've been that happy lately is around him. He says I light up a room, but *he* lights *me* up.

"Thank you," I whisper, unable to say much else right now, but it doesn't feel like enough. This gift, what he's done for me, that he knew I needed this, there are no words strong enough to convey what this means to me.

He picks up the necklace and brushes the hair from my neck, letting his fingers linger as he clasps the necklace on me. He doesn't move his hand when he's done and I shiver, turning back toward him and throwing my arms around him.

I hold on tight to my friend who seems to know me better than anyone else. My friend who always knows exactly what to say or do to cheer me up. My friend who does more for me than a friend should.

My friend who I want to be more than a friend.

"Seriously, Adam, thank you," I say into his shoulder. "This means more to me than I could ever express in words."

I pull back to lean my head on his shoulder, his arm still around me, and we listen to the crowd inside start the final countdown to midnight.

"Three!"

"Two!"

"One!"

"Happy New Year!" they cheer.

I take a deep breath.

Just like that, everything changes and the first year I'll spend alone begins. Adam's arm moves from around me to find my hand, interlocking our fingers and squeezing.

Well, not completely alone.

My eyes find his and both of our breaths catch. The sounds of the party fade away until all I hear is my racing heart. I bite my cheek nervously before I softly say, "I think it's bad luck not to kiss at midnight."

His lips twitch up into a smile. "Is that really a thing?" he asks, but he's already leaning closer.

I raise my shoulders slightly as my eyes flash down to his lips just long enough for him to notice and start to tremble. I look back up into his eyes. "I don't care. I just want to kiss you."

He must want this just as much as I do because he doesn't even ask if I'm sure before pulling my face to his like he'll die if he doesn't kiss me this second. It isn't gentle or sweet like our first, it's hungry and desperate and echoes everything I've felt these past months. Everything I'm sure he's felt too.

We lay back on the blanket that fell off our shoulders at some point, but neither of us noticed as his hands trace down my back and anchor my hips to pull me closer. I don't even remember telling my leg to move, but it's sliding up his legs and hitching around his waist so he can move even closer, and he does. We're getting lost in this kiss, in each other—not caring that if anyone looked close enough out the back windows it'd be obvious what was happening out here.

His hand slips beneath the hem of my shirt and I suck in a breath because his hand is *cold*. A shiver runs across my body and it's enough for us to find ourselves again. His lips leave mine and tears well in my eyes, so I keep them shut. He rests his forehead against mine as we both gasp for air and try to steady our breathing.

"If we don't stop now, I don't think I'll be able to stop at all." His hands tighten on me, emphasizing his point and I arch into him.

"I don't want to stop," I choke out and he chuckles. "But, I don't know if tonight is the right time for this."

"It's definitely not." He chuckles again and pulls back to look at me, but when I open my eyes, tears slip out and all humor fades from his face. "What's wrong?"

"I don't know. Nothing. Everything."

"Rylie," he rasps, and wipes the tears from my cheeks. "Talk to me, what are you feeling?"

"T-terrified," I admit, knowing I owe him some explanation and wanting him to understand me and my twisted mind. "I'm fucking *terrified*."

His eyes widen but his hands never stop comforting me. Moving from wiping my tears to smoothing my hair and pulling the blanket over us again to shield us from the cold. In order to be fully covered we have to lay on our sides, almost pressed together from chest to hips and purposefully tangled together from hips to toes. It has the effect of feeling like we're in a bubble, like nothing else exists outside of him and me and the gentle, caring way he's watching and listening to me.

"What are you so afraid of?" he whispers, almost as if he's afraid of what the answer will be.

"How much I want this, want you," I start, and he goes completely still. "I see you and I'm dying inside because all I want is to run into your arms and seal any space between us. And when you kiss me, it's like that's all I need to survive in this world." I blink the tears from my eyes so I can see the stunned look on his face before I continue. I almost don't want to continue, because I don't want to wipe this beautiful look off his face, so I close my eyes to continue. "But then, when I come back to reality, I feel guilty because she hasn't even been gone a full year yet and it's the last day of the last year she was alive, and for a moment, *I forgot* about all that. We have so much history with this dock—*good* history—but that history only happened because she was sick. It's like anytime I try to be happy again, the darkness taints all the light."

He finally moves again and it's to pull me to his chest while I cry. All the while cooing sweet words in my ear, as if I'm not the one who's hurting him. I don't know why he cares for me enough to put up with this rollercoaster I've put him through. I just know that I need to tell him everything now, so I won't have any regrets if he ever decides it's too much.

"I'm scared to let you in completely, because I know that the second I do, that's it." He keeps up with the comforting movements but stays quiet to listen. "I know that the moment I allow myself to love you the way I know I will, it'll be an all-encompassing type of love. It's inevitable, hell, I'm probably already there, but I'm too scared to let myself accept it. I'm terrified to love you like that, because it's how I loved her, and when she left, she took so much of me with her. I won't survive that again."

"Oh, Rylie." He holds me tighter, and I think he's crying too. "I can't imagine how complicated this is for you. Please know, there's no pressure from me at all to rush your healing. I'll be here as your shoulder to cry on, your friend to confide in, anything you need me to be for as long as you need."

"How can you be this understanding?" I tighten my arms around him, grateful for his heart, his care.

"Because I know what you've been through. I've had to watch you go through it all, all the while wishing I could do anything to take a sliver of your pain away. So I will wait as long as it takes for you to feel safe enough to let me in, because I know that when you do, it'll be more than worth it. *You're* worth it." He tilts my head up until we're looking in each other's eyes. "But just so you know, I'm going to love you in that same, all-encompassing way." A smile pulls at his lips, and he leans in to whisper, "Hell, I probably already do."

I stop breathing and he pulls back to look at me with the sweetest grin. My eyes widen as they absorb the truth behind his words. I can't stop the words from tumbling out. "I really want to kiss you again."

His face softens and he leans in to plant a short and sweet kiss on my lips that's nowhere near enough but is also everything I could ever need.

The pressure of his lips is gone as fast as it arrived. "Happy New Year, Rylie."

"Happy New Year, Adam," I whisper, the echo of a smile on my lips.

We sit there, with my head resting on his shoulder and his hand in mine, until our glasses are empty, and the sounds of the party die out inside.

chapter twenty

"RYLIE? YOU HOME?" Caleb calls as he enters the apartment.

"You're finally back," I say, running over to give my best friend a hug. I haven't seen him since two days after Christmas and classes start again tomorrow.

When I pull away, I see Jess standing in the doorway behind him and my smile grows. I walk over to her, and she doesn't hesitate to hug back. I'm still not used to how great of a friend she's become in such a short amount of time.

"How was the time with your family?" I ask.

"It was so nice seeing them again." She smiles. "It's been a while."

I lead them to the couch. "I want to hear everything."

As Caleb launches into a story about how he thought Jess's mom hated him for most of the trip, I can tell how serious they are about each other. There's no denying the way they look at each other, the love and happiness there.

My hand strays to the gold locket around my neck, and the person who gave it to me. Remembering the way he looked at me with such care and tenderness, and how we basically spoke our feelings with words that were just shy of the life-changing, world-stopping ones I know I feel and want so desperately to hear him say one day. It also gives me an idea of a sort-of present I can give him to make sure he knows he's always the one I'll want even if I can't have him right now.

"So, where's that necklace from?" Caleb asks that evening while we're catching up on episodes of *The Bachelor* that we missed while on vacation. I don't realize I'm touching it again until he mentions it.

It's already developing into an instinctual habit whenever I think of Adam. A habit that will too easily give away when I'm thinking about him, which happens an embarrassingly large amount of the time.

"It was a late Christmas gift," I say, avoiding his scrutinizing gaze.

"From?"

I don't bother answering that, he already knows his guess is right, so I just open the locket and shift closer to him. He leans in to look at the picture and the name and his eyes go wide. Slowly, he lifts his gaze to mine in question.

A sad smile crosses my face. "New Years was rough for me. I couldn't stand to be at the party, and he sat out with me in the freezing cold." I close the locket and run my thumb over the design on the outside. "He said it's to remind me that a piece of her will always be with me and that I still deserve to be as happy as I was in the photo.

"And I needed that reminder because I've felt so guilty being happy without her. I think I've unintentionally been sabotaging myself because I didn't feel like I should be happy since she's gone. I know it's stupid, but I didn't know how to deal with the fact that I was entering a year she'd never be able to see." I had these realizations shortly after New Years and Caleb is the one I wanted to talk about them with. I look down with a small smile. "It's still hard, but not as hard as I expected because of this.

When it starts to hurt too much, I can look down at this and some of that happiness comes flooding back."

While touching the locket and running my thumb over the etching is a sign I'm thinking of Adam, I open it when I'm thinking about my mom. It really has helped me get through these first couple days of the new year. When the darkness comes, this reminder of the happiness and love we shared is my light. My thoughts always end up back on Adam though, because he gave me this incredible gift. It's as if it's imbued with a part of him since he's always been a light for me too.

How will I ever be able to thank him for the comfort he's given me?

"It's not stupid, Ry," Caleb squeaks and I know he's crying too, but when he reaches out to grab my hand, I feel his appreciation that I shared this with him. He pulls me into a hug. "He's right, you know. You do deserve to be happy and having known your mom, I truly believe your happiness was most important to her."

Of course, he's right, but knowing the truth doesn't make it any easier to move past the fears still clouding my mind.

* * *

A NEW SEMESTER IS HERE, and classes are in full swing. Unfortunately, my schedule doesn't line up with either Caleb or Adam, so I'm left eating alone on days I'm on campus for lunch. Caleb was officially offered, and accepted, the research position, but it doesn't start until summer so he's still at the deli for now. And my schedule at The Split Bean takes up most of my free time during the week because I work almost every evening after classes.

Adam is doing a TA program offered to the business majors, where any juniors or seniors can assist professors in entry level courses with grading and administrative tasks for a weekly pay.

Other than weekends, I almost never see anyone anymore. It's not until Friday that Adam even stops by The Split Bean.

"Hi, sorry I haven't stopped by sooner," he says, approaching the counter. "I'm helping with two courses this semester and both professors wanted to spend extra time going over schedules. They've been a lot more hands on than the one I had last semester. It's been exhausting."

I smile and hand him the coffee he never ordered. "I know. You've texted me every day saying you wanted to stop by but have been busy."

"I wanted to make sure you knew I'd have been here if I could've been, and that I was still thinking about you even though I was gone." He shrugs like it's no big deal, but the words are so casually sweet, they steal the air from my lungs.

"I appreciate that." I smile at him and it's full of more emotion than I usually show but it's hard to hold it back. "I'm glad to see you, I've missed our lunch dates."

"Me too," he says, eyes shifting from my face and catching on something that causes a huge smile to spread across his face. "You're wearing it."

My hand immediately stays to the locket, realizing that's what caught his attention. "Of course, I wear it every day."

His eyes don't leave the locket and the smile doesn't leave his face, I'm not sure he even heard my response when he snaps out of it and changes the subject. "When are you done here?"

"We close in an hour, so not long after that."

"You hungry?"

"Starving."

"Great, I'll be here when you get off." He smiles again, eyes flashing to the locket once more with a look of pride, or relief, before he walks out. Usually, I don't enjoy working without Angie, but right now I'm grateful she's not here because I'd never hear the end of this.

The last hour feels like it lasts a lifetime as I count down the minutes until I can leave. I sigh in relief when I finally lock the door and head out toward the last car in the parking lot—Adam's.

"What's for dinner?" I ask as I sit down in the passenger seat. I'm starving and, as if in agreement, my stomach grumbles loudly.

"I thought we could just pick something up and eat back at your place," he says as if it's a question, even though it's not phrased as one. There are no objections from me, I'd rather not go out somewhere smelling like coffee after hours of work anyway.

"Can we do Chick-Fil-A?" I suggest. "I've been craving their waffle fries for days."

He laughs. "Chick-Fil-A it is."

Thirty minutes later we're parked in front of the ugly high-lighter yellow of my apartment building, and the car is filled with the smell of freshly cooked chicken and crispy golden waffle fries that are half-gone already. They're best hot so I started snacking on the way home and alternated between feeding myself and feeding some to Adam, who used the opportunity to nip at my fingers each time he took a bite.

Jess's car is parked out front but when we walk in the door, the living room lights are off and the door to Caleb's room is closed. I try to give them as much space as possible when the door is closed, so I lead Adam to my room and shut the door behind us. They'll have heard the front door, so they know I'm home and they'll come find me when they're ready.

This isn't the first time he's been over when Jess is here, and we have our routine perfected. I turn on the small TV in my room to whatever reruns I can find, which happens to be *Grey's Anatomy* tonight, while Adam goes to the bathroom closet to grab a towel and sets it up on the ground like a picnic. There's only one chair for the desk and I don't want food getting on my bed so this is what we came up with.

Adam has seen enough reruns to understand what's happening, and I practically have the script for this show memorized with how much I've watched it. It just so happens to be the episode where Meredith builds the house of candles for Derek. The irony doesn't escape me that we're watching her overcome her fear to finally choose to be with him when I'm still not able to. But Adam doesn't make any comments about how this pertains to us, even though I'm sure he's thinking the same thing with how he keeps glancing over at me.

We're just finishing our food when a light knock sounds at the door.

"Come in."

I grab the remote and mute the TV just as the door swings open to reveal Caleb's smiling face. "Hey guys. What are you up to in here?"

But the way he asks suggests we were up to no good and I glare at him even as a light pink flushes my cheeks. Adam looks between us, and I can see the lightbulb go off in his head that Caleb knows everything that has happened between us and is okay with it. We've both brought up the concern of his family not being okay with us, but I dropped that concern long ago when I told Caleb, and he was happy for us. Although I can't help but wonder if it's still weird for him—having his long-time best friend and his older brother interested in each other and having a first-hand account of their time together.

"We just finished dinner, if that wasn't obvious," I finally answer, with a planted smile on my face.

"More than that is obvious," he says, and I choke on the sip of sweet tea I just took. He's getting bolder with his comments, and he looks smug about it.

"You're good for Wednesday still, right?" Adam is the first to speak and it shuts Caleb up immediately. I can't be sure, but I think he changed the topic to protect me from Caleb's teasing, which I really don't mind all that much even though it always draws a reaction from me. Wednesday is a day I've tried not to think about, even though I should've reminded Caleb of it, I just couldn't bring it up. I think he knew that too and brought it up for me.

"Yeah, I took off work and made sure I'm not missing anything in my classes," he replies softly.

Jess speaks up for the first time after looking between our suddenly sullen faces in confusion. "What's Wednesday?"

I swallow my tears because I feel like I need to be the one to say the words first. "Wednesday is the one-year anniversary of my mom's death."

My hands are shaking but I've managed to keep from breaking down crying . . . for now.

"I'm so sorry," she whispers, and I know she's remembering what it felt like to be where I am now. She knows exactly what I'm feeling, and I can't look away from her because of that.

I don't even notice Adam scoot closer to me until his hand gently comes to rest on my lower-back in support. "We're going to go back to Lockney for the day," Adam explains.

I momentarily feel bad that we're talking about this in front of her when she's not invited, but she just nods like she gets that I need to do this surrounded by people who knew her and loved her too.

The conversation moves back to happier topics and the four of us hang out for hours until Adam is the first to head out. I run to my room quickly before walking him out, hiding the item I grabbed behind my back.

"Goodnight, Rylie," he says, pulling me into a hug that keeps me warm even though it's still winter and I'm in a short-sleeve shirt.

I'm nervous as we pull back and I hold out the CD case for him. His eyebrows pull together as he looks down at the unassuming gift. "What's that?"

"It's for you," I say, pushing it closer to him until he takes it.

"I know this situation is less than ideal and that it isn't easy for you, and still, you've always been there for me. You never waver, never show any frustration. You're patient and thoughtful and always show me how much you care about me. I hope I've been able to show you the same, but I'm sure not everything has come out right. That is a playlist of everything I want you to know. Songs that remind me of you, of us. Songs that say words you deserve to hear but I'm afraid to say. Songs that convey everything I feel. So you'll know I'm always thinking about you too."

"Rylie," he squeaks, and looks up at me on the verge of tears. "This is the best gift anyone's ever given me."

I look down, embarrassed and reach for the necklace he got me. "Not as good as a locket," I mumble.

"No, it's better."

My eyes shoot back up and I can tell he truly means it. He wraps me in another hug that somehow pulls me even closer into him than before and I squeeze as tight as I can.

"Thank you," he whispers into my hair, and I can't help my smile.

"Goodnight, Adam." I pull back, stretch onto my tippy toes to plant a kiss on his cheek, and turn to run inside before I don't have the strength to walk away at all.

Inside, Caleb and Jess are back in his room—she's staying the night—so I head into mine and try not to think about the songs Adam's probably listening to right now. Most are sweeter songs that convey how thankful I am for him always being there and how much he means to me, but I slipped in a few songs that go deeper into my feelings. I wonder what he'll think of those, of all of it.

I don't have to wait long to find out.

Just over an hour and a half later my phone dings, indicating a new text.

ADAM

Glad I didn't listen to this around you. You might have taken it back after seeing me cry like a baby.

I laugh, thinking it's a joke until a picture comes through that's a close up of his eye, red-rimmed with tears spilling over.

ME

I want to be your shoulder to cry on, especially when I've caused the tears.

ADAM:

These are good tears. You can cause these tears any day.

Before I can reply another text comes through.

ADAM

But seriously, this means so much to me. Thank you.

And another.

ADAM

And I definitely have a favorite, btw.

Now that intrigues me, and my mind is running through each song on that CD wondering which it could be.

ME

Which is?

ADAM

Guess.

I know which one I *want* his favorite to be, because it's my favorite too. It's one of the deeper ones that I almost didn't put on there but it's probably the most truthful song on the CD— "Dress" by Taylor Swift.

Before I can overthink anything, I send the dress emoji to him. Less than a second later three successive texts come in.

ADAM

NO WAY!!

THAT'S CRAZY!

How'd you know??

I laugh and there's a huge grin on my face. Him choosing that song as his favorite is almost like confirmation that he feels the exact same way about me as I do for him, and what a feeling that is.

ME

Because it's my favorite too.

ADAM

I guess that makes it our song.

My heart stutters.

ME

It's perfect.

When I wake the next morning, I see he sent one last message, long after I'd fallen asleep.

ADAM

Yes, you are.

chapter twenty-one

THE DRIVE to Lockney is quiet. We all know if any of us says a word, we'll all start crying—again. The sun has barely risen above the horizon line, yet there are six, red-rimmed, puffy eyes in this car. Mine are worst of all, and considering I didn't sleep at all last night because I was up crying, they're likely bloodshot too. Caleb came into my room around three in the morning when my echoing sobs woke him and he laid there with me until morning, although we barely said two words that entire time. What is there to say on a day like today?

When Adam pulled up to pick us up before dawn, he found us huddled together on the steps in front of the apartment. He shut the car off, came to sit on my other side, and started to cry with us.

That moment made me glad of everything that has happened the past few months, no matter how hard it's been. If I had stayed closed off, and kept pushing them away, we never would've had that moment. I might not have allowed them to be part of this day. I don't know how I would make it through today without them both by my side.

I break the silence when, once in town, Adam turns down a

road that takes us away from the cemetery. "Where are we going?" My voice is scratchy and hoarse.

Both boys just smile at me in answer. A few minutes later, we pull up to the local coffee shop and I feel stupid for having asked the question. Lockney is a small town, I should've known we were making a coffee stop the second he turned right instead of left—there's not much else this way.

"You coming?" Adam already has my door open and is offering me his hand.

I nod and glance over to see Caleb making no move to come with. "What about you?"

"This surprise was all Adam." He nods to his brother with a smile. "I'm going to wait here."

That confuses me. "Surprise?" The words slip out in a breathy whisper as I take Adam's hand. He doesn't give anything away as we walk up to the small brick shop.

I'm studying him as I walk through the door he's holding open, so I don't notice what's going on until I step inside. Even when I do look, I don't understand what's going on. If I didn't know better, I'd assume it was some sort of surprise party—or surprise mourning?—with a small group of people gathered inside, obviously awaiting our arrival.

"What is this?" I ask, turning back to Adam but it's the coffee shop owner, Bill, who steps forward and speaks.

"A few weeks ago, this young gentleman"—he gestures toward Adam—"called me up to make sure I'd have lavender in stock to make your mom's favorite lavender lattes today when you came."

I shift my gaze to Adam, who's looking away as if he's embarrassed when that is the sweetest thing he ever could've done. I reach over to grab his hand as Bill explains the rest of the people here.

"Word spread quickly about what today is, and that you'd be stopping here in the morning." Bill smiles sheepishly, obviously he's the one that told everyone else. "So many shop owners in town remembered your mom and had such lovely stories about her. They wanted to share those with you, along with all of her favorite things."

I look around the room, recognizing some people immediately—like Windy, the owner of my mom's favorite flower shop—but not recognizing even half of them. One by one, they take turns telling me stories about my mom. Windy says she always kept calla lilies in stock just for her, and still does just because they're a reminder of her. A man I don't know, who identifies himself as the owner of a café near the hospital says she stopped by his shop every time she left the hospital, and that he'd never allowed her to pay but she'd pay for the person behind her each time to spread the joy. Even her doctors, who couldn't be here for obvious reasons, left an envelope with kind notes about how much they all adored her and included some polaroid's they'd found of her with her doctors, or giving a thumbs up to the camera.

We must be in there for an hour listening to story after story and accepting gift after gift. We've amassed a bouquet of calla lilies, lavender lattes, a box of her favorite macaroons, three of her favorite sandwiches from the café near the hospital, a plethora of notes from people who couldn't be here, and the promise of her favorite Chinese food delivered to us for lunch. It's such an overwhelming experience of community and belonging.

I'd wanted to keep out of Lockney for so long after she passed because I thought it couldn't be the same without her. But she's alive here. She changed this place with her heart and left a lasting impact. Now, this town feels like magic because she's sprinkled across every corner of it.

I sob and laugh and *smile*—holding tight to Adam's hand the entire time—and when it's time to go, I hug each person in that shop and thank them personally for this incredible gift.

And after we load everything into the car, I hug Adam longest of all.

"Thank you," I whisper. "That was so special."

"It was mostly them," he says, and I pull back to look him in the eyes.

"The fact that you even thought to call to make sure they'd have the lavender lattes, means the world to me."

He smiles like making me happy is all he cares about before opening my door for me.

"How was it?" Caleb asks, yawning. He was napping in here but I still feel bad he stayed in here the entire time.

"I wish you were in there with us, it was magical." Tears still stream down my face, but they're different because they're happy tears.

* * *

WHEN WE GET to the cemetery, Caleb lays out a large blanket and some pillows as Adam and I unload the drinks, food, and flowers we'd been given. I lay the flowers at the base of her tombstone and kiss my fingers before touching them to her name, Lydia Lewis. I try to shut off the math part of my brain that automatically wants to calculate the years represented by the dash because I know it's much too small of a number.

We sit for hours and talk to her. Between the three of us we recount everything that happened in the past year, and everything that's changed about our goals for the future. We talk and occasionally snack on sandwiches or macaroons until the sun is high in the sky. Just as our stomachs all start grumbling for more substantial food, Claire and Phil pull up with bags and bags of Chinese food in hand. As the five of us eat, it's Claire's turn to update my mom on everything that's changed in town the past year and make sure she's up-to-date on the current gossip circling the moms group. That part sends us off on tangent after tangent, trying to dissect whether it's the truth or not.

This day, which I thought would be one of the worst days of my life, has turned into one of the most special days I've ever experienced. It's easy to realize how much I've changed and grown in the past year. I hope she'd be proud of me.

When I voice as much, Claire grabs my hand and assures me she *is* so proud of me and is watching down on my every move. The five of us sit there until the most beautiful sunset I've ever seen in my life has faded to black and it's time for us to head back to campus. As we all hug Claire and Phil goodbye, I can't help but feel like everything is exactly as my mom would've wanted it to be.

chapter twenty-two

THE WEEK AFTER, I'm eating lunch on campus alone when someone calls out my name. I look around, searching for familiarity in the sea of faces.

"Rylie, hi!"

This time, I find the source and I start smiling.

"Jess," I call back as I stand up to give her a hug. "What are you doing here?"

"One of my classes got canceled so I'm grabbing an early lunch. Can I join you?" Her smile is always so genuine.

"Of course, I'd love that."

I shift my bag out of the second chair at my table to make room and we both settle back in. I'm almost finished with my food but she's just beginning. I give her some time to take a few bites before speaking. "Thank you again for your message last week, it meant a lot."

On the way back from Lockney, I finally looked at my phone and amongst the sea of condolences, was the sweetest message from Jess. It must be because she knows what it's like that her message was so meaningful and thoughtful. Most people stuck to the general messages of *"Sorry for your loss,"* or, *"You're in my thoughts today,"* or, *"Your mom was amazing, I'll remember her always."* Those messages are kind, and I appreciate that people remembered her, but sometimes it feels like people are too afraid to write something truthful or real, or they're afraid if they say too much it'll upset me. But the truth is I'd rather read a memory of her than a basic message.

"Caleb told me what the town did," she says, softly. "It sounded beautiful."

"It was." If anyone else had used the term *beautiful* to describe that day it wouldn't have made sense, but that gesture *was* a beautiful display of humanity that not many get to experience. Beautiful is the perfect word for it from someone who's gone through the same thing. I hesitate for a moment but decide it can't hurt to ask and she's always offered to talk if I wanted to. "Can I ask you something personal?"

"Of course." Her expression mirrors mine in sudden seriousness.

"How did you know you were ready to move on after your dad died?" My face scrunches together realizing that didn't come out quite right. "I mean how did you start allowing yourself to live again . . . if that makes sense?"

She smiles a small, sad smile and nods. "It makes complete sense, but it's a complicated answer. Some days his loss still feels fresh, even though it's been many years. Some days I feel normal. The more time that passes, the more normal days I have, but I don't think the hard days will ever stop coming. There will always be things that come up that remind me of him, or that I wish I could share with him, and those things will always be hard. But I realized that being sad and closing myself off from the world—closing myself off from happiness—was the opposite of what he would've wanted for me. Just because he wasn't here to see it, doesn't mean he wouldn't want me to experience it. That's what finally allowed me to begin living my life again."

I'm nodding as she speaks.

"Yeah, I think I've been realizing that same thing, but that doesn't make it easier to actually start doing it."

"I hate to break it to you, but it'll never be easy. You have to wake up each day and choose happiness, choose life. I almost didn't go to that Halloween party because I was struggling that day." She gives me a pointed stare as she says, "Look at everything I would've missed out on if I let the negative thoughts win that day and stayed home."

I know she's talking about me and Adam now, and I know she's right. I need to stop letting the negative thoughts win.

* * *

THE END of January is Caleb's 21st birthday and we spend the morning at the mall, shopping for new outfits for Hydra, a low-key bar and club just outside of town that Caleb wanted to go to tonight. It's some much-needed time alone together. Since he started dating Jess we haven't had as much friendship time and it's nice spending this time just us. I take him to his favorite Italian restaurant for lunch and by the time we get home, it's time to start getting ready for the night out.

I put on the emerald top I bought today. It's a solid tank top with a mesh, skin-tight long-sleeve top over it. It's thin enough to see my skin through the green mesh covering my arms, but isn't overly revealing. I pair it with black heels and a black skirt that's form-fitting through the waist and hips but is A-line the rest of the way, down to my mid-thigh. I curl my hair into soft curls that cascade down to my mid-back and keep my make-up natural except for a defined eyeliner that Jess taught me how to do, and a dark blush lipstick.

It's almost embarrassing to admit, but the reason I bought this shirt for tonight is because I remembered the way Adam reacted to the emerald dress I wore on Christmas Eve, and I'd like to see him react like that again. After my conversation with

Jess last week, I feel closer than ever to being ready to be with him. I'm both nervous and excited for what might be in store for us tonight.

"Happy birthday!" I practically scream at Caleb when he walks out of his room all dressed up in cream pants and a blue short-sleeve button up. I throw my arms around him and feel his chest shake as he laughs.

"You know, that's the hundredth time today you've said that."

"And I still have a few more hours to say it a hundred times more," I say. "My best friend is finally twenty-one, it's time to celebrate!"

"Thank you for a great birthday." He squeezes me before pulling away.

There's a light knock on the door before Jess enters, looking radiant in her light blue silk dress that matches Caleb's shirt. They look stunning together.

"You ready to go? Adam's pulling up now too." She moves to give Caleb a kiss and whispers something in his ear that makes him blush.

I grab my purse and head towards the door. "I'll see you guys there."

I'm going to ride with Adam, while Caleb rides with Jess, just in case groups of us want to leave at different times. I'm halfway to the street when Adam gets out of the car and walks around to lean against the passenger door. My breath catches and I stumble on my next step.

"Well, aren't you looking handsome," I call, a smile spreading across my face. He's in black pants and a beige short-sleeve button up with a large, black palm leaf pattern on it. With his sunglasses still on, he looks like he walked right off a movie set. He's the leading man, of course.

He takes off his glasses and smiles up at me. When I get close, he holds out his hand to help me down the steps to the street and then uses our joined hands to slowly spin me around.

"Me? Look at you. You look incredible." While his one hand stays holding mine, the other runs over the emerald material on my arm which had caught his attention. His smile turns soft and reminiscent, I hope he's remembering Christmas Eve too.

"You know, I love this color on you," he mumbles, caught up in memory.

"Oh, really? Why's that?"

"It brings out your eyes and I love your eyes," he says, looking up into them and I might as well be glued to this spot. He laughs a little, still more in memory than in the present. "Sometimes I think I'd like to spend a few hours lost in them, trying to decipher exactly what color they are. I can never quite put it into words, their color, but I think it might be my favorite."

I stare at him, mouth open in shock and eyes locked on him. That's the first time he's told me he loves my eyes. My eyes, which are my favorite feature too, because they're her eyes.

"Ready?" Caleb yells as he and Jess walk out the door, heading to her car. I didn't even realize the door had opened.

We're silent on the fifteen-minute drive there—the only sound is the music playing—and, after the second song, I realize it's the playlist I made for him. I beam at him and lace our fingers together on the center console, but we still don't speak until we're out of the car and walking into the building.

"After you," he breathes, his hand grazing the exposed skin of my lower back. A breathy gasp escapes me and I quickly walk through the door, hoping he doesn't notice the effect his touch has on me because knowing him, he'll use it to drive me crazy tonight. But from the dark chuckle that rumbles from behind me, he definitely noticed.

When we get to the table I take the seat next to Caleb, while Adam sits across from me. We're at one end of the table and there's four of Caleb's friends on the other side of him and Jess.

After ten minutes of trying and failing to keep up with the conversation at the table and keep my eyes off Adam, I barely notice the waitress asking for drink orders.

"I'll just have a Pepsi," Adam says, not breaking eye contact with me. "I have a feeling I'll be needing all my wits about me this evening."

At the suggestive smile that grows on his face, my heart skips a beat and I can't help but return it. We're both drunk enough off each other that we don't need alcohol to make it even harder to keep our hands off each other. Although, I'm beginning to question if I still need time to figure things out. I feel like I've been good lately, but am I truly ready? How am I supposed to know when it's the right time?

With a laugh I counter, "Apparently, I'll be needing my *wits* as well. Better make that two Pepsis."

While the rest of the table orders, Adam and I just sit there staring at each other and grinning like idiots.

"I'll be right back," Jess says, breaking the silent conversation between me and Adam.

I take a deep breath and smile at her before she goes. I need this distraction and with Jess away there are some questions I have for Caleb that I didn't bring up earlier.

"You and Jess seem really happy." I turn to Caleb, trying to ignore Adam for a few minutes but constantly aware of his eyes always on me. "How are things going?"

He blushes and my heart warms with happiness for him. "Things have been great. I really like her."

"Have you said, 'I love you' yet?" I prod, as any good best friend does.

He blushes and looks down. "No, I haven't said it yet."

"You haven't *said it*, but you do, don't you?"

"Ry!" he whisper-yells at me, looking around to make sure she isn't close by.

"Oh. My. Gosh!" I gush over this new bit of information. "I think you guys are great together."

"I was a bit worried in the beginning because I could tell she wasn't sure what to think of you—it made her uncomfortable at times. I'm glad you guys are such good friends now." That seems to remind him of something else because his face twists. "You know, she never did tell me what you two talked about that night before Thanksgiving."

I hear the question in his words and shrug my shoulders. "I told her the truth—about our friendship, about my mom, and about how your family is all I have left. I saw how uncomfortable she was and would've hated myself if I stood in the way of your happiness. With her dad . . . well you know . . ." I trail off and he gives me a sad smile. Understanding washes over him. "We bonded over that hardship, and I think knowing more about my past helped her see me and the situation in a new light."

"You didn't have to do that for me," he squeaks, glassy-eyed.

My hand strays to the locket that's as good as welded around my neck at her mention. "You deserve happiness and I wanted to make sure she had no reason to doubt you, at least about me."

He pulls me into a side hug. "I love you, Ry."

"I love you too, Cale." I pull back to smile at him. "And no crying on your birthday, Jess is coming back now."

He chuckles and straightens himself out while Jess makes it back to the table. I turn back to face Adam and find him staring at me with a look that borders both quizzical and awestruck. He stands, a smile growing on his face and all eyes at the table shift to him.

"Would you honor me with a dance?" he asks in a chivalrous tone, extending a hand towards me. The look he gives me sends chills down my spine and makes me forget about the six pairs of eyes on us.

"How can I say no to a gentleman such as yourself?" I barely manage to get out and take his hand.

As we reach the edge of the dancefloor, Adam uses our joined hands to twirl me—similar to how he did at the apartment, but much faster—and pull me in. In my clumsiness, I can't keep up with the faster spin, especially in heels, and I stumble, slamming into him, clutching at his back to keep myself from falling before his arms wrap around me and tighten to support me. I finally regain my footing and burst out laughing from embarrassment.

"Are you okay?" I can feel him trying to hold back laughter but his shaking chest gives him away.

"Only slightly mortified. Maybe it's safer for me to go sit down again." I turn my head up towards him. His grip tightens as we freeze, faces centimeters apart. In an instant the mood switches from light-hearted fun to electric, burning heat.

"Please stay here with me." His voice is barely a whisper.

I swallow and nod, *I'll always stay with you.* He only holds me tighter as we sway side-to-side in tune to the slow song playing. Our eyes never leave each other.

The song fades out and I step away from Adam and release a breath so I don't inhale his scent and lose my mind more than I already am. I regain my composure faster than he does and smile as I hear the song that fills the room now. The song that not long ago he dubbed as *our song*.

"What are the chances," he shouts, a wicked grin on his face before he spins me and pulls me back, so his chest is against my back.

My eyes close and my hips start to sway as I let myself give into this, into him. As the first chorus plays, I interlock my hands with his on my hips and push back against him with more force.

After a few more of these forceful sways, I think I hear a desperate groan before his arms snake around me further, crisscrossing across my stomach. My hands move to rest on his forearms and squeeze when his hands settle on my sides, thumbs teasing the hem of my top before slipping just beneath.

I'm going to go insane, it's all too much. His hands on my skin. His breath on my neck. Our hips moving together in perfect synchronized movements. And as if it's not enough, and he's trying to drive me over the edge, his hands drift down to my thighs. Ever so slowly his fingers inch up my skin, following the time of my movements, until they reach the hem of my skirt.

My right-hand reaches behind me to run through his hair and my left-hand rests on the side of his leg, wanting to pull him closer. His breathing speeds up and he leans down to run his nose down the side of my neck, pressing his lips to the chain of the necklace he got for me.

I can't stop the moan that slips through my lips, and I tug gently on his hair, leaning my head to allow him better access to the length of my neck. His fingers start circling on the inside of my thigh, ever so slowly daring to creep up, bit by bit, beneath my skirt. I lean against him, not trusting my legs to support me with his hands on me like that.

My blood is boiling. I want more, I *need* more.

I forget we're on the dancefloor in a bar. I forget about everything except him and every point of contact between us. I rotate my head until my lips are at his ear and I'm about to beg for his hands to move faster, for his body to be closer, and for his lips to claim mine. I'm about to beg for him, all of him, everywhere.

Just as my mouth is about to form the only word I can think, *"Please,"* the music abruptly stops.

"We're taking a short break to fix some equipment issues." A voice rings over the speakers. "Go grab a drink and be ready to dance again soon."

His hands move to wrap around me, instead of remaining under my skirt, but other than that, we don't move. I can feel his chest rising and falling just as fast as mine is. I don't want to step away from him. I don't want this moment to be over.

"Well, now I need to know," he teases, trying to soften the

fall for both of us. "Did you buy this dress just so I could take it off?"

I laugh at his use of the song's lyrics in what sounds like a serious question. "This isn't a dress, but I did buy this shirt because I remembered how you looked at me on Christmas Eve when I wore this color."

He chuckles softly against my shoulder and kisses it before finally releasing me, and only once he's stepped away do I add, "And I'd quite enjoy you taking it off."

I walk away before his heated expression burns a hole through me. We rejoin the group to scandalous looks from Caleb and Jess, but when everyone moves to the dancefloor later that night, Adams hands stay glued around my waist.

chapter twenty-three

"YOU LOOK GREAT, JESS," I compliment her when she shows up on Valentine's Day. Caleb's finishing getting ready. He at least told her it was more casual of a date because she's in black, skin-tight jeans and a light pink satin tank top.

"Thank you." She gives me a quick hug. "So . . . did he tell you where he's taking me?"

I laugh. "I won't say anything except you're going to have a good time."

He's taking her to a drive-in movie that's showing the Harry Potter movies in memory of the night they met. He even picked up her favorite dinner and snacks. I think it's a sweet plan that's more personal than just a normal dinner out. I hope she loves it.

"I guess I have to trust you," she jokes but I can see the apprehension behind the teasing. "What are you up to tonight?"

"You're looking at it." I gesture to my outfit of gray sweatpants and a black tank top. "Chick-flick marathon and all the food I can eat."

She laughs with me but turns serious and lowers her voice. "He's probably not doing anything tonight. You could invite him over, I'm sure he'd come."

Caleb walks out and I don't have a chance to reply, not that I know what to say. Jess is distracted by the flowers Caleb gives her and I'm distracted by the sudden fear that he *is* doing something tonight, even though I try to tell myself that after everything, there's no way he'd make other plans.

"Enjoy your night," I call after them before shutting the door.

I stare at my phone, thinking about what Jess said. I should text him and see what happens. I grab the phone, thumbs hovering over the keyboard, the message forming in my mind, but I don't type a single word. I don't know what stops me, but in the end all I do is sigh and throw my phone to the other side of the couch as I settle in for the first of many movies on the agenda.

* * *

IT'S ONLY six p.m. when the first movie, *27 Dresses,* ends. Next is the aptly named *Valentine's Day*, before my favorite chick-flick, *Dirty Dancing*, starts at eight.

I'm in the kitchen, searching for something to heat up for dinner when the doorbell rings. Slowly, I creep to the door, trying not to make a sound in case it's a stranger on the other side. Not that it'll help much if anything were to happen, but it makes me feel better when I'm home alone.

When I look through the peephole I freeze, my eye locked on the nervous boy outside my door. He's shifting his weight from foot to foot, eyes flashing to every window in view trying to gauge whether anyone is home or not. My heart starts racing—excitement, happiness, and relief course through me.

He's here.

He doesn't have other plans tonight.

I finally remember that we're standing on opposite sides of the door when his face twists into pain because I've left him standing out there for too long. He doesn't think I'm home. I open the door so fast I'm out of breath for a moment, or maybe that's because I'm finally looking at him without the fisheye effect of a peephole between us.

His hair looks like he spent hours getting every piece to lay perfectly, and he's wearing a cream button up shirt with jeans—*the* jeans. The ones that fit him perfectly and cause my eyes to wander too far south too often. I almost laugh at how under-dressed I am compared to him—no makeup, hair thrown into a bun, and in sweats.

But when I force my eyes to move up his body to his face, he's looking at me the way I imagine my husband will when he's standing at the end of the aisle, like he only has eyes for me and he's never seen a more beautiful person in all his life. My lips shake as we just stare at each other. I'm leaning against the door so I don't fall over because my legs are no longer strong enough to support me on their own.

"You're home," he breathes, surprise and relief identifiable in his voice.

"Did you think I had plans?"

"I wasn't sure." He looks away, but his eyes flick back to me almost immediately. "I mean, I hoped you'd be here but wouldn't have been surprised if someone as amazing as you had plans today."

"You should know by now the only person I'd want to have plans with is you," I say, and step aside. "Are you going to stand there all night or are you coming in?"

The corners of his mouth twitch up, and that look in his eye, I won't be able to stay away long if he keeps looking at me like that. After I shut the door behind us, I feel it's been a respectable amount of time for me to ask about the multitude of items he has with him. "What's all that?"

"Have a look." He smirks, setting everything on the table.

I pull the items out one-by-one. A box of chocolates, all with caramel centers. Containers from the best Chinese take-out in town and . . .

"Are these . . ."

He nods before I'm even done asking. "Rose lattes from the coffee shop in the arts district? Yes."

All my favorites.

He steps up behind me, close enough that his warmth radiates through me. He leans down and whispers in my ear, "What? No questions about how I knew these were your favorites?"

I fight a shiver, glancing back enough to see his smug expression. "At this point, no, I don't have questions. You've proved, beyond a shadow of a doubt, that you know me better than anyone else."

"Good." His lips are at my bare shoulder, planting a kiss like he did at Hydra and my breath noticeably stutters.

"And these?" I ask, lifting a small bouquet of flowers out of the bag. It's composed of roses in white, pink, and yellow. The stems on them are shorter than you'd expect from a normal bouquet, the petals showing more wear than usual too.

But I don't care about any of that, all I care about is that *he* got them for me. They're perfect for that reason alone.

He clears his throat before speaking. "It's all that was left at the flower shop. I didn't think they'd actually run out of flowers, I'm sorry it's not a real bouquet or anything."

I spin around to face him. With how close he moved earlier, we're now standing chest to chest, faces inches apart. I swallow, remembering why I turned around and lift my hand to rest it against his cheek. "Don't you dare apologize. They're beautiful. They're perfect."

I loop my arms around his neck and that's all the encouragement he needs to wrap his arms around my waist and pull me close. We hold onto each other tight, bodies melting together. Each time I think we can't get closer, we do, until I no longer can tell where I end, and he begins. There's simply us, together as one.

"Thank you," I say into his chest, not wanting to let go. "For all of it. For coming."

"I just want you to be happy," he says as we pull apart. He seems unwilling to pull his hands away, slowly retracting them but holding contact with my back and sides for as long as possible. Just before he's forced to break contact, I cover his hands with my own, holding them to me.

I look him straight in the eyes. "You make me happy."

It's a day for love and the person I love is standing here in my living room, looking at me like he loves me too.

For the first time, I think I might be ready to let him.

"I hope you're in the mood for a chick-flick marathon." I grin at him and walk over to the couch, bringing the flowers with me and giving them a place of honor in the empty vase that's only free because I accidentally killed one of Caleb's plants last week.

"There's nowhere else I'd rather be." He follows behind me with the food, trying to hide his happiness that I put his flowers on display, but it's shining bright in his eyes.

* * *

"I'M STUFFED," I declare, slumping back onto the couch at a weird angle with my legs still hanging off the side.

It's almost the end of the next movie and we spent the past two hours talking and eating more than we should have. Empty white boxes that held flavored chicken and rice dishes only an hour ago are scattered around the flower vase on the coffee table.

Adam shifts, leaning forward to grab another chocolate from the open box also in the mess. "Want another?"

"Is that even a question? Yes." We both laugh at how contradictory it is from my previous statement. I shift so I'm sitting against the corner of the couch and lift my legs up to lay straight instead of bent like a broken stick. Adam moves closer to hand me the chocolate so when I lay my legs out, they end up resting on his lap.

I assume he's going to move back to where he'd been, a few feet away on the couch, but I'm glad when he doesn't. His left-hand drops to rest on my knees while he eats his chocolate, settling in like this is a normal position for us to find ourselves in. My hand betrays my thoughts and moves to the locket at my neck. His eyes lock onto the movement of my thumb running back and forth over the etching. My movement grows faster in time to my heartbeat the longer his eyes are on me.

Nervous, I say the first thing I can think of. "What do you think of Jess?"

I haven't asked him this before, but he's met her plenty of times now. I'm sure he has some opinion of the girl dating his younger brother. He's always been a protective older brother over Caleb.

"She's very sweet, exactly what Caleb needs," he says, looking down at his hands that have started tracing circles around my knee. "I'd ask what you think, but seeing as how you two are best friends now, I think I know the answer."

I laugh. "She's just genuinely kind. Did you know she's going into nursing because she wants to help people the same way the nurses helped her family when her dad was sick. She's gone through some tough times but has come out of them thinking about how she can make those times easier on others experiencing the same thing."

I can't say the same for myself.

It's as if he hears the words I didn't speak aloud. "Rylie," he says, forcefully, and I look over at him, getting trapped in the intense look in his beautiful brown eyes. "You can't look at it like that. She's had a lot more time to process the passing of her dad, you can't expect yourself to be at the same stage of healing she's at. Plus, everyone deals with grief differently."

"Yeah, some destroy themselves and some help others," I grumble.

He gives me a disapproving look. "Neither of you is handling it better than the other. You're both handling it, and that's enough."

I never thought of it like that, but I feel the truth of his statement and it rattles me a little bit. I continue, "I also like her because she treats him right and seems to like him as much as he likes her. Caleb deserves that. Did he tell you what they were up to tonight?"

"Yeah, it sounds very thoughtful and personal to them. I think she's going to love it."

I remember the night they met in excruciating detail. It was the first time I saw him with Olivia. I'm not likely to forget the earth-shattering, heart-breaking, sickening wave of emotions I felt that night any time soon. I hesitate for a moment, wanting to bring up something light-hearted from that night but not wanting to bring up memories of Olivia, but this is Adam. I don't need to be afraid of hard discussions with him, I don't want to be afraid, so I push on.

"You should've seen the horrific costume I had on that night." I laugh. "Luckily the robe was long enough to cover my butt, because the skirt sure wasn't and the shirt was cut so low it wasn't even cute."

Intrigue clouds his features and I swear he's trying to picture it as his eyes rove over me. "You wouldn't happen to still have that, would you? Because I'd happily wait here if you wanted to go change."

I lean forward and swat his chest, unable to hold back a laugh as his faux seriousness cracks into a bright smile. "You sound like every other idiot that couldn't stop ogling me that night."

His mouth drops open, and he raises a hand to his chest, feigning insult. "How dare you compare me to those other imbeciles."

I turn my head back to the TV just as the movie ends and mutter, "If the shoe fits."

Because I'm looking away, I don't catch his mischievous smirk as he leans in toward me, and I'm unprepared when his hands descend on my ribs, tickling me and I shriek. I try to still his hands with my own, but don't push them away because I want him to keep his hands on me. I want to keep feeling this warm electricity that's coursing through me—just without the strangled sounds of shrieks and jarring movements that resemble a fish out of water.

He's stronger though, so the tickling continues until I'm crying and hiccupping from non-stop laughing. I can't even appreciate the way his body is leaning over mine to get the best angle. He only stops because he's also laughing so hard he's starting to cry and can't keep going. We're both catching our breath when *Dirty Dancing* starts.

"This one's my favorite," I say, glaring at him but suddenly wondering if he already knew that too. The look on his face makes me think he did. "No distractions."

He pretends to zip his lips together, giving me a look of pure innocence that's so far from the temptation he is that I laugh. His eyes light up at the noise and I force myself to look away, or else I don't know if I'll ever look away. My legs are still draped over him, and I settle in for the movie with a smile that won't go away as I replay the way he looked at me over and over in my head.

I try to keep my breathing steady as his hands continue circling my knees and get brave enough to trace lines up my thigh but even through the thick material of my sweatpants every movement leaves a path of heat on my skin. Multiple times I catch him looking at me, but when I meet his eyes, he doesn't look away. Instead, when he looks at me, time seems to stand still. I lose track of what parts of the movie I do and don't see because my mind is jumbled by his stare until the final dance scene triggers a forgotten childhood memory and I laugh.

Adam glances over. "What's so funny?"

"Once, after that movie night where we watched all those chick-flicks with the moms, I forced Caleb to try to recreate the big lift with me." I can't stop laughing as the details come flooding back.

"Did you?"

"Try? Yes. Succeed? Absolutely not. I'm lucky I didn't break a bone that day."

He laughs. "Was it really that bad?"

"I almost took down the built-in shelves in the playroom." I give him a pointed look and we both laugh.

"I bet we could pull it off," he says nonchalantly.

I laugh because I'm sure he's joking until I look over at him and he's expecting a reply. "Wait, you're serious?"

He shrugs. "Why not?"

"Because I'm perfectly content without any broken bones, that's why."

"I guess that's fair." He chuckles but it sounds like there's a hint of disappointment.

I half scoff, half laugh at the fact he was truly serious about that.

"How about just a dance then?" He holds out a hand to me, gently lifting my legs off him and pulling me up when I take his hand. I can't help the smile on my face, I'll indulge him in his crazy ideas any day.

As the characters dance on the screen behind us, we dance in the living room. One of his hands holds mine and the other is wrapped around my waist holding me close to him. I let happiness and laughter consume me, free from everything—except his closeness and the memories of the last time we danced together when I got lost in his touch. This time, as I get lost in his eyes, looking at me like I'm the only thing that matters in the world, I can't help thinking it's a beautiful place to be lost.

On the TV, the characters perform the famous lift and Adam whispers, "Ready for our big lift?"

"What? No, I—"

Adam moves quickly, his arm tightening around my back as the other sweeps behind my knees, pulling me off the ground and holding me to his chest. I laugh, dazed and joyous as he spins us around and around. Nothing else matters in this moment but him, *us*.

When the credits roll across the screen, we collapse onto the couch still laughing happily and wrapped up in each other. Another chick-flick starts, and I curl into Adam's side, starting to get tired and thinking of no better place to rest my head. He lays his arm around me, and his fingers run through my hair as I slowly drift into a peaceful sleep in the comfort and safety of Adam's arms.

* * *

A DOOR SLAMMING SHUT jolts me from my sleep. My eyes flutter open and as the world slowly comes into focus I realize I'm still on the couch, curled up against Adam who also fell asleep. Caleb and Jess stand near the front door looking intrigued at the scene they walked in on.

"Did you have a good time?" I ask through a yawn, purpose-fully ignoring the topic of me and Adam cuddled up on the couch. A picture is worth a thousand words, and there's nothing to say that they wouldn't have assumed already.

"It was perfect." Jess beams.

Good. I don't know if I say the word aloud or just in my head as the world turns blurry again. I'm too tired to have this conver-sation now.

"I think I'm going to head to bed." I'm barely awake and

won't be able to keep my eyes open much longer. I ask Jess, "Will I see you in the morning?"

She nods. Good, I want to hear all about their date when I'm coherent enough to remember the answers.

I try to stand but the world spins and my legs give out. Suddenly, I'm off the ground, floating. No, not floating, I'm in Adam's arms and his laugh shakes me. A shiver runs through me and I'm just tired enough that a small groan leaves my lips. I open my eyes enough to see his gaze locked on my lips and all I want is to surge forward and close the distance between us. Lock my lips to his and never come up for air again.

"Let's get you to bed." He sighs, and I stop breathing when his breath hits my face. I'm starting to shake, and he must know that it's because of him.

As he lays me in my bed and tucks the sheets around me, I try to form a coherent thought but all I manage is, "Stay here tonight."

His tired laugh rattles me. "Rylie, are you asking me to get in bed with you?"

But the way he asks is like he assumes I'm going to say no and he's already planning to be a gentleman who sleeps out on the couch. Instead, I reach for his hand and firmly say, "Yes," before pulling him down onto the bed with me. He's wide-eyed and breathless as he lays on his side facing me and a huge smile pulls at my lips because *holy shit*, Adam Dey is lying next to me in my bed.

I can see the words forming on his lips, the question of *are you sure* that he always asks me. Before he can speak, I set expectations and simultaneously answer his unasked question. "Sleeping only," I clarify, and he nods in acceptance of these limits, but something in me makes me add, "I'm tired."

His eyes cloud with intrigue and a question I don't have the answer to, *what if I wasn't tired?*

I kind of wish I was going to learn the answer, because after the night we had, it'd be so easy to fall into this feeling and explore this connection. We're getting closer and closer to colliding, whether I'm ready or not, but I think I am . . . or at least extremely close to it.

Neither of us has moved, but we're laying sideways on the bed and he's still in his clothes. At this rate, we won't sleep just because we can't stop staring at each other, and even though just that is sending my heart into overdrive, I really am tired.

"You going to sleep in jeans?" I tease and he begrudgingly gets up, but he doesn't move to the bathroom. He stands merely feet from the edge of the bed and doesn't move his eyes from me as he slowly unbuttons his shirt and hangs it over the back of my desk chair. In the dark I hope he can't see me fisting the comforter, so I don't reach out and help him undress him faster because it's torture when he smirks and takes his time with his belt and jeans.

I'm too mesmerized by him to care that he can probably hear how deep and rapid my breaths have gotten and probably see my eyes roving over every new exposed bit of skin. The moonlight flashes across him as he passes the window and *fuck*, he's perfection. It's almost unfair that someone can look as good as he does, but boy do I enjoy the view.

Just sleep, just sleep, just sleep, I keep mentally reminding myself as he crawls under the covers next to me. I'm suddenly not as tired as I was earlier, but no, I set the boundaries of tonight. He wouldn't let me change them even if I tried—damn him for being too much of a gentleman—but this is a good step for us.

"Goodnight, Adam," I whisper, once we're laying side-by-side, rolled in toward each other. Even in the dark, my smile for him is shining bright.

He reaches up to brush my hair off my shoulder and his bare skin on my bare skin, while we're laying in a bed together changes something in me permanently. I suck in an audible, desperate breath and his hand freezes, realizing what he's doing to me. He closes his eyes and whispers, "Goodnight, Rylie."

He shifts like he's about to turn over so I grab his arm, turning to face away from him and scooting back until I'm nestled in the curve of him. Without my prompting, his arms wrap around me and hold me tight.

Just sleep includes cuddling, right?

Within minutes, I'm fast asleep.

chapter twenty-four

WHEN MY LAST professor of the day dismisses us on Thursday, it's officially the start of my spring break. I head to the on-campus gym for a last workout before leaving for Florida tomorrow. The four of us spent months planning our spring break trip and decided on Disney World because none of us had ever been. It's crazy that it's here already.

Since I first asked Adam to be my trainer, I've tried to consistently make it to the gym two to three times a week and have slowly gotten more comfortable being there by myself. Adam's finishing up some of his TA work so he can leave tomorrow, and I mentally rearrange my routine to cut out any machines that I need a spot on—like the chest press that I almost beheaded myself with the first day.

I can't help but think of him as I go through my exercises and on each one, I'm doing at least five to ten pounds more on each rep. I've never felt as capable as I do when I'm here, testing my limits and measuring my progress in weight and reps. I built a whole Excel worksheet to model my improvement on each machine and I constantly marvel at the steady rate of improvement, knowing that I'm the one driving the increase, that it's directly correlated to what I can do. When I showed it to Adam, he chuckled and muttered, "Of course you made this a math problem." But his grin gave away how excited he was that I was this into it.

As I finish my weight training, I start to head towards the stairs to hit the elliptical for a bit, but as I walk past the chest press, a familiar face pops up wearing a cheeky grin.

"Fancy seeing you here," he says, looking around. "Where's lover-boy?"

"Blake." I roll my eyes at his comment. Our banter has become a welcome treat to look forward to at the gym since he and Ryan are often there at the same time as Adam and I. Adam doesn't seem uncomfortable with his teasing comments anymore like he was at the beginning. It quickly became obvious the goal of his banter was to push Adam and I closer together, not tear us apart, so he just enjoys the show as Blake and I chew each other out. "Adam's not here, although I'm sure you already knew that."

He flashes me a grin and stands, gesturing to the chest press machine. "Need a spot?"

I hesitate for a second thinking of saying no, but it's the only machine I don't have a viable work around for without a spotter, so I just sigh and sit down on the bench.

"How much?" He's de-racking his plates and I have to think for a second.

"I think we bumped it up to ten on each side last time," I finally say, and he moves again to get the bar ready for me.

I haven't had a scare like that first day since. I quickly learned to judge when I could handle more or not, so Blake's job is easy, but I can tell he's taking it seriously by the scrunched look of concentration on his face as he monitors my movements.

Between sets he asks, "You're into Adam, right?" and I'm

glad I don't have the weight in my hands because I might've dropped it from the shock of the casualness of the question.

I laugh nervously, but answer truthfully, "Yes."

"And . . . well—" He hesitates but seems to decide it's worth asking. "You know he's into you too, don't you?"

I smile at that. If my face wasn't already red from the workout, it would be now. "Yes, I do know that."

He nods at the bar, and I begin my second set.

"So, why aren't you together?" he asks as he helps me get the bar back in place.

I sit up for this, no longer afraid of telling my story and wanting him to understand. He is one of Adam's best friends after all. I want him to approve of me. I want him to know that I'm not playing some game with Adam's heart.

"What has he told you about me?"

"Mostly just that you're Caleb's best friend and he's known you for most of his life." Blake clears his throat as if there's more that he doesn't want to say but I'm pretty sure it's not related to why I asked the question, so I just nod and move on.

"I met Caleb in fourth grade," I begin. "And in fifth grade my mom got diagnosed with cancer."

His entire face drops, it's the first time I've seen him without humor as his main expression and I know for sure Adam never told him this part of the story.

"That day in January when Adam skipped class, it was the one-year anniversary of her passing." I try to state this as matter-of-factly as possible, so emotions don't take over this conversation. I take a deep breath. "This is the abridged story, of course, but the point is we have a complicated history that's wrapped up in some of the worst moments of my life, and this past year has been hell for me.

"When Adam and I first admitted that we have feelings for each other, I was in no state mentally to be in a relationship. It wouldn't have been fair to either of us, for him to have to constantly be helping me through a breakdown, and for me to feel guilty that I couldn't give him everything he deserves in a relationship. But he would've done it, without complaining, without feeling like he was on the losing side of the deal, because he's always been there for me on my worst days. It was me who suggested we wait, because I wanted to be able to give him everything in return, instead of just taking everything he was ready to offer."

Blake drops down onto the bench beside me but is still speechless. I don't think he bargained for all this when he asked, but there's one last thing I need to say. I turn to look at him.

"I need you to know, I'm not playing games, I'm not stringing him along. I see a future with him, I see my entire life with him. I just needed to heal on my own first, so I could give us the best chance at becoming everything I hope we'll be."

He considers this for a long time, his face shifting through a variety of emotions as he processes everything I've just told him, and finally says, "Does you sitting here, telling me this, mean you're ready to give it a shot?"

If it wasn't Blake, I might be a little surprised at the question, but compared to some of the things that he's said in the past months, this is tame. I can see that it's all in the protection of his friend and it makes me happy that Adam has someone looking out for him like this.

I think back on my conversation with Jess when she said she still gets sad years later and consider what it really means to be healed—or at least healed enough to be ready. I've been so worried about healing that I never really spent time to consider what that actually means. I've come to realize that healing doesn't mean you don't cry anymore or aren't sad still. It just means you're not debilitated by the memories. It means you're ready to try to live again and not feel guilty about it. It means you're ready to look toward the future and find happiness in what's to come.

Healing isn't forgetting, it's finding joy in remembering.

"Yes," I say softly, a smile growing. "I think it does."

"Finally," he teases, but with genuine joy behind the words. "You know, the three of us are going to Freddy's Bar tonight to watch the game and have a few drinks. You should come with."

Something in my heart settles that Adam's friends want me around.

"I appreciate the offer, but I still have to pack. And I should let you guys have your time before I steal him away for the week," I joke, and he laughs. "Next time," I promise.

* * *

WHEN MY PHONE rings around 1 a.m. I know who it is without even needing to check the caller ID.

"How was your guys' night?" I ask as soon as I pick up.

"How'd you know about that?"

I laugh. "Oh, did Blake not tell you that we ran into each other at the gym today?"

"Oh yeah, he said that he invited you to come."

"Yeah, I thought you should have your guys' night before you're stuck with me for the next week." I grin at the thought of a whole week with almost 24/7 access to him. It's an intoxicating thought.

"Then you sorely miscalculated my priorities," he teases, but there's truth behind the words that sets my heart racing. "But seriously, you're welcome to come with us in the future."

"I'd like that." I smile at the thought of being *more* involved in Adam's life.

"Eager to get to know Blake and Ryan more, huh?" He tries to pass it off as a joke, and I know it mostly is, but I hear the genuine interest behind the question.

"I'm eager to get to know your friends more because it'll help me get to know *you* more," I respond, honestly.

"You know so much about me already."

"Yes, but I want to know everything."

I want to be there for everything. I want to be everything— his everything.

chapter twenty-five

THE FOUR OF us drive down to the Dey's house first and then Claire drops us off at the Charlotte airport to catch our flight to Orlando. Caleb and Jess sit together across the aisle from me and Adam. They watch a show together, sharing headphones and huddling together to watch off one phone. I love watching them together—it's clear how happy they are.

Adam and I sit closer than airplane seats really allow, so our legs touch and our hands lay linked on the armrest. I keep stealing glances at him from the corner of my eye, but from the smirk that grows on his face it doesn't go unnoticed. I wake when we land, my head resting on his shoulder and his head resting on me.

An Uber drops us off at the Dolphin Resort—we're spending four nights here before heading back to the Dey's for two nights before classes start back up again. We've had this planned for months but it's not until we're standing outside the doors of our two rooms that I really consider the sleeping arrangements of this set-up.

We all agreed to only do two rooms and I knew one of those was for Caleb and Jess, but I always managed to not think about the fact that Adam and I would be sharing a room for four nights. I might get the answer to our question on Valentine's Day:

What will happen if we're not tired and in bed together?

"Are you going to be alright?" Caleb asks when it's just us left in the hall.

I put my hand on his shoulder and smile, probably too big that it gives away my line of thinking because he raises an eyebrow. "We'll be fine. Have a good night."

"See you in the morning."

"Bright and early." I smile one last time before entering my room.

The room is clean and spacious. The carpet is an ocean blue, the walls a lighter shade of blue, and the beds are crisp white. There's two queen beds, and I'm almost disappointed because the thought of being forced to share a bed is something I've thought about more than I care to admit.

In the corner there's a small table with blue chairs, and a TV rests atop a wooden dresser. The room is simple but classy, and the far wall is mostly a window, overlooking an excessive pool. Adam is unpacking on the bed closest to the door.

"You can shower first, if you want." Adam breaks the silence, actively avoiding looking at me.

"Sure, thanks," I reply, and quickly open my suitcase and grab my bag of toiletries, eager to escape the tension that's already overwhelming the room. We're both unsure how to act being in such confined quarters when we already have a hard time keeping away from each other when we're *not* in a small room.

I take my time under the scorching water, letting myself unwind and relax after a long day of traveling. When I finally start to feel like myself again, I step out of the shower, leaving the water running. Only then do I realize that in my haste to get out of the other room, I forgot to grab clothes to change into.

I sigh but there's no other option here, so without further

delay I wrap the towel around myself and open the door. The towel covers everything it needs to, but I still feel Adam's eyes clinging to me as I walk across the room, trying to act confident instead of embarrassed.

"You're up," I remind him without turning around. I can't stand to see whatever look is there in his eyes right now because I'll lose all control of myself if that fiery look is staring back at me like I'm all he could ever need. My hands start shaking, because I realize that I want to turn around and I want to see that look on his face. I want everything that comes after it too.

I let out a long sigh when the bathroom door finally clicks shut again. After a few calming breaths, I rummage through my suitcase for undergarments and my pajamas which consist of, as always, my Hawaii t-shirt and a pair of gray cotton shorts.

Once my underwear is on, I let the towel drop, feeling comfortable that Adam won't be coming out any time soon. I'm facing the window that's now covered by the blackout curtains, and just lifting my t-shift to my head when the sound of the shower gets louder. The bathroom door swings open.

I glance over my shoulder just in time to catch Adam freeze mid-step when he sees me. His eyes run up my bare legs, widen fractionally when he gets to the cheeky black lace underwear that's on display and linger there a few seconds longer before drifting up my bare back. When his eyes finally reach my face his cheeks flush, realizing I've been watching his slow exploration of my body. But even then, he isn't shy about staring and I'm sure my whole body is turning red as he looks at me with the exact look I pictured earlier.

"I, uh—" he stammers, not able to find the words he's looking for.

I smirk to myself as I finally pull the shirt over my head, the oversized fit covering enough on its own, and turn to face him. He's usually the one disarming me, it's a powerful feeling being on the other end, being the one to render him speechless.

"I, uh—" he tries again. "Forgot . . . that." He points at his toiletry bag sitting on the edge of the bed. His eyes never leave me, and while he tries to keep them on my face, I catch them, multiple times, roaming over my mostly bare legs.

I walk forward slowly to grab his bag for him because he seems unable to move and I have an undeniable need to be closer to him. With every step I take, his fists clench tighter at his sides, knuckles growing whiter by the second. By the time I'm standing in front of him I can hear his heavy, ragged breaths.

The rest of the room fades when our eyes meet and I find myself instinctually moving even closer. My heart pounds against my chest, trying to propel me even closer, wanting no distance between us. The A/C unit rumbles on, pulling my focus away from him just long enough to stop myself from taking that last step. I let out a long breath and hold out the bag.

"Thanks," he breathes but it takes a few seconds before he actually moves to grab it.

"You're welcome," I whisper, sucking a breath as his hand grazes mine. I let the touch linger as long as I dare before I need to pull away and take a step back. Any longer and I might give in to the thoughts running through my head of what I want to do. To him. With him. Right now. "We haven't even been here an hour and I'm already about to lose my mind."

His eyes light up and a blinding grin breaks out across his face. "Me too."

I turn and walk back to my bag, body shaking from the restraint required to walk away from him. It's not until I'm back on the far side of the room that I hear the bathroom door close again. It's a long time before it reopens.

By the time he reemerges, I'm fully clothed and composed, sitting on my bed surrounded by the uneaten snacks from the plane ride earlier. Currently, I'm wrist deep in a bag of trail mix, while he's rummaging through his bag—avoiding my gaze again as if he's unsure if we should be leaning into this pull between us. I smirk at the idea before chucking a peanut at his head. He looks around, unsure of what hit him, and I throw another one. This time it hits him square in the cheek. I try to hold back my laugh, but a snort escapes. I clap my hand over my mouth as his gaze narrows on me, trying but unable to contain his growing smile.

He takes a step toward me, and I sneakily throw the last peanut I've been holding for precisely this moment. Just before it hits its mark, his forehead, he snatches it out of the air and swiftly closes the distance between us, smile flowing freely now.

Leaning over me, his hands descend on my waist, and I cry out in laughter. Squealing as his fingers continue to dance across my stomach, hitting every ticklish spot with such precision I'm convinced he has a map. He only stops when he has me caged in, his legs on either side of mine, forearms on either side of my head, and body hovering only inches above me. I'm consumed by his closeness, mind racing about how and when is the right time to tell him I'm ready.

Is it now?

We stay frozen like this, breathing heavily and eyes locked on each other for a long time. But before I can decide, he says, "Are you going to share those or continue using them for target practice?"

He's close enough that I feel the rumble of his chest with each word and my back arches up into him. He smirks before pushing away and taking the bag with him. The breath comes whooshing out of me and I relax back against the bed, I don't know how much more of this I can take before I break. I settle my racing heart before grabbing the rest of the food and joining him on his bed.

After flipping through the channels, I gasp, eyes-widening because it's fate, it has to be. *Baywatch* is on—the very movie Adam said inspired him to workout because of how I watched Zac Efron.

"No way." He laughs, reaching for the remote and I throw it over onto my bed.

Zac Efron's character is running, shirtless, in slow-motion and I sigh. "This movie is fucking incredible."

He shoves me and I fall over on the bed, laughing. As he glares at me, I rotate so I'm lying on my side and looking right at him. My eyes take in every detail on his face—his sharp jawline, the way his eyes shine when he's looking at me, and they linger on his lips that are just slightly open. He licks his lips, and my eyes shoot back up to his.

Now. It has to be now. I can't wait any longer or it'll make me insane.

"Want to know what's even better than this movie?" I whisper, scooting closer to him.

"What?"

"You." I can't stop smiling as I say it and his brows raise in curiosity.

"And why's that?"

"He might be attractive, but my heart doesn't skip a beat when I see him because all I want to do is run into his arms and never leave again. And he wasn't the one who held me together on my worst days, or was the reason for some of my best days. He's not lying in front of me, looking at me like I'm all he could ever want in this world and driving me crazy because he's all I want." The wonder in Adam's eyes as I speak almost brings me to tears. "So, you see, he's not any of that, but you are. You're all of it. You're everything."

His eyes darken, and before I know what's happening, he grabs my arms and rolls us over so he's lying on top of me—my arms are pinned above my head. I stop breathing. Every tether to sanity I have snaps. I don't care about anything except every place our bodies are touching, a connection I never want to break.

The fire in his eyes burns low in my gut as his lips brush

against my ear. "You have no idea how much I want when it comes to you. How much I've thought about exactly what I'd do when you were finally ready."

My eyes flutter closed, and a trembling breath escapes me. "Then show me."

He moves closer in what feels like slow-motion, and my body arches into him, trying to seal the space faster. Our mouths are centimeters apart and moving closer.

A moan freezes us both, faces not even an inch apart. The moment is fracturing but we're trying to hold it together. Another moan, louder this time, and the moment shatters. My back relaxes back onto the bed, body trembling as cool air replaces his touch.

"Is that . . ." My question trails off and more noises come through the wall behind us, the wall that separates us from Caleb and Jess's room. I squeal, "Oh my God, it is. Ew!"

We sit up on opposite sides of the bed and break out laughing in a mix of discomfort and disappointment.

"Turn the TV up or something," I say when the noises get louder and faster. "I'd rather not hear . . . that."

Adam complies but counters with, "Aren't you used to this? You do live with him."

"Yeah, but I make myself scarce when *that* is happening." We laugh again, trying to act like our perfect moment wasn't just shattered, but I wanted that so badly it hurts. Adam was just on top of me, about to kiss me and maybe do even more than that. I want him back on me, I want everything. I want him.

I move to pack the snacks away that are still strewn out across the bed, needing to breathe air that isn't contaminated with him and his intoxicating smell. But when I finish and turn back, he's under the covers and is holding them open in invitation. My eyes widen in amusement as a thrill goes through me.

I eagerly crawl in next to him, letting his body curve around me like it did the time he spent the night. We fit perfectly together, like we were made to connect in just this way. I let myself get lost in the feel of him as his hand settles on my waist, beneath my shirt.

"Hey, Adam?" I whisper, voice shaking. I can't forget that look in his eyes, those words he said, and I want it. I'm ready to want it, to let it happen. To let *us* happen. Even if I have to manufacture the moment to make it happen.

"Mm-hm?" His body rumbles with the noise and I shiver at the feeling.

"What would be one of those things you want?"

His hand twitches on my waist and I suck in a breath, trying to suppress the urge to pounce on him right now. "What do you mean?" He's stalling but I can feel the restraint in his tightening grip.

"Like, right now, what's something you want when it comes to me?" I use his wording, just to be overly clear exactly what I'm asking. He stays silent and I know it's because he still assumes I'm not ready, because I haven't said I am. But I am so I push on. "Oh, come on. Just tell me."

He sighs in resignation, understanding that I'm not going to let this go.

"What I want right now," he says in a hushed voice, lips at my ear, "is to take this hand"—he squeezes my waist again and my eyes flutter closed—"and slowly move it up your body, taking your shirt with it—"

He stops talking when I move, laying my hand on top of his and guiding it through the exact movement he just described.

"Rylie—"

"Please, continue," I gasp out.

I feel his breathing stutter against my back. "Then I'd wrap my other arm underneath you so it could slip up underneath your shirt."

I lift my body, just slightly, to allow him to slide his arm through and gasp as it slides up my stomach and under the shirt.

"Then, I'd slowly creep this hand down toward the waist of your shorts." I guide his hand there and the tips of his fingers slip beneath. Growing impatient with the slow progression, I try to guide his arm down further, but he holds firm. "Then, I'd ask to make sure this is what you want."

I let out a dark, impatient chuckle. "I'm trying to shove your hand into my pants and you're still asking to make sure I want this? Yes, Adam, I want this. I want you."

He still isn't moving, so I turn my head back to look at him. Our eyes lock only for a second before we both surge forward, locking our lips together and kissing with a desperation and passion that puts every other kiss we've shared to shame.

His hand finally lowers to exactly where I need it and I cry out in pleasure, reaching back for him.

We're a tangle limbs and lips, gasoline that's finally been set ablaze. There's not a single thought in my mind other than him and how glorious this long-awaited moment is as we both fall over the edge.

chapter twenty-six

I WAKE up with a smile on my face and pull Adam's arms tighter around me.

"Good morning," I mumble as I kiss his shoulder, his arm, anything I can reach. He moves his arms in a way that forces me to turn over, so we're face to face, and my hands immediately move up and over his chest. I pull myself flush against him and hold on tight.

He kisses my forehead. "Good morning, beautiful."

I blush and bury my face in his chest.

"Last night was . . ." He trails off and I pull back to look at him. His eyes are wide with wonder as he searches for a word.

"Incredible, amazing, worth the wait?" I smile, giving him options that also reflect how I feel.

Just the thought of the pure ecstasy his hand caused sets my body buzzing all over again. We didn't even do anything more than that, but it was earth-shattering. We could never do anything else, and all the waiting would've been worth it just for that . . . although I really *want* to do more.

His hand moves to my cheek and his expression softens. "It was all of that and more."

He gently touches his lips to mine. It's sweet and loving, and when he pulls away, I'm left smiling. But that only lasts a second before we're colliding again. These kisses are long and slow, drawn out like he wants me to remember every detail, like I'm going to be tested on it later.

My leg slides up and over his hip as his hands move to my lower-back and he rolls his hips against me. It's unlike anything I've experienced before and sends my body into an instinctive reaction that consists of my hands tightening on his shoulders, my eyes closing, and a gravelly moan escaping my lips. When I open my eyes, he's staring wide-eyed at me and I think I feel his hands shaking on my back.

He rolls his hips again, and even though I know it's coming, it yields the exact same result. Before my eyes open this time, his lips are back on mine and he whispers between kisses, "*That* is the most glorious sound I've ever heard in my life."

I laugh because that sound doesn't even seem like it should be able to come from me. "Yeah, right."

"I'm serious," he says, this whole conversation still taking place in gasps between kisses. "I could listen to that sound all day and never get tired of it."

For emphasis, he rolls his hips again. The same sound—that I couldn't recreate if I tried—comes tumbling out as he's still kissing me, like he wants to capture it for himself. I'm left panting for air afterward.

"As much as I'd love that plan . . ." The words fade off in little gasps as his lips move across my cheek and down to my neck. "I think we both know Caleb is more likely to kick down the door than let us skip out on today."

He chuckles against my neck and every muscle in my body tightens. "You're probably right." He groans, sitting up after giving me one last kiss. "I guess we should get ready."

By the time he comes out of the bathroom, dressed and ready to go, I've changed into my blush pink biker shorts and sport bra set with a white short-sleeve crop top over top and I'm almost done braiding my hair. I can see in his eyes that he's remembering the last time I wore this—our first gym session, when he told me he wanted to strip it off me. My hands shake as I finish the braid.

When I get close to him, he hooks an arm around my waist and pins me against the wall. "This outfit again? You remember what happened last time you wore this, right?"

"How could I forget?" I laugh softly and he smiles. "But this time, the intent is that you will take it off. I made you wait so long for this, the least I can do is fulfill one of your fantasies."

"Firstly," he says breathlessly, pushing against me more and looking right into my eyes, like he's trying to make me melt right here. Like he wants to deadbolt the door and spend the whole break in this room, and I would let him. "You don't owe me anything. I only want you to do something because you want to, not because you think you owe me it, okay?"

"Okay," I breathe, and keep talking when he looks like he's going to say something. "But Adam, I want this, too."

He breaks out into a grin and moves in until his lips are just barely touching mine. "Secondly, if you keep saying stuff like that, I'll decide to take my chances with Caleb knocking down the door."

As if on cue, there's a knock at the door and Caleb's voice calls through, "You guys ready?"

We chuckle and he whispers, "How long do you think we have?"

I shrug. "At least long enough for this."

Then I kiss him, deep and long enough that Caleb knocks again and yells, "Hello?"

Smiling, I grab my bag and go to open the door, hoping the flush of my cheeks isn't noticeable even though I know it is.

✳ ✳ ✳

THE PLAN for the day is to take the shuttle from the hotel to Animal Kingdom to begin the day, and head to Magic Kingdom after lunch where we'll stay to watch the fireworks over the castle. We solidify our plans on the ride over and chart the quickest path to the Everest ride, hoping to head there first so we can avoid the long wait time it's known for during the day.

As we run through the park that day, everyone's joy is palpable as we soak in all the magic this place exudes. Caleb and Jess are the perfect Instagram couple at Disney—complete with matching ears, sharing Dole Whip and churros, and taking the cutest photos that rival any influencer. And Adam isn't shy about wrapping his arm around me and holding my hand. It makes me melt. Even when Caleb obviously notices something's different between us and keeps shooting me looks that make me blush.

It only gets worse after Caleb walks in on us kissing in the locker area after riding the Kali River Rapids, but I'm too happy to care about the teasing.

After we're done with dinner, Caleb tells Adam and Jess to go grab us a spot to watch the fireworks while we wait for the bill, although I know he just wants to talk. The second they're out of earshot he turns to me practically bouncing.

"Okay, you need to tell me everything," he says, and I realize how lucky I am that I have a best friend who cares so much about my happiness in whatever form it takes. That instead of being mad or weirded out by me being with his brother, he's happy for us.

"I'm going to tell him that I'm ready."

His lips press into a flat line, and I know him well enough to see he's holding back some teasing remark.

I roll my eyes. "Just say it."

"I just thought that you two about to rip each other's clothes off by the lockers meant you had told him that already." He laughs.

I ignore the ripping clothes off part because even though he's my best friend, it doesn't feel right talking to him about that stuff when I'd be doing it with his brother. "I did, but I didn't say everything I wanted to."

"Because his tongue was down your throat? Or was it another body part that was there?" he deadpans, and I choke on air. My eyes go wide and my mouth drops open knowing that he's the one conjuring those images in his head . . . and now mine.

Fine, he wants to play like that? I narrow, challenging him "Well, we all know what your body parts were up to last night." I wasn't going to bring it up. I was going to give him a free pass on this until he started with the cheeky comments first. "Maybe tonight you could try to remember that the walls are thinner here, and your best friend and brother are on the other side of the wall."

His mouth pops open and his face turns dark red. His lips move like he wants to talk but can't find a single word. It's too funny of a look and I can't stop my laugh from sputtering out, but I put my hand on his shoulder and squeeze.

Slowly, his face fades back to a normal color but there's a timid smile on his face. "Could you try to remember that tonight too? I'm happy you two are finally getting together but hearing that would be a little too weird."

I laugh and hug him tight before we walk out of the restaurant. "What did I ever do to get lucky enough to have you as a best friend?" I squeeze before we break apart. "You're the best, Cale."

"I know," he says, and we both laugh. "But don't forget that you're amazing too."

We walk arm in arm over to the area where Jess texted saying they found a spot. Jess stands towards the front of the crowd, at a railing, but Adam is nowhere to be found. I look around, until a hand laces with mine and pulls me over a bench that's behind the crowd and more private.

"Well, hello." I grin.

His eyes twinkle from the streetlamps and I stare at him in awe. How does he keep getting more handsome?

"This feels vaguely familiar." He smiles and sweeps my grown out bangs that fell out of the braids over the course of the day behind my ear.

"A full-circle moment for us." We've come a long way since that day. *I've* come a long way since that day. "Adam," I start, "I know I asked you to wait for me to heal, and you've been so amazing as I figured everything out. But I don't think I knew what healing meant when I said that. I thought I couldn't love you and grieve her at the same time. And I don't regret waiting because I wasn't in any position to be in a relationship back then, but . . ." He looks up at me and my smile grows before I finish. "I am now."

"Rylie." He sounds excited, reaching over to grab both my hands with more happiness than I've seen on his face before.

"I know now that I'll never be completely healed, but I also know that I never want to be. I want to be able to remember her, and that means I might be sad sometimes. But when I'm sad, you're the person I want to cry with. You're the person that can make me smile and remember the good when all I feel is the bad. You know me better than anyone else, and I love you for it."

He goes completely still and squeaks out, "What?"

I can't stop my grin. We may have almost said these words a hundred times, but it's not the same as finally saying them, as finally hearing them. I mean every word with my whole heart.

"I love you, Adam. I love you now, I loved you on Fourth of July, and I've loved you for a lot longer than that too. Many things in my life have changed, but that never has, and it never will."

He blinks and a tear drops down his cheek. My heart constricts, tears coming to my eyes as I move to wipe his as he's always done for mine.

"Rylie, I would've waited a lifetime to be with you even if just for a moment." His voice is shaky and raw, and his words only cause my tears to spill over. "I have loved you since middle school when I saw how you always brightened everyone's day, even when yours was full of darkness, and I wanted, more than anything, to be the person to brighten yours. I love you, Rylie Lewis."

He fell in love with me in *middle school?* My head is spinning. I fell in love with him in high school when we were having our late-night dock conversations regularly. I'd been intrigued and interested in him before that, but I didn't love him then. And he's saying he loved me in middle school? Middle. School.

We didn't have stolen moments back then, there wasn't much time we spent just us. But what he's describing would've happened at school when he wasn't around. So he was watching me, *noticing me* for that long?

I'm speechless.

So, I lean forward and press my lips to the man I love. As our lips touch, I feel the tenderness and love in overwhelming abundance. The firework show starts and this time we don't get scared. This time it feels as if it's celebrating just for us. I can't help the short laugh of happiness that comes out and my fingers move to run through his hair. I pull back and grin at this incredible man who loves me.

I rest my forehead against his, savoring the feel of his skin against mine on purpose. It feels like a dream with the fireworks creating the most beautiful background song just for us.

With a huge smile, I give him a lingering kiss before saying, "I love you, Adam."

"And I love you, Rylie." His returning smile is radiant.

I groan. "I could listen to you say that all day."

"Maybe tomorrow," he says with a kiss. "Or the next day." Another kiss. "Or the next." Another kiss. Then the words stop coming but the meaning radiates through the kisses that don't stop.

"I like the sound of that." I begrudgingly pull away. "But we are in a public place, so maybe we should watch the fireworks now and later you can take all this off me."

"Well, it's no dress, but I guess it'll do."

I laugh at his joke referencing our song, knowing full-well that he's dying to take it off as much as I'm dying for him to. He pulls me in for one last, long kiss before we walk, hand in hand, over to where Caleb and Jess stand. Caleb flashes me a look that's more fitting for a five-year-old than a twenty-one-year-old but I just grin back.

As the firework finale reaches its peak Adam's arms wrap around my waist, pulling me closer into his chest. His nose moves against my cheek, shifting a lock of my hair out of the way so his mouth can reach my ear. "You are radiant, *my* Rylie."

A tear of happiness runs down my cheek. My heart has never felt so full.

* * *

WE RUN, hand in hand through the hotel lobby, yelling "goodnight" to Caleb and Jess who are far behind us, and dart into an elevator, laughing. He presses the door close button until they shut and we're finally alone. I've been waiting for this moment since this morning when we had to leave our hotel room, but it's been agonizing since our conversation during the fireworks. Finally telling him my full, true feelings, and hearing his in return has opened my heart in all the ways I was afraid of months ago. It's still scary, knowing someone holds that much of you—loving someone this deeply and completely. But I wouldn't trade this feeling for the world.

Our room is on the eighth floor, but we only pass floor two before his lips crash into mine in desperation.

"This thing moves too damn slow," he grumbles between kisses, and I laugh against his lips.

His hand threads into my hair as the other wraps around my waist, leading me back until I'm against the side of the elevator. And thank god I am, because when he deepens the kiss, I'm sure I would've fallen over if it wasn't for the wall supporting me.

When the elevator doors open, he groans and without breaking the kiss, sweeps my feet out from under me and carries me to the door, only setting me down when we realize both keycards are in my bag. Opening the bag, I expect to not be able to find the card as is typical when you're in a rush, but it's right there in the front pocket like it knows I need that door open this second or I might be the one to kick it down.

I push him in the door once it's open and don't waste a second throwing my bag on the bed and sealing myself to him. This isn't like the movies, where the first time is slow and sweet. This is a culmination of every long-awaited want we've had for each other. In no time at all, our shirts are off, but he pauses just before pulling my sports bra over my head.

"I've been dreaming about this exact moment for months now." He's shaking his head like he still can't believe it's actually happening now.

"Really?" I say, breathlessly, shifting, impatient for him to continue. "Only months?"

He laughs, finally complying. I suck in a breath when his hands run up my bare back. This is actually happening. This is *finally* happening.

His lips move to my neck, and he mumbles, "Okay fine, much longer than a few months, but a few months ago the dream changed to include this exact outfit."

I laugh but there's no more talking after that other than the occasional whisper of, "I love you," which we can't seem to stop saying as the rest of our clothes end up thrown across the room before Adam carries me over to the bed we shared last night, *our* bed.

253

chapter twenty-seven

I WAKE in the morning in nothing but Adam's t-shirt and a skimpy pair of underwear as I'm wrapped in his arms. Last night was the best night of my life, but as I roll over to wake him with a kiss, his hands slide up my legs and under the shirt, and I know this morning is about to be better.

In every way that last night was desperate and rushed, this morning is slow and sensual. I savor every gentle movement, every lingering kiss. These are the arms I want to hold me for the rest of my life, the lips I want to kiss, the eyes I want to look into.

This is the person I want to fall asleep with each night and wake up to each morning.

"I know I'm asking this a little late," he says as he kisses my shoulder, putting off getting out of bed for as long as possible, "I want this to be official though. So will you, Rylie Lewis, be my girlfriend?"

My heart skips a beat and I kiss him so hard that we roll over. "I thought you'd never ask."

He chuckles and rolls his hips against me, which draws out an even more guttural sound than before because there's nothing between us this time. His eyes light up with mischief and he does it again as he asks, "So, is that a yes?"

"It's a . . ." I start but he does it again and I can't think straight. I shift my hips so he has a clear angle for another round before we have to go. He doesn't move, he just stares at me, waiting until I say, "It's a hell yes."

Then, his lips are back on mine, his hips roll perfectly into me, and I feel complete.

* * *

"CAN I ASK YOU SOMETHING?" I whisper as I trace circles on his chest with my fingers. We haven't left the bed since we got back to the hotel this afternoon.

"Hm?" His chest rumbles. His eyes are closed, like he's never been this comfortable, this relaxed in his life.

"Did you really fall in love with me in middle school?" I've been thinking about that statement often, and wonder how that even happened.

His eyes open and he smiles at me with a nod. "I used to despise you at the beginning."

I almost choke on a laugh. "What?"

"When you started staying over at our place on weeknights, and joining us on some family vacations, I was so mad." His eyes are sad even though he's sporting a smile. "I didn't understand why Caleb got to bring a friend along to everything, but I couldn't. And then when mom started decorating the guest room for you, I threw a tantrum. My parents obviously knew about your mom, and Caleb knew because you'd told him, but no one ever told me."

My eyes grow wide and my heart drops into my stomach. That was the time we referred to as his *"too cool for us"* phase, but it wasn't that at all. He was rightfully angry.

"It wasn't until I threw that tantrum that my mom sat me

down and told me what was happening. Not long after that was when we both got sick and talked for the first time." His bottom lip trembles and I reach out to place a hand on his cheek. He leans into the touch and closes his eyes. "I felt like the biggest jerk in the world. Your life was so hard already and here I was, making it harder for you. So I vowed to look out for you after that.

"But I had no clue that I'd fall for you. I would watch you at school, especially on days you were staying at our place because I knew those were hardest for you and I noticed that you were kindest on your worst days. You were always lifting everyone else up, being a light for everyone in your life, but you never let anyone do that for you. I saw how your smile faded and the light left your eyes when you thought no one was looking. I saw how you never let others see the darkness growing inside you. I wanted to be that person for you."

I'm shaking, tears steadily dropping from my eyes. He's always seemed to know things about me that no one else did, but he was always watching even when no one else was.

"So when you started joining me on the dock in high school . . . ?" I ask.

"I already loved you—your kind heart, your strength, your generosity. You were all I thought about." He looks at me with those eyes that have seen me—truly seen me since the beginning —and have always been my safe place. "So when I was up late one night and saw you out there I went without hesitation. I knew you were going through a lot so I just wanted to be a friend, someone you could count on when nothing else made sense in your life. Every time you'd stay over after that I'd be up all night waiting to see if you went out there so I could join you. I didn't want you to feel alone ever again."

And I never did, except for when he was with Olivia . . . I want to ask more about that but he keeps talking.

"You have no idea how happy I was on Fourth of July when

we kissed, and when I learned you felt the same way I did. I'd always kept my hopes low because I wasn't sure if you saw me as more than a friend. But I was so excited I went overboard, even though I knew you needed space still. I couldn't stay away."

"To be fair, that was both of us," I interrupted because he shouldn't have to feel responsible for that. "I was so excited you felt the same way too that I didn't let you stay away. I wanted you around every second."

He nods but then looks away, his smile dropping. "But then I panicked and did a complete one-eighty. Olivia had been into me for a while and I never gave her the time of day. But she was nice, and I started second guessing everything. I wondered if you and I weren't working because we weren't meant to be. I was worried I was hurting you by not being able to stay away, so I removed myself from your life, thinking it was better that way. And to distract myself, I gave her a shot.

"But I was horrible, to both of you. Everyday I woke up wishing it was you I was going to see that day, and I was disappointed when it was her walking with me after class. I ignored the feelings, but deep down I knew I was just stringing her along. I knew it would never work between us because you were all I could ever think of and I knew I'd made such a huge mistake. I went to see you before Thanksgiving because I missed you, and I lied and acted like I thought you didn't know about her."

He doesn't look at me as tears drop down his face. He's still beating himself up over this, but I'm just glad to finally know why he did it—what he was thinking. "I sat in the car in the parking lot and cried after seeing how bad I'd hurt you. I wanted to break up with Olivia right then, but her family was gone for Thanksgiving, and she had nowhere else to go so I thought I'd wait until after. No one should be alone for Thanksgiving—that's what my mom always told us—but there was no competition once the two of you were in the same space. You were all I could look at, all I could think about. You were still all I wanted, and she obviously saw that. It's why she chose to sleep in the guest room, on her own.

"When I saw her the Monday after, she was so nice about it all, which only made me feel worse. I never should've been with her. I wanted you. I've only ever wanted you, Rylie."

"Hey." I slide up his body so I can hold his head in my hands and press my forehead into his. "Good people still make mistakes. You weren't trying to hurt anyone, right?"

His breath stutters on the way out. "No, never."

"You were trying to do what you thought was best, in the moment. You're not a bad person, Adam." I kiss his forehead and pull back to look him in the eyes. "You have to be able to forgive yourself or else the pain will become darkness that festers into something uncontrollable. Take it from someone who knows what that's like."

"I'm just sorry that I hurt you—that you ever had reason to question my feelings."

"I forgive you." I lean forward and kiss him, kiss the pain away. "Anyway, we ended up together in the end. If you ask me, all the chaos only made us stronger. And just so you know, I've only ever wanted you too, Adam."

He holds me tight to him, cocooning me in his love, in his heart, and in his presence. Even when I fall asleep, I never let go of him.

I will never let go of him again.

chapter twenty-eight

CLAIRE WRAPS each of us in a hug when she picks us up from the airport two days later. We spent the rest of the trip jumping between parks and taking in everything Disney World had to offer. Adam and I also used the time to explore our new relationship and explore each other.

We're both willing to admit that we were insufferable to be around, but we've been waiting years for this moment. We're doing our best to tone it down around others, but it's still so new, it's hard to fight back all the pent-up emotions that we repressed for so long. Even on the ride back to the house, Adam keeps a firm grip on my hand in the backseat, running his thumb back and forth across the side of my palm. There's a goofy smile on my face and I keep glancing over at him.

Claire eye's us suspiciously through the rearview mirror as Caleb and Jess recap the trip. Adam and I jump in every once in a while to add details, but we mostly leave the story to them, happily distracted by just sitting next to each other.

When we get back to the house, Adam grabs our bags out of the car last, everyone else is already inside. I try to take mine from him, but he moves it just out of reach and looks at me like I offended him.

"I got it, *babe*." He smirks and I laugh. We haven't used pet names before and honestly, it's a little weird hearing it. I'm not sure I like it. I love saying his name, so it hasn't even crossed my mind to call him anything else.

"That bad, huh?" He reads my expression like a book.

I smile and lean in to give him a peck on the cheek. "I could get used to it, but it's not nearly as thrilling as hearing my name from your lips."

He takes it as a challenge and leans in until our lips are just barely touching. "Ry-lie," he whispers slowly, accentuating each syllable and it sends shivers down my spine. I close my eyes but still feel his smug smile. "Better?"

"Much," I breathe into him and close that last little space between us. "We better head in, you still need to tell your mom about your new girlfriend."

I head up to my room while Adam goes to find Claire, not wanting to wait another minute to tell the world about us—he actually said that—and I haven't stopped smiling since he did. He's perfect. He is actual perfection. I know everyone says there's no such thing as perfection, but those people have never met Adam Dey. They've never been *loved* by Adam Dey.

I'm still in my room, pulling the laundry out of my suitcase to do a load of wash before heading back when a light knock on the door startles me. I look up and Claire stands in the doorway, a sad smile on her face.

"Is it alright if I come in?" she asks, always polite, even though it's her house.

"Of course," I reply, warmly.

She sits beside me on the bed, her expression unreadable but it feels like something's wrong.

"I just talked to Adam . . ." she starts, and I suddenly realize that she might not be okay with this relationship, even if Caleb is.

"Oh, I'm sor—" I start to say but she cuts me off.

"Oh, honey, no. I'm thrilled that the two of you have finally realized what you have in each other, and are happy together." She reaches out to grab my hand. "I want to tell you a story about your mom, if you'd like to hear it."

I freeze, only able to nod.

She squeezes my hand. "When you and Caleb first became friends, your mom and I used to joke about our two families combining if you and Caleb grew up and developed more than a friendship."

I laugh. Of course, the moms gossiped about us. I can picture it in my mind—picture her laughing and smiling as she watched us run around. I can already tell I'm going to love this story and it's a relief to not feel like I'm going to fall apart at the mention of her.

"Obviously, we quickly figured out that plan wasn't going to work." She laughs, starting to get emotional. "You and Caleb are soulmates—soulmate friends—of that I'm sure. But that's all you ever were so we dropped it, until, years later, we were watching a group of you kids hang out on the lake and we realized we had you paired with the wrong brother."

She smiles and I huff out a strangled laugh. How long ago was this? She said only years after we met. Was that late middle school or early high school? Either way, I hadn't even realized I loved him then.

"We watched you and Adam steal glances at each other all day. You two lit up around each other. We weren't sure if either of you had realized it yet, but what we saw was two kids in love." Tears form in her eyes. "Over the years we watched you two fall more in love and wondered when, or if, you would come to realize it."

The gravity of this story hits me then, and tears start to form.

But they're more happy than sad. My mom knew. She *knew* I loved Adam. She knew he loved me.

"The week before she passed, I went to visit her." Claire pauses, getting choked up. "And she told me . . ."

Tears stream down my face and I have to take deep breaths so I don't pass out from lack of oxygen. Claire's trying to pull herself together enough to finish the story. I squeeze her hand and she smiles.

With a deep breath, she tries again. "She told me that if you and Adam were to ever get together, I should tell you she approves wholeheartedly and couldn't dream of a better match for you."

I stop breathing. It feels like I stop living, like there's nothing holding me to Earth as I float up towards the sky. Towards her.

"All she wants for you is someone who makes you as happy as she saw you with him. Someone who looks at you like you're the light of their life like he did, and if I may add, still does."

Of all the things she wanted me to know after she was gone, this is what she left me—her approval of the person I love. It means everything to me, that she knew how I felt before she left, how *we* felt. That she saw how special he was and would've loved him as her own if she was still around. She would've welcomed him as family in a heartbeat.

I give her a hug. I've loved Claire like a mother for a long time, but I'm only now realizing just how special our relationship is.

"She loved you so fiercely," she whispers. "She hated that she was leaving you all alone."

"I've never been alone," I say, more sure of this statement than anything else said. "She knew she was leaving me with you."

* * *

AFTER CLAIRE LEAVES, I take a few minutes to commit every word she told me about my mom to memory. I don't want to forget a single thing. I splash some water on my face, smile at my reflection when I see her in it, and head for the stairs where I run right into Adam. He holds my arms to steady me as we laugh.

"I was just coming to look for you." He runs a hand across my cheek. "What've you been up to?"

He's looking at me like he hasn't seen me in months, even though it's only been fifteen minutes. My heart is just as frenzied to see him. I kiss him, already missing the way we fit perfectly together and answer, "I was talking to your mom."

"About?" His curiosity is piqued.

My hand strays to my locket and I smile. "My mom." I sigh.

He looks surprised and apprehensive because the mention of my mom usually brings me into darkness. "Are you alright?"

This time though, the memories of her bring light into my life. "I've never been better."

And it's actually the truth.

I head down into the kitchen with Adam right behind me.

"Want anything, *babe*?" I jokingly emphasize the pet name he tried to call me earlier.

I glimpse over my shoulder with a grin then open the fridge to look for something to drink. He doesn't answer but his arms wrap around my waist, and his chin rests on my shoulder.

"I could get used to this," he says, flirtatiously.

I chuckle, planting a kiss on his temple. "I've offered to get you things before, why's it any different now?"

"Because now"—he turns to kiss my neck and holds me tighter to him—"when you ask, I'm allowed to think, *Damn, this incredible, beautiful woman is going to make a great wife.*"

"Wife?" My eyebrows raise with intrigue. Butterflies bloom in my stomach and my heart skips a beat at the thought. "Dating less than a week and already using the word 'wife'? Quite presumptuous of you," I tease because we both know we've thought about our future for much longer than a week.

"What can I say, I know what I want." He still stands behind me, holding me, but we turn our faces toward each other. He doesn't hold back the love and admiration that shines in his eyes, it's heart-stopping. "The girl of my dreams has somehow agreed to be mine, I'm not going to let her go that easily."

I hope I never get used to hearing him tell me his feelings—of not hiding my own. "I'm glad to hear that." I brush the back of my fingers across his cheek and run them into the hair above his ear. My smile grows when he leans into the touch. "Because the guy of my dreams is standing in front of me, telling me I'm the girl of his dreams, and I'd like to keep hearing that forever."

He fits his lips to mine, kissing me sweetly and deeply, leaving me feeling cherished and loved beyond measure. As we stand there looking at each other, in front of the forgotten, open refrigerator, I can't recall a time I've ever felt more love for someone, or more loved by someone, in all my life.

I know it's early in our relationship but when I look into the eyes of this man, who I've loved for years and love now more than ever, who has helped me through the worst days of my life and given me some of the best days of my life, who, by some stroke of luck, loves me beyond reason, I know I'm looking at my future. I know he is my forever.

"I love you, Adam Dey."

"And I love you, Rylie Lewis."

epilogue

2 YEARS AND 4 MONTHS LATER

I STAND in the kitchen of our new apartment. Unopened boxes lay strewn around, covering every open space in sight—it's overwhelming. I let out a sigh, not wanting to think about how much work we still have to do to finish moving in. That's a problem for a different day, though. Today is July 4th, and we need to get going so we'll make it to the party on time.

"You look incredible."

I spin around to find Adam smiling at me from the bedroom door, eyeing my white strapless dress with approval and a darker, but familiar, expression that lets me know we won't be leaving any time soon.

"You say that every time." I grin at him as he crosses the room, looking handsome in his blue shorts and cream, button up shirt. He got a haircut earlier this week, so it's freshly trimmed—shorter on the sides but still longer on top.

He reaches me and my arms habitually wrap around his neck as his snake around my waist, pulling me into a deep kiss.

"That's because it's true every time," he mumbles between kisses.

Without warning he picks me up and sets me on the countertop. I laugh, knowing exactly what his plans are and I don't plan on stopping him. I wrap my legs around his waist and tug him closer as his hands move to the zipper on my back. Our kisses grow more desperate by the second.

There's a pounding on the door, but neither of us move from our position.

"Just ignore it," he whispers against my lips, but I don't need any encouragement. I unbutton his shirt in response.

"You better not be ignoring me!" Caleb's voice echoes through the door and we both groan. "Your car is still here; I know you're home."

"Go away," I yell loud enough for him to hear, and it draws a chuckle from Adam whose lips have moved to explore my neck. My head drops back and my eyes close. I still get butterflies every time he kisses me or touches me, and this is only the beginning of what I want right now.

"If you guys are naked in there, I'm going to kill you both! You promised you'd be there on time!"

Caleb isn't going to stop.

I want to kill *him* right now, but he's right, we did promise not to miss the party.

We've developed this bad habit of being late for almost everything because anytime we get dressed up, this happens. I wish I could say I'm sorry, but we've been together for almost two and a half years and we still can't get enough of each other. I will never have enough of Adam.

After Adam graduated a year ago, we decided to move in together while I finished up senior year. He found a job nearby and while it wasn't exactly what he wanted to do, it was only temporary until I graduated two months ago, and we could move somewhere else. Our new apartment is in Charlotte, close to our hometown, where Adam got an offer from his dream company, and I was able to find a job I'm excited for too.

We went through the trials and tribulations that accompany

living together for the first time, but we never lost sight of the love we share. We put in the work to resolve any issues that arose and made it through stronger than ever.

Caleb and Jess moved in together the same time we did, but the stress of finishing school and working proved to be too much and they split shortly after. Caleb's research with his economics professor turned into a full-time job after graduation so he's still in Kasper. Last I heard, Jess got an offer to work at a local hospital and stayed in town as well.

Apparently, they've been reconnecting the past few weeks and she's coming to the party tonight too. Caleb and I still speak most days, and it sounds like things are going well between them.

Adam groans and gives me three quick kisses before zipping my dress back up and helping me off the counter.

"To be continued," he sighs.

I pull him into a passionate kiss and whisper against his lips, "I'll hold you to that."

"Still here!" Caleb yells again and I move to open the door before he tries to kick it down. "If you don't open this do—" He stops when we're face to face.

"I'd say I'm glad to see you, but I'd be lying." I frown at him.

He only laughs, unfazed, and pulls me into a hug. "It's good to see you too, Ry."

It takes me all of five seconds to start laughing with him, and all of my anger fades away. He's still my best friend, no matter how much of an annoyance he can be at times.

"Jess is by the car, she's excited to see you."

"I've missed her." I smile. "I'm glad you guys are talking again, you were always a great couple."

He gives me a pointed glare and I go off to find Jess, while Caleb enters the apartment, presumably to find Adam and hurry him along.

"Jess!" I run over and give her a hug, we stayed in touch a little after she and Caleb broke up, but things were never the same. I miss having her around. "How have you been? How's work going?"

She laughs. "I'm doing great, loving the job so far. How are things with you? Seems like you and Adam are still going strong."

I blush. "We're doing great. We both start our new jobs after the holiday weekend."

Before she can respond the boys walk out, looking like they're discussing something serious. When Adam's eyes meet mine, his face brightens and he rushes over, wrapping his arms around my waist and spinning me.

"Come on, beautiful. It's time for us to go," he says, carrying me to the car, "before Caleb yells at us again for being late."

He winks at me, and we laugh, not having to look to know Caleb is staring daggers at us for the teasing comments. Adam opens the door for me, but before I get in, I lean in and give him a quick kiss.

"Are you two going to be able to keep your hands to yourself long enough to get there safely?" Caleb calls out.

Just for the snarky comment, I deepen the kiss until it's just past what's appropriate in the presence of your boyfriend's brother. I laugh against his lips when Caleb grumbles to Jess, "Remind me why I put up with this?"

"Because you love us," I say, shooting him a cheesy smile.

"I can't recall why, at the moment," he shoots back and all four of us fall into laughter.

This is how it's always been between us, and I hope it'll always be this way. This is what it feels like to belong to someone, to something. This is what family feels like.

* * *

"RYLIE, you are glowing. Love suits you well." Claire squeezes me tight when we finally arrive, and I laugh at her comment. She loves to make cheeky comments, not-so-subtly hinting that she hopes we'll get married soon.

"I'd have to agree." Adam walks up and Claire is beaming. "Hi, Mom." He hugs her and then settles his arms around my shoulders.

"Oh, honey. You're glowing too." She pats his cheek but her eyes flick behind us, to Caleb and Jess walking up the driveway and she frowns. "Why is Caleb glowering? What did you two do?"

"Nothing," we chime in unison, trying not to laugh.

"You two go find Phil, I think he's at the grill. I'll deal with grumpy over here."

We walk away laughing, knowing that Caleb is acting this way purposefully so he can tell Claire we would've been late again if it wasn't for him.

"Jess, hun, it's so good to see you again," I overhear Claire say before we're out of earshot.

Adam claps his dad on the back with a greeting before he's pulled in for a hug. Phil gives me a hug next. Over the years we've gotten closer—he's not quite so quiet anymore when I'm around. I've learned he has a dry sense of humor that I can't help but laugh at. He's truly become the father I never had.

The party passes in conversation, most of which includes questions of if we're engaged yet, to which I smile and say, "No."

But each time my heart screams, *Hopefully soon.*

I spend a lot of time with Caleb, reminiscing about all the Fourth of July's we've spent here over the years and how, while so much has changed, so many things are still the same. It's some much needed time with my best friend since we don't get to see each other face-to-face as often anymore.

Just before sunset I'm chatting with Claire and Jess in the

kitchen. "Where's Adam and Caleb?" I ask, looking around. I haven't seen them in a while.

Claire and Jess glance at each other nervously before answering. How odd. But then Claire smiles and answers, "I think Phil needed some help with the fireworks setup."

I laugh and forget all about my earlier suspicions. Phil told me he went bigger than ever for this year's fireworks show and I'm excited to see it.

I catch a glimpse of the three of them walking through the door and heading towards us, all looking excited about something. My heart warms, seeing them together and knowing that while I consider them family now, one day they might officially be.

Caleb smiles as he passes me on his way to Jess, and Phil smiles, inclining his head as he heads off with Claire. Adam walks right up to me, threads his hand in my hair and kisses me.

My heart sighs in relief. We've been separated most of the evening and I've been craving his comforting presence. The moment he's near I feel complete again—calm and serene.

"Walk with me?" He extends his arm and I nod, taking it.

While we walk towards the door, I try to ignore the feeling of being watched, like the whole room's eyes are on us as we exit the house. He leads me down the same path we took three years prior, the beginning of the crazy journey that brought us here. I smile, remembering how scared I'd been to love again after losing my mom. That fear almost kept us from this incredible love story we've written.

When we step out of the trees and onto the little piece of beach, I freeze, taking in the transformed space around me. There's a white blanket laid out in the middle of the sand, and other than a thin walkway to the blanket, it's the only open space left. The rest of the sand is covered with candles, flickering and bathing the space in a warm glow that perfectly compliments the sunset sky, and vases of roses in colors of red, pink, and white. Scattered rose petals cover every bit of sand in-between.

Tears burn my eyes. "You did this for me?" I squeak, looking up at him and his face is a picture of love.

He only smiles and holds out his hand.

I half-laugh, half-smile in disbelief as I take his hand, letting him lead me to the middle of the blanket. I'm speechless. It's a magical feeling standing here in the middle of this set-up. It's like being in a dream or a fairytale, only it's better because it's real and I'm here with Adam.

"I love you," I insist, needing to say something, but not finding any other words.

He holds my hands in his and takes a deep breath. "Rylie, from the moment you entered my life, I knew nothing would ever be the same, and while falling for you happened slowly, once I saw your heart, your kindness, I knew. I felt the gravity of my world shift. This world and all of its possessions had no hold on me anymore as long as you were by my side.

"Three years ago, when we first kissed in this very spot, I knew that every last piece of my heart was yours and I'd wait a lifetime if it meant getting to be with you at the end. I've made many mistakes since that day, but loving you has never been one of them."

He gets down on one knee and I clap a hand over my mouth —which is hanging open in surprise—tears streaming down my face. My stomach is doing backflips, while my heart is trying to remember how to beat.

"Rylie Lewis, it is the greatest privilege of my life to be loved by you. Your kindness, your strength, your unwavering love and support . . . there is no one like you. You make me a better man every day and I would not be the person I am today without you.

"I promise to never take your love for granted, and to love you with everything that I am, for as long as I live. Even long after we've left this earth, I know that my soul will be forever intertwined with yours. You are my past, my present, and I hope you will forever be my future." He pulls out a red velvet box and opens it, but my eyes never leave his. "Rylie, will you marry me?"

I can't speak, I can't remember how to breathe. I sink down onto my knees, head nodding up and down, non-stop. I put my hands on his cheeks and kiss him until I'm finally able to speak again and even then, I can only whisper, "Yes," between every kiss I continue to give.

I finally pull back and look at my fiancé, his face is lit by candlelight and the last rays of the setting sun. I don't think he's ever looked so handsome. "You are the best thing that has ever happened to me and I will cherish you as long as I live. I love you with everything that I am, Adam Dey."

He's getting choked up, tears of joy scattering his cheeks. "I can't wait to spend the rest of my life with you."

I've been so caught up in him—his words, his emotions—that I haven't even looked at the ring yet. I finally shift my attention to it as he slips it on my finger and all the remaining strength leaves my body.

I stare in pure, utter shock. The tears that were just starting to ease up come back in full-force. "Is . . . ." I bite my lip. "Is that . . . ?"

"Yes, it is."

"But—" I can barely form words, my head shakes of its own accord. "They said it was lost, no one knew where it was . . . how?"

His warm smile steadies me. "Apparently, it was left with my mom. Along with this." He reaches into his pocket and pulls out a folded-up envelope. My eyes widen and ask the question I can't find the words to ask. He only nods and hands me the note. I unfold it and start to read. Familiar handwriting stares back at me and my hands shake.

Dear Adam,

My eyes shoot up to him in shock, confusion, and too many other emotions to process. I'm glad I'm already on the ground because my legs would've given out if I'd been standing. I have a guess as to what this is, and I don't know if I'm strong enough to continue.

"Just keep reading," he encourages.

Dear Adam,

I know as I write this that you and Rylie are not yet together. In fact, I don't think either of you have quite realized that you're in love with each other yet.

My head is shaking, unable to comprehend what I'm holding in my hands, unable to comprehend the words I'm reading, and trying to figure out when she would have written them. Then I remember my conversation with Claire when we first started dating . . . Did my mom give this to her during that last conversation, or before? Adam's hand rests on my cheek, wiping tears as they fall, giving me the support I need to keep going.

You might not realize it yet, but I see it every time the two of you are together. The way you look at her like she's the center of your universe, the way you care for her, and the way you light up in her presence. Not only that, but she looks at you the same way and I've never seen her smile as big as she does when she's with you.

As a mother, that's all I could ever ask for.

I don't know what your future holds, but if you and Rylie end up together, I want you to know that you have my blessing, and I couldn't have imagined a better man for her to end up with.

I'm leaving my ring with your mother until the time that someone is considering proposing to my daughter. If that someone happens to be you, she is instructed to give you this note and the ring for you to decide what you think is best. You, and only you, have my blessing to use this ring to propose if you wish. You're the only one who will truly know what this means to her.

I guess that if you're reading this, then that means it is you and congratulations are in order. I want you to know I'd have been honored to have you as a son-in-law.

I AM honored.

I wish you two all the happiness in the world.

Love,

Lydia

P.S. If you hurt my girl, I swear I'll come back just to haunt you.

I huff out a laugh through my tears. That's my mother, through and through.

Adam's arms wrap around me, and I turn into his chest.

The trouble she went through to set this all up on the off-chance things played out this way . . . I'm shaking, still not believing it. Her love is still reaching me, even now. I place a hand on the locket around my neck, the same one Adam gave me years ago that I still wear daily and say a silent thank you that my mother's kindness and compassion have passed onto me.

I still miss her every day and I know she'd have loved to be here for moments like this. But her memory is no longer a darkness weighing me down, it's a light guiding me on my path to love as fiercely and live as selflessly as she did.

I'm grateful Adam knows he has her blessing—that he knew her and how much she meant to me. And I'm grateful her ring isn't lost after all. I pull back to look at it again, admiring the pink oval diamond in the center, with rectangular, white diamonds shooting out around it like a sun. I've always loved my mother's ring. She wore it even after my dad passed away, she wore it all the way up to the end and now, I will too.

I was heartbroken when they told me it was lost but it was never really lost, it was waiting. For this, for *us*.

"We can get you a different ring, if you'd ra—" Adam starts, but I'm shaking my head before he can even finish.

"No," I breathe, "it's perfect."

When I look into his eyes my heart swells at the love there, the love that's always there.

"I love you, Adam."

"And I love you, Rylie."

As our lips touch, the first fireworks light up the sky, but we don't notice. The light in our hearts shines brighter than any real light ever could.

Memories of the Fourth of July that started this all flash in my head. I wasn't ready to follow my heart at the time, but luckily, we still found our way to each other. I smile against his lips. "You know, I seem to recall we started something on this beach all those years ago that we never did finish."

He pulls back wide-eyed, and my answering smile is a challenge he's eager to meet. I laugh as he lays me back on the blanket and seals his lips to mine. Surrounded by candles, flowers, and the gentle sound of waves, underneath a never-ending array of multi-colored explosions, we finally rectify the wrongs of our past.

* * *

THE FIREWORKS ARE COMING to a close but as I lay beside Adam, wrapped in the blanket, I can't tear my eyes away from him.

"You know, I used to curse the world for the hand I was dealt —for the pain and suffering I had to go through. But I've realized that every bit of pain, every hurt, led me to this moment right here, with you," I say, smiling, as Adam reaches over to brush the tears from my cheek. "And I want you to know, I'd endure it all a hundred times over if it meant getting to be with you at the end. Every bit of heartache was worth it for the happiness I feel, in this moment. My world was full of darkness until you came along and lit it up. You lit me up."

His kiss is sweet and tender and when he pulls back there's a tear in his eye. "Rylie, I know you always say I'm the one who saved you, but it's the other way around. You saved me. The moment you entered my life you made me a better man."

"I've heard you say before that you tried to be better so you were deserving of my attention, but I want to make sure you know, you've always been enough. You've always been what I wanted, *who* I wanted. It's always been you, Adam." I stare into his eyes, eyes that I've always felt safe in. "I used to be so lost after my mom passed, I felt like I didn't have a home. But I see now I always did. My home is here in your arms. My home is you."

Our kisses turn long and lingering, each moment of our history woven into their fabric and every hope for the future spoken, without a word.

Between kisses he says, "Now that the fireworks are over, we might want to head in before someone comes looking for us."

I wrinkle my nose and pull him closer. "I'll throw anyone in the lake who tries to pull me away from *my fiancé* right now."

Adam's laugh is music to my ears and the realization sets in, I'll get to listen to that laugh for the rest of my life.

This time, as we make ourselves presentable and fold up the blanket, it's with hope and not fear. This time, as we walk back to the house, it's hand in hand, and not in hesitation. This time, we enter the house as future husband and wife.

THE END

acknowledgments

When I started writing again in 2022, the last thing I expected was to have a completed manuscript five months later. But after my grandma passed away, Rylie's story burrowed into my head and grew by the day until I had no choice but to finally write it down. In a lot of ways, Rylie is me. She was my way of dealing with my own grief because—like her—I tend to keep my emotions buried. Writing her healing from her grief helped me heal from mine. This story will always be close to my heart because the emotions are all real and raw and true—and mine.

One of the things I really wanted to portray in this book is that grief and healing aren't linear. Even once you think you're "healed" you still have hard days, and the closer to publishing this I get, the harder it gets. My grandma was the biggest cheerleader for her grandkids, and I know she would be gushing about my book to everyone that would listen if she was still here. I hope more than anything that she knows this is for her as much as it's for me.

I know my family picked up on a lot of the real-life references in this book, but for those who don't know, I hope it made the characters feel more real to you. Because they feel so real to me.

Speaking of family, I want to thank all my family and friends who made this book possible.

To my incredible fiancé who one day said "you should write a book" when he didn't know I was already considering it, thank you for always believing in me (and always being ready to play video games when I needed writing time). I couldn't have gotten this far without your support. I love you!

To my parents who have read every draft of the various book projects I'm working on, thank you for always supporting me, even on my wildest dreams. Our book discussion facetime sessions have kept me excited about these stories.

To all the friends and family who read the early drafts of Rylie and Adam's story, thank you for reading an absolute mess but still believing in the story beneath it. A special thank you to Maddie who read this book chapter by chapter as I wrote it—your constant desire to know what happened next helped this book reach the finish line and your excitement for this story means the world to me. And another special thank you to Hailey who was the first person to read this book from start to end once it was completed (and for talking about dragons and faeries with me when everyone else at work wanted to talk about self-help books!).

To everyone who has alpha and beta read this story through the iterations, your feedback has been invaluable. A special shout-out here to Jess, whose insightful comments helped me see what wasn't working in the story and led me to the realization of what I really wanted this story to be. You Light Me Up would not be what it is today without you!

To Caitlin, my amazing editor and one of the sweetest humans, thank you for helping me bring Adam and Rylie's story to the next level. Your comments and reactions made me smile and laugh, and your suggestions helped improve this story. It was such a joy to work with you!

To MiblArt who were an absolute pleasure to work with on the cover design, you took my vision and brought it to life better than I ever could've imagined. I'm so in love with the cover of this book.

Last but certainly not least, to you—the reader—I would not have achieved my childhood dream of being an author without you. I am so incredibly grateful that even one person took the time to read words that came from my head. Thank you, thank you, thank you!

I'm sure I'm missing someone here, so please feel free to yell at me if I missed thanking you! But to everyone who helped me along the way, in big or little ways, I thank you from the bottom of my heart. It all has meant so much to me.

Brooke Noel is a romance and fantasy writer. You Light Me Up is her debut novel. She currently lives in Southern California with her fiancé and ragdoll cat, Roku. Much like the main character of her book, Rylie, she is a math nerd and holds a degree in Actuarial Science from Florida State University with minors in Business and Economics. You can find her on Instagram @brookenoelauthor and learn more on her website www.brooke-noel.com.